FREEING LINHURST

INTO THE TUNNELS

LILY —
ENJOY THE
BOOK!

Al Cassidy

AL CASSIDY

Published 2018
ISBN: 978-0-692-13864-9

E-ISBN: 978-0-692-13940-0

Library of Congress Control Number: 2018906947

CONTENTS

Chapter 1 1

Chapter 2 15

Chapter 3 29

Chapter 4 48

Chapter 5 65

Chapter 6 80

Chapter 7 92

Chapter 8 113

Chapter 9 130

Chapter 10 154

Chapter 11 171

Chapter 12 199

Chapter 13 224

Chapter 14 245

Chapter 15 276

Acknowledgements..285

About the Author 287

For Grady & Wyatt

Chapter 1

As Jack stood helpless, the scream was coming from the darkness. Faint at first, growing louder.

"Who's down there?" His voice echoed for only a second before being swallowed by the void ahead.

Why isn't my light working?

He stared into the pitch black, the scream barreling toward him as he stood frozen in place. He looked down at his feet—they felt swallowed up by the darkness that surrounded him, as if his sneakers were sucked into invisible quicksand.

How many times do I have to do this?

He had to try and move out of the way of this thing, because he already knew it wasn't planning to stop. He reached to his side to feel for the wall, his arm stretched out full length. It was farther than he remembered. He yanked his feet from the floor, like pulling out of a thick mud, and moved a few inches to get closer to the wall. His open palm met the damp, brittle facade of the tunnel. It felt real, as always, like it was really there, like he was really there.

The scream was barreling out of control toward him.

"Stop!" Jack yelled desperately toward the voice, hoping to give it pause. Jack's shrill scream was no match for the deafening wail forging relentlessly toward him.

One hand still on the wall of the tunnel, he feverishly reached inside his sweatpants and hoodie with his free hand and felt around, hoping to find the flashlight he was sure he must have brought with him. He figured he would pull it out, click it on, and blind whatever was coming at him.

Alas, he was unarmed.

He reluctantly pulled his hand from the wall and felt inside the other pocket.

Empty.

What was he thinking, coming into the tunnels completely unprepared? It was pitch black down here!

The air around him grew very cold as he tried to move his feet, again without success. The scream was nearly on top of him when he let out a blood curdling, "STOP!"

The sound of his own voice chilled him to his core as it slammed hard against the opposing force. Then he was violently swept off his feet, and the thing stopped howling and began carrying him backward down the tunnel in the direction he must have originally entered.

As he was raced along, a freezing wind at his back, he became terrified that whatever had hold of him wouldn't stop. And at the speed they were traveling, they would come to a turn soon, and surely, they wouldn't make that turn and would crash hard into the tunnel wall.

Jack attempted to push and tug himself away from whatever held him, methodically and forcefully at first then more fiercely when it became evident this thing was far too strong for him to escape. Jack desperately needed a way out of its arms… and fast.

"Let me go!" Jack shouted, struggling against the thing with all his might, ever furious he couldn't be freed.

Just then, the thing made a sharp and dizzying turn, rapidly ascending a stairwell out of the tunnel. Light shined brightly through the tall windows from the landing above. At every turn, they shifted violently, quickly, yet somehow with great ease. Jack was pressed so tightly to whatever this thing was that even as he continued to struggle against it, his energy to fight it equally deteriorated.

With the light coming through the windows, he tried to get a look at this thing that had him in order to make sense of what was happening. Though he could feel the bondage around him, all Jack could see below him was the staircase winding away with speed.

He was carried—apparently by nothing—to the top of the stairwell, out onto the ground floor, dashing ever rapidly backward through a great open room filled with boarded windows and busted furniture, then blasting through the front doors of an abandoned building on the Linhurst campus—backward down the short, busted staircase at the front entrance they raced, then backward through the tall weeds and overgrown brush. He was carried several feet a second from the face of the decaying brick building with broken windows and covered in ivy. If not for the tight, invisible bonds that held him a foot off the ground, Jack would have thought he was flying perilously through the air.

Without warning, Jack was let go and tossed onto the ground, and skid another ten yards across the dirt to a full stop. Dust kicked up all around him into a cloud of debris, chasing dead leaves into a whirlwind around him. The sun was sitting low overhead in the sky; it appeared to be late evening.

Jack was stunned, breathing hard and sweating profusely. His arms were aching both from the struggle to escape and from the excruciating tightness by which he'd been held.

But more than anything, he was angry. No, infuriated.

This had happened before—countless times—and he couldn't stop it. But he was more frustrated that he couldn't prevent it, change it, or escape it.

A glowing orb of hot, red-orange light took shape amid the dust in front of him. It burst into a fiery sphere and darted away from him, dashing within the portico at the entrance of the abandoned building twenty yards away. The orb hovered several feet above the busted wooden planks of the porch for a moment—looking heavenly and menacing all at once. Above it, the broken windows of the brick building stared down at Jack like a great skull preparing to swallow him whole.

"What do you want from me?!" Jack pleaded for the umpteenth time. He was defeated. Again. The ball of light innocently floated above the floor boards.

"Is it something I have done?" Jack asked desperately. "Something I have that you want? Something you want me to do?"

Problem was, he knew he would get no response. He never did. He was simply brought to the depths and darkness of this place, bonded and bound, then carried out to the Linhurst grounds and left alone in despair—night after night, over and over again.

Jack huffed. His chest moved up and down more rapidly as he dug his clenched fingers into the dirt around him, wanting to grab a great pile and hurl it at the unseen force, hoping to destroy it forever.

"Why won't you answer me? What do you want?!"

A voice growled and shrieked from within the building, echoing as though coming from the belly of the tunnels. The body of red-orange light vibrated madly several times then exploded into a fiery hot disc that dwarfed the front of the building. The ball of light folded into itself, popped like a bubble just inside the entrance door, then all was quiet.

Jack looked around at the overgrown woods surrounding the abandoned building, one of the many still on the Linhurst property. The sun shone through the dense trees high above, scattering leafy shapes of orange light across the ground around him. Birds chirped unassumingly through the gentle breeze.

Suddenly, something new appeared, something he hadn't remembered from dreams past. An audible howl grew from within the building. Only this time it was more definable and clearly human.

There was something else—from the darkness of the building appeared two people, one Jack recognized immediately. Suzanne—the tour guide for Linhurst hired by Dr. Moseley—and a man he couldn't make out. Jack had often seen Suzanne around campus as she worked so many hours showing guests around the buildings and tunnels on the property. She had become immune to the psychological terrors that newcomers worked up in their minds, but he could clearly see she'd never looked quite as terrified as she did now. She was scrambling to get out of the building as she hopped over the broken floorboards of the porch.

The man, who was hot on her heels, appeared to be middle-aged—wearing a sharp button-down suit and tie, with dark slacks, shiny pointed shoes, and hanging on tightly to a briefcase. He looked ten times as terrified as Suzanne. His face was pale as an apparition, and sweat beads laid like a thin blanket across his forehead.

The pair ran straight toward Jack.

"You are the only one who can stop this!" Suzanne called out to no one in particular.

Then they ran past him as if he wasn't even there.

"Suzanne!" Jack hollered, but when he turned to look, she and the man were no longer there.

Where did they come from? Where did they go?

Jack was enraged. *This is the last time I let this thing control my dreams.* Even though he was solidly asleep, Jack knew he was trapped in a nightmare he was determined to escape.

But he played along. He pushed himself off the ground that wasn't there. Got to his feet and kicked the dirt that wasn't there. Brushed off his pants then clenched his fists. He stood firmly in place, leaning resolutely toward the building and staring into the hollow blackness.

"You don't scare me!" he cried out, hoping his voice would carry inside where the thing had retreated into the belly of the tunnels. "I want answers, and I'm coming to find them!"

He expected no reply because there usually was none, which enraged Jack even more. This time, however, something called back.

"GO AWAY!" a loud, strong male voice wailed, echoing from within and falling dead against the trees around him, scaring a flock of crows into the evening sky.

Jack was stunned. His clenched fists relaxed, and his stance retreated in surprise. He'd never before received a response to his demand for answers, especially not a response as clear and blood curdling as this.

He screwed his face up, pondering what to do next. Before he could utter another word or think how to reply, a blinding white light blast from within the building, so bright he couldn't see a thing. He put his head down and shielded his eyes.

When he looked up again, he saw a familiar image for an instant—a sun and peace symbol. Or at least he thought he had seen it. His jaw dropped as his eyes widened.

The light withdrew so rapidly it brought on a sudden and complete darkness. He widened his eyes to try and take in his surroundings, try to see where the symbol went. It was pitch black.

Am I in the tunnels again?

His breathing was intense, his chest rising and falling rapidly. Then he realized he was in a seated position again, the ground beneath him feeling pillow soft. He sat up straight, arms stretched out behind him and propping him up. He clenched his fists in frustration, suddenly realizing he had a handful of bed sheets balled up in his tight fists. The darkness surrounding him began to lift and he could make out familiar objects—first his desk, then his chair, then the posters on the walls.

The light from the half moon cast faintly through his bedroom windows. A bead of sweat turned to a stream down the side of his face, and he rhythmically controlled his breathing, trying to calm himself. A breeze blew warmly through his open windows, bringing late autumn air into his lungs.

I'm in my room. It was a dream. It was that damn dream again. That nightmare!

He irritably wiped the sweat off his face and the back of his neck, then pulled the sheets off to provide cool relief to his overheated body.

What does this dream mean? Why do I keep having it?

He looked over at his alarm clock shining a brilliant blue— 3:13 a.m. Just three hours before he would need to be up for school.

Jack fell back to his pillow, soft but damp from the sweat. He flipped it to the dry side for cool relief, hoping it would settle his rattled and put him to sleep instantly. No such luck.

He laid awake for another hour, his racing thoughts consuming him. He heard a thump outside his bedroom door and down the hall. *Just a thump. Nothing more and nothing less.* He was unconvinced—every unexplained sight and sound seemed to have him on edge these days, his body and mind replete with stress.

He thought of how he and his dad still weren't getting along well. *He needs to chill out and get a life.* He thought of how much he wanted to be done with high school, but he was only in eleventh grade and still had two years to go. *I'm sick of being treated like some idiot who supposedly imagined the Linhurst campus being completely overrun with ghosts two years ago.* And, as if having one too many AP classes wasn't enough to consume his 16-year-old mind, he had to deal with his recurring nightmare.

He tried to shrug it off, but the thump out in the hall had him thinking that whatever haunted him in his dreams might be haunting him now... just outside his bedroom door.

He looked over at his alarm clock again—4:07. The room suddenly felt chilly, and he pulled the covers up over his body and peeked out over his knuckles into his barely lit room. Still scared, he pulled the sheets over his head, convinced it would protect him from whatever was lurking outside his room. He told himself over and over it was only his imagination.

What felt like another hour passed, and he finally fell asleep again. Until...

"Jack! Wake up, buddy!"

He sat up suddenly and found himself staring at his dad. They were nearly nose to nose.

"Henry?" he said dumbly, his eyes full of crust.

"*Dad*, you mean?" his father replied.

Jack shrugged. He had taken to calling his father by his first name, a somewhat common thing among his classmates. It was Jack's way of retaliating for his dad's constant pushing and prodding at him.

"Are you getting up today or sleeping in?" Henry replied softly.

"What time is it?" Jack asked hazily.

"It's almost 7:45, bud," Henry replied sharply.

"Are you kidding me?" Jack screeched. "I gotta go!"

"Yes, you do," Henry added.

"*Yes, you do,*" Jack mocked his father after he left the room. He madly ripped the blankets and sheets off and leaped from his bed.

"Remember, you have a four o'clock appointment today," Henry called matter-of-factly from halfway down the hall.

Jack didn't reply. He knew his dad wanted him to continue the counseling sessions, but he had grown very tired of them after going three times a week for so many months and hearing the same questions about his dead mother, the night at Linhurst when an explosion didn't happen, his overload of school work, and so on and so on. He just found the appointments repetitive and condescending. He felt like no one really understood him or listened to him anymore.

He raced through the bathroom, brushed his teeth, combed his hair—best he could, of course, with a little over four months buildup of uncut curls—and dashed back to his bedroom to pull one of his many plain gray t-shirts off a hook in his closet.

He ran down the hall and into the kitchen, yanked open the fridge, grabbed his bagged ham-and-cheese sandwich lunch off the top shelf, nearly pulling the half gallon of milk with it, slammed the door, yanked a banana from the fruit bowl, then darted for the front door.

He scooped up his backpack, slung it over his shoulder, and no sooner reached for the knob when a hand snagged his wrist to stop him.

"Jack," Henry said in an attempted calming tone. "Let me give you a ride."

"No," Jack said firmly.

Henry froze. Jack waited impatiently for him to step aside.

"When are going to get your license?" Henry asked.

Now Jack was annoyed. *Go ahead, keep asking…it will just take longer until I want to do it.*

Henry just stared at Jack from behind his thick framed glasses. His face looked kind and apologetic, but Jack was simply tired of him.

"Take it easy and have a good day, buddy." Henry forced a smile and released Jack's arm. "No need to get stressed, okay?"

Jack stared a hole right through his father.

"You all right?" Henry replied nervously. "Did you have the dream again?"

"No, I'm fine," Jack replied, staring at the wall behind his dad.

Henry slowly stepped back. "Okay, bud." He sighed deeply. "Just don't be late for your appointment, please?"

Jack smiled unconvincingly then spun on a heel and pulled the door shut ever-so-gently—though he wanted to slam it shut—and stepped out into the hallway.

"Get off my case already," he said under his breath.

Jack peeked at his phone—7:51. Less than ten minutes to get to school. He growled at the thought of being late again. He stuffed his phone into his jacket, took in a deep breath, and took off down the hall at full sprint.

"Good morning, Jack!" his neighbor, Mrs. Jacobs in 2C, said as she opened her door to go out for her morning paper.

"Hello," Jack replied.

"Running late today?" she asked.

Jack grumbled under his breath and moved on. He dashed down the stairs to the first floor, making the quick turn at the half landing and skipping the last three stairs to the bottom as usual. He slid across the tile floor past the large round table in the lobby that held the massive vase of fake flowers.

"Mornin', Jack," called Mr. Edwards of 1D, who was in his usual spot in the lobby sitting area, reading his book and sipping his coffee.

"Hi, Mr. Edwards," Jack called out without looking back. He raced to the front doors and barreled through, nearly knocking over Bill Williams—dressed in his usual winter gear though it was a warm autumn morning.

"Watch where you're goin', dude!" Bill snapped.

"Sorry, Bill!" Jack chirped.

Bill snorted irritably at him.

Jack raced down the front set of stairs, out into the courtyard, past the fountain spraying a glimmering stream of droplets from the twin cherubs.

"Morning, Mam and Pap," he called out to the old Saunders couple picking up miniscule bits of litter around the fountain. They didn't reply—they never did.

Out of the courtyard, he hurried past the cemetery at the edge of the woods.

"Hi, Heather," he whispered in solemn recognition of Dr. Moseley's daughter, who may well have saved his life just two years before.

Jack continued his feverish pace down the recently repaved main road that led to the generating station and out onto Main Street. Jack could just picture the bus flying past the entrance only minutes earlier, leaving him stranded again.

Can't believe I missed the bus. Fourth time this month. And his run to school wasn't getting any easier. *Maybe a ride from dad wouldn't have been as bad as this.*

As he neared the generating station, Jack spied Dr. Moseley opening the doors to the Linhurst Care Center where Jack and his friend Celia volunteered a few days a week after school. He enjoyed working with Mose and helping out wherever he could. He always felt like he didn't do much, but at least enjoyed coming back to see the people who visited regularly and would have otherwise been prisoners at Linhurst decades before.

As he jogged along, Jack saw a nurse coming from the care center's parking lot at the side of the building. She looked distressed and was in a terrible hurry. As she approached Dr. Moseley, she looked frantic. She ran right up to Mose and grabbed his arm, then began rambling incoherently. Mose attempted to calm her. As Mose began to speak to her, he caught glimpse of Jack, then gave him a wave and a smile.

"Good day, Jack!" Mose called out. "Late for school?"

"Yes, sir!" Jack replied breathlessly, slowing down to say hello.

"Do you need a ride?" Mose hollered back. Jack was relieved to hear this—he would definitely take a ride from his old friend.

"I must speak with you now!" the nurse pleaded with Dr. Moseley.

"I'll be all right," Jack replied, deflated. Noting the concern in the woman's voice, he figured she needed Mose more than he did.

Mose nodded to Jack then turned back to the nurse, inviting her inside the care center.

"Come inside, Janice, and let me make you a cup of tea while you tell me what's going on," Mose said as he gently placed his hand on her shoulder.

The pair disappeared through the automatic glass doors of the care center, and Jack continued on to school—very curious about what had Janice so worked up.

Chapter 2

As Jack ran along, he recalled that, not long ago, the entire campus was shuttered and awaiting demolition. Now, people came from all around to see Dr. Moseley and his staff. It seemed like overnight the popularity of the idea behind a Linhurst Care Center allowed them to raise the funds to build the $2 million facility that was now a hallmark of the Linhurst campus. A beacon of Spring Dale and the subject of so many media stories, it became the inspiration for similar care centers popping up around the country. The care center was purposefully placed near the entrance of the property so that it could be seen from Main Street. It was also built just across the road from the generating station, as Dr. Moseley felt it was critical to be close to the most important piece of equipment on the property—the fusion reactor that powered the campus.

As the care center and generating station fell behind him and he neared the entrance, Jack checked his watch—7:58.

Half a mile to go. Maybe I should just get my driver's license.

By Jack's quick calculations, he would have to run over ten miles an hour to get to school on time. He was going to be late for sure—time to pick up the pace.

Out on Main Street, Jack stopped to catch his breath just under the brand new iron Linhurst sign that curved between the two ten-foot tall stone columns on either side of the road.

What once held the moniker of the tarnished Linhurst State School and Hospital now read *Linhurst Gardens and Care Center*. He looked up and down Main Street in hopes that someone he knew would be running as late as him and want to give him a ride to school.

As he ran along Main Street, he began to think how his town had changed very quickly in recent years. He had lived in this same town his whole life and, for most of his upbringing, Spring Dale was a depressed area without much hope for the future. Since the revitalization of the Linhurst campus, Main Street had become a bustling hub with new shops and stores popping up every month in a once vacant space.

Suddenly, just across the street, he spied Pete Sawyer leaving Brewed Awakenings with his backpack in one hand a cup of coffee in the other. His dad, Mark, had opened the store only months before and gave away free brew to Pete and his classmates. Relieved to see his friend running late, Jack ran across the street, knowing Pete would give him a lift.

"Hey, Pete!" Jack called out to Spring Dale High School's state golf champ. "Can I get a ride with you?"

Pete slung his bag over his shoulder and paused mid-sip. "Jack, you know I would, but I have a doctor's appointment in the opposite direction. Maybe tomorrow?"

"Oh, it's cool," Jack said, hiding his deflation and frustration. "Thanks, though!"

Pete disappeared around the back of the coffee shop, and Jack was stranded again. He checked his watch—8:00.

"Why can't Dad just let me get a car?" he growled under his breath. *Then I would get my damn license.*

"Can I give you a ride?" a voice called out behind him. It was like the clouds lifted and the heavens opened up. Jack turned around with a huge smile of relief on his face.

"Dad?" he blurted out when he saw where the voice came from. Henry was leaning over to open the passenger door of his thirteen-year-old orange PT Cruiser.

"Come on… get in!" Henry pressed, responding to the hesitation on Jack's face. "You still have a few minutes before Wilson nails you for being tardy."

Jack rolled his eyes and grumbled under his breath, then hopped in. He desperately wanted to remain stubborn toward his dad, but was far less interested in racking up any more tardies.

They rode in silence the entire half mile. Henry cleared his throat every so often as if he was going to make some statement or ask some stupid question—but he never did. Jack just watched the houses go by, counting down the seconds until he could escape his overbearing father for the second time in one morning.

Henry stopped in front of the long sidewalk leading up to Spring Dale High School, where only a few stragglers hurried up the front steps. Thankfully, being a few minutes late saved him the embarrassment of being caught getting a ride from his dad. Jack pulled on the door handle, cringing, thinking that his dad would have one last piece of advice or a final word to add. He knew it was coming. He grabbed hold of his backpack strap firmly, slung the door open, stepped onto the pavement, and slammed the door shut.

Still waiting.

Here it comes.

Any minute now.

But nothing. To Jack's complete and utter surprise, his dad had nothing to say.

Jack turned to his father, sheepishly and cautiously, to see that Henry was only smiling. Not sinister and not condescending. He was just smiling—kind and calm and, well, fatherly.

"Thanks, Dad," Jack said.

"Have a nice day," Henry replied, then pulled away.

Jack was stunned. He couldn't believe his dad had let him go without some warning or speech or I-told-ya-so moment—or, god forbid, a hug.

He flipped his backpack over his shoulder and ran like mad to the front of the school.

Once inside, Jack spied the large clock hanging over the main hallway. He was three minutes late. He headed right for the student check-in area and found Mrs. Hagstrom tapping away on a laptop.

"Name?" she said without looking up.

"Jack Alexander," he replied.

"Good morning, Jack," she replied without looking up. "Reason for tardiness?"

"Uh…" Jack hesitated, "car trouble."

"Car trouble?" Mrs. Hagstrom looked up. "Do you own a car?"

"No…that's the trouble," he replied, chuckling nervously.

Mrs. Hagstrom looked down and began typing again. "You're good to go," she said without looking up. "Know where you're heading?"

"AP Physics," Jack replied.

"Okay, you're all set," she said, her attention still fully on the laptop.

Jack walked away, completely flustered at being possibly the last student to arrive to class that day.

What has gotten into me? I'm acting like a complete idiot! I have to get my life together!

"Running late, Alexander?" a voice called out behind him, interrupting his thoughts.

Principal Reginald Wilson was the toughest, meanest, hardest principal in the history of Spring Dale High School. At least in the minds of the students of Spring Dale High School today.

"Y-yes, sir...I am checking in late, sir," Jack said, spinning around to catch his heat.

"Won't this make the second time this month?" Wilson asked firmly.

He can't count. Thank goodness!

He didn't know what to make of Principal Wilson other than that he was more like a prison guard than a principal. He was constantly lurking about the hallways looking for someone to make a mistake, be it big or small. Drop a piece of paper unknowingly, he was on you. Close your locker too loudly, he had something to say. Walk too fast or too slow, and who knows, it could land you in detention!

"Do you feel this is becoming a problem?"

"N-no, sir, I don't think so."

"You don't think so?" Wilson asked.

"I mean, maybe."

"Maybe?"

"I know it's a problem. Just need to work on getting my license."

"How about managing your time better?"

Jack dropped his head and shuffled his feet. Wilson was right, though he hated to admit it to himself.

"You have a problem looking at me when I'm talking?" Principal Wilson demanded.

Jack his gaze to Wilson. "No…sorry!"

Principal Wilson was a tall man with a bristly black mustache and male pattern baldness. He wore a brown suit snugly around his thick frame, rolling along the contours of his bulging belly. Etched on his forehead was a permanent set of horizontal lines that may as well have been an angry equals sign. Jack kept his gaze on Wilson.

"That's better," Principal Wilson said. "Now, I hope you will work on your lateness. The word from your teachers is that you are a good student, and I personally know so because I have seen your records."

Wilson smiled devilishly. This made Jack a bit queasy.

"You seem to have some issue with authority, though," Wilson continued. "Where I come from, that's not tolerated."

Wilson's equals sign got a bit madder.

"I may seem much older than you, Mr. Alexander, but not long ago, we respected our elders, unlike you teens today. In my day, our elders were to be listened to and looked up to. We didn't ignore them or curse them or, worse, go around trying to set them up for prison time, if you know what I mean."

Jack immediately knew Principal Wilson was insinuating that Jack was personally responsible for former Spring Dale High School Principal John Thomson currently serving time for involuntary manslaughter and his partner in crime, Coach Eric Slater, doing eleven years.

"But they were guilty, sir," Jack replied hastily. "I didn't set them up."

Wilson scowled. "I wouldn't know the facts, only what I read."

Jack thought quickly—he needed to appease Wilson and find a way out of this conversation. "I wish nothing more than to do better at respecting my elders."

Wilson's eyebrows raised, his equals sign sharpening in his forehead. He pierced his gaze upon Jack and opened his mouth, but before he could utter a reply, Mrs. Hagstrom appeared behind him.

"Mr. Wilson, I gave this student a tardy slip and he is running late for AP English class. Is there anything else I can do?" She gave Jack a wink.

Principal Wilson's firm stance loosened as he looked at Mrs. Hagstrom, pondering her approach. "No, Shirley, we're all set. Morning announcements should be getting started soon anyway."

"That's correct," Mrs. Hagstrom replied. "We have less than a minute, then we have a meeting following announcements."

"Right," Wilson replied, then turned his cold, steely gaze back on Jack.

"You mind yourself, son," Wilson said quietly and coldly. "I have my eye on you."

Jack gulped.

"Understand?" Wilson added with consternation as he leaned in uncomfortably close. "I...have...my eye...on... you."

Jack nodded. Wilson pointed a long finger down the hall. Jack turned slowly, maintaining eye contact with

Wilson until he was fully facing the other direction, then vanished—tail between his legs.

Luckily, the first class of the day was Mr. Urbach. Jack enjoyed AP Physics, even though the material was tough. And thankfully for Jack, Mr. Urbach was one of the few people remaining in his life who didn't question his mental stability.

* * * * * *

Things had changed quite a bit in the time since Jack, Celia, and their friend Nate were freshmen at Spring Dale High. No longer were they bullied outcasts—they had their own table and were respected by lower classmen. At least, that's how they wanted to see things, though they suspected most of the ninth and tenth-grade students barely knew they existed aside from knowing the nickname "Ghost Boy," as Jack was labeled.

Principal Wilson was on lunch duty and standing watch over the entire room like a sentry from a medieval army.

"Isn't Wilson terrifying?!" Jack's friend Nate belted out as he slammed his tray of food on the cafeteria table.

"He's more like a nosy jerk than he is terrifying," Jack replied, irritated as he spied the principal from his seat in the far corner of the room.

"I like Principal Wilson," Celia said casually as she peeled her banana. "He brings a sophisticated and intelligible presence to the leadership of the school."

Nate screwed up his face. "I don't know where you get that impression—I think he's a complete dictator!"

"Well, he's no Thomson or Slater." Celia smirked.

"You had to mention them," Nate replied.

"I'm just saying I think Spring Dale High finally has someone leading the school in the right direction."

"Not hard to pull something out of the dumps," Jack added glumly.

"You really think it's that bad?" Celia asked.

"Yeah, why are you hating on Spring Dale?" Nate asked, his mouth half full of mashed potatoes.

"I'm just ready to be done with all this," he replied, waving a hand around in the air.

"All this?" Celia questioned. "What is all this?"

"This school… this town… this whole area!"

"You are unusually grumpy today," Nate said.

"I've just...you know...had enough of it," Jack said.

"Enough of what, Jack?" Celia replied with concern in her voice.

"Just, you know,everything!" Jack replied.

"Well, isn't that terribly non specific?" Celia grumbled.

Jack chewed on his ham and swiss sandwich as if it was made of dirt and vinegar. He showed little expression.

"You worry me these days," Celia said after a few moments of silence, only the clatter of silverware and chatter of students breaking the air between them. "What's gotten into you?"

"I just feel like I'm cut out for more than this," Jack replied.

"More than what—high school?" Nate laughed out loud. "We're all trapped here!"

"I just feel like, you know, ever since the whole thing with Linhurst went down, nothing has been the same," Jack said.

"It hasn't been the same for me, either," Celia replied, annoyed.

"And me," Nate added, swallowing hard.

They both screwed up their faces at Nate, thinking he'd had little to do with that night.

"A lot happened that night, though—how could things be the same?" Celia said.

"We don't live in the old house, for one thing," Jack replied sadly. "At least that much could have stayed the same."

"I thought you wanted to move to Linhurst," Nate said.

"I guess I was wrong," Jack replied.

Celia frowned.

"And besides that, it's just getting old—all the attention I still get. Being called Ghost Boy for being some kid who went inside and found a bunch of ghosts. Most people don't believe it and the other half just think I'm crazy!" Jack said, dramatically waving his arms around his head.

"That was years ago," Celia replied, agitated. "Get over yourself. Move on."

"I can't get over it—no one will let me!" Jack replied.

"Just ignore what everyone says!" Celia punched back.

"My dreams won't even let me forget it!" Jack raged.

His outburst caught the attention of everyone in the lunch room, stopping conversation and creating an awkward silence.

"Don't mind him—he's just going mad," Nate merrily told the gawkers, his mouth full of food.

Jack shook his head furiously, completely ignoring everything else around him. "Whatever. You have no idea what my dreams are like."

"Why don't you talk about it in therapy?" Celia pleaded.

"Do you know what it's like sitting through those sessions every week?" Jack snapped.

"Yes, Jack—I finished mine," Celia replied.

"You had it easy!" Jack yelped.

"Easy?" Celia cried. "How do you figure it was easy for me to convince a shrink, week after week for over a year, that I saw a bunch of ghosts starting up some machine in some abandoned mental hospital and that one of the ghosts helped us get out because she was the daughter of one of the doctors who worked there?!"

"Shhh," came a loud voice from a nearby table.

"Oh, shush yourself!" Celia snapped back.

"I get that you had a hard time with it, Celia, and I'm sorry I dragged you into it," Jack began apologetically.

"Well, I am still going through it."

"Then tell someone about it!" Jack said.

"I already did, every time I went," Celia replied. "But she never listened to me! She tried to tell me that it's a dream and I can work to control it and understand it."

"Well, that's exactly how I feel every time I go," Jack said.

"Then maybe you should just stop going," Celia said.

"Good luck convincing my dad of that!" Jack replied.

"I have no idea what you two are going on about," Nate added foolishly, chugging his chocolate milk. "If you just don't talk about it, no one can give you a hard time."

They both ignored Nate's comment.

"Look," Jack said, face to face with Celia. "If there was some way they could fix me, they would have fixed this by now. But they can't. I'm broken. Something inside me broke that night, I swear to you, and there's no going back."

Celia sat dumbfounded.

Principal Wilson was suddenly lurking in a nearby corner, arms folded, spying on their table and listening in on their conversation. He had a stern look on his face that made the equals sign on his forehead a solid downward pair of arrows.

"I appreciate the sentiments, Celia," Jack said glumly. "I'm afraid there's nothing you can do for me this time around. I'm on my own."

"You say that every time," Celia replied in reassurance. "We're still with you."

Jack scooped up his trash and pushed himself away from the table.

"Jack, I'm your friend," Celia cried out after him. "I'm here for you. I— I—"

Jack turned abruptly. "You what?!"

"I—" Celia hesitated longer. Jack waited. She couldn't get the thought out.

Jack snorted and turned to go.

"Jack, wait!" Celia cried out. "I care for you!"

The nearby tables erupted in laughter.

"Oh, Jack!" a tenth-grade boy cried out in a mocking voice as he fell into his buddy's lap. "I care for you!" His peers burst into laughter.

"Ghost Boy—I would travel to the ends of the earth for you!" a boy at another table called out before the entire row broke into complete chaos and laughter.

"You're my everything!" a girl cried out mockingly.

"Enough!" Principal Wilson roared.

The entire lunch room fell silent immediately. The only sound in the vast space was a dropped fork that rang out like a car wreck.

"Get cleaned up!" Wilson added. "We're changing periods in one minute!"

As proof of Wilson's dominance, students began clearing their places at record speed. Jack slipped away and stopped just outside the lunch room to see Celia lock eyes with Principal Wilson for a moment, and he gave her a kindly nod of affirmation. Jack wasn't sure to believe Wilson's attempts to help.

Chapter 3

The bell rang at the end of the day, and Jack was halfway down the hall toward the front of the school before most students could leave their classrooms. He pushed madly through the doors and out onto the sidewalk, hurrying to escape the grip of Spring Dale High School.

He made it to the end of the walk and turned onto Main Street just as a rusty gray sports car came flying wildly down the road toward him. The decade-old beater had lost most of its paint, and the muffler sputtered almost as loudly as the bass poured out the speakers through the open windows.

At the wheel was Danny Slater, who hardly ever showed up to class these days. But when he did, he made his presence known.

The car came to a screeching halt at the curb by Jack's side.

"Hey, Alexander!" Danny hollered from the car.

Jack tried to ignore him and kept walking. It was no good. Danny put the car in reverse and stayed with Jack.

As he walked along, head down and trying to ignore the bass-pumping beater rolling at his side, Jack suddenly recalled his long history with Danny. Starting on the kindergarten playground all the way through high school, he had been a target of Danny's senseless bullying on a regular basis, with the assistance of his partner-in-crime, Tommy Thomson.

"Yo, Jack!" Danny called again over the blaring music.

Jack ignored him still. He just wasn't in the mood today, even if Danny had softened since the night at the generating station when his father, Eric Slater (then coach of the high school basketball team) was taken away in handcuffs after authorities were told of the bodies of former Linhurst residents who may have been buried under decades-old rubble in the tunnels due to his neglectful leadership. The allegation was quickly confirmed when they investigated the abandoned property's tunnel system and found the men decayed to bones inside a collapsed section underground.

Since that incident, Jack saw in Danny a change of heart and a new direction. Even though the bullying stopped, it didn't make Danny any more eager to become a star student.

Danny stopped the car, then jumped out and ran up onto the sidewalk, blocking Jack's path.

"What gives?" Danny belted out as he stood right in front of Jack, a hand out against his chest.

"What's up, Danny?" Jack asked indifferently.

"Need a ride?" Danny replied excitedly, like a lost dog needing a friend.

"I don't need a ride," said Jack. "I need a walk to clear my head." Jack tried passing him, but Danny simply followed him.

"Where are you off to?" Danny asked.

"Home," Jack said.

"Come on!" Danny said in a chipper tone. "I'll give you a lift. It's no sweat!"

Jack looked to see Danny's expression unusually bright and playful.

What does he want from me?

"Fine," Jack caved.

"Sweet!" Danny replied. "Hop in!"

Danny dashed back and jumped into the driver's seat then leaned over to open the passenger door. Jack reluctantly climbed into the bucket seat and closed his door just in time for Danny to peel out, leaving a trail of smoke and burnt rubber in their wake.

The ride was rough and bumpy. The seats were stained and held an odor that had to be years old in spots. Jack attempted to find a place for his feet amid the fast food wrappers and empty Gatorade bottles lying on the floor.

"Remember when you said Mr. Moseley was looking for help at Linhurst?" Danny started before they reached the end of the block at twenty miles over the speed limit.

"Dr. Moseley," Jack corrected, holding tight to the door's grab bar.

"Sorry, Dr. Moseley," Danny replied sheepishly. "You said he was looking for security help, right?"

"Yeah, he mentioned that high schoolers could apply as well," said Jack. "There's been a lot of vandalism and theft with all the people sneaking onto the campus since everything went down. Lately, they've found a rash of graffiti inside the abandoned buildings and underground tunnels. I guess people just want to leave their mark. Mose says some strange things have been going on, and he could use a few feet on the ground, keeping an eye on things for him."

Jack paused, recalling the events of that night in his mind. It was hard to believe that just two years ago he was all over the media along with Celia and Dr. Moseley. The attention earned him the nickname Ghost Boy after he'd told the story of that night in such great detail. His dad suggested they pack up the only home he had ever known to move to the renovated Linhurst Gardens for a fresh start. And he was now riding with Danny Slater, who had bullied him his whole life.

It was a lot of change in just a short time.

"So, you want me to talk to Dr. Moseley about it?" Jack offered.

"Heck, yeah!" Danny replied, overly excited and mostly out of character. "Beats working fast food or delivering newspapers or whatever. Does it pay good?"

"Didn't ask," Jack said.

"My mom keeps hounding me to help out with stuff at home. Things are tight. She's working two jobs, but I guess she's okay with that since it keeps her mind off things. Been tight since Dad...well...you know…"

"I can ask him if he still needs help," Jack interrupted, saving Danny from his thoughts.

"Could you talk to him now?" Danny urged.

"Right now? I suppose," Jack replied. "We're going that way anyhow."He suddenly realized Danny's motivation to give him a ride.

"You rock, Jack!"

Jack felt a small sense of relief that he could somehow repay a debt that even Danny didn't seem to recognize. Although Danny had stood up to his dad and questioned his actions that night, it was still puzzling the way things turned out.

Danny floored it, blowing through every stop sign until they reached the entrance to Linhurst. He took the turn fast and was soon met by another car coming down the road toward them. He slammed on the brakes and veered off the road, skidding across the muddy lawn just before the woods.

Danny put the car in park and jumped out. Jack followed and turned to see a police cruiser half off the road opposite them. The officer opened the door and stepped out. Captain Hadaway looked rather perturbed as he approached Danny.

"In a hurry, Slater?" Hadaway asked with surprising calm.

Jack could see the many fine lines streaking across the captain's face. A veteran of the force, he looked strong for his age, though the age was starting to show.

"Sorry, sir!" Danny replied. "I was just...I took the turn and didn't think...I…"

"Slow down, Danny," Hadaway interjected. "You kids are always in such a damn hurry. Where are you off to?"

"I was going to see Mr. Moseley about a job, and I just wanted to get there so he could…"

"He's not going anywhere," said Captain Hadaway. "Trust me, whether you go 20 or 100 miles per hour, he will still be there."

Hadaway pulled out his pad and jotted down a note, then handed it to Danny. "You're lucky we didn't punch bumpers just now. I'll let you off with a warning this time—slow it down and watch those turns."

Danny nodded as he took the note. Hadaway turned and walked back to his cruiser, checked the front and rear of the vehicle, hopped in, threw it in gear, then pulled out onto Main Street.

Danny opened the note and read it.

"What does it say?" Jack asked curiously.

Danny crumpled the note and stuffed it into his back pocket. "Oh, uh...you know…" Danny began, stuttering, "Nothing. Just slow down, you know."

Jack screwed up his face. *Why would Hadaway write a note about what he just said aloud?*

Danny ran back to the car and hopped in, fired it up, then slammed his door shut.

"You coming?" Danny called to Jack.

Jack shook his head and got back in the car, and they headed up the road to the care center.

Danny pulled up quickly to a stop just in front of the main entrance. He practically leaped out of the beater then dashed for the entrance. Jack jogging up behind him, up the short set of concrete stairs alongside the handicap ramp and through the double automatic doors. He walked up by Danny, who paused just inside the building and began to look around in awe.

"Whoa, this place is amazing!" Danny said, his mouth hanging open.

Jack took in the place he visited several times a week, almost forgetting how grand it was. The lobby was a vast open space, architecturally stunning in design, bright and colorful, with colorful abstract art hanging amid the four-story vestibule where the upper floors looked out from balconies high above. The space was inviting and calming, the high windows at the front of the building casting warm sunlight down onto the visitors seated in plush, colorful chairs and sofas awaiting their turn to see a doctor.

Having seen all this a few times a week, Jack let Danny soak it in as he walked up to one of the several check-in desks.

"Hi Jack," said a pleasant woman in her mid-thirties seated behind the desk. She had soft features and a glowing face illuminated by the high windows. "What brings you in so early?"

"Hi Andrea," Jack replied. "I'm not volunteering today, but is Dr. Moseley around?"

"He's in his office playing catchup," Andrea replied. "Been a bit crazy around here today. Captain Hadaway was just here filing a report. Suzanne went to the hospital last night. A lot going on! Let me call him."

Hadaway was here to see Mose? Suzanne is in the hospital? That's odd. Wonder what's going on.

"Hi Charles, it's Andrea," she said into the phone. "I have Jack here...Okay, I'll send him back. Thanks."

She looked up at Jack."You can go back to his office."

"Thanks Andrea!"

Jack started for the door beside the check-in area, but before he could reach for the knob, she called after him.

"Is he with you, Jack?" Andrea asked, pointing to Danny still standing in the middle of the lobby.

"Yes, Danny is looking into the security job."

"I'll need him to sign in."

"No problem," Jack replied, and they made their way back to the desk where Danny picked up a pen and began filling in his info.

Andrea winced.

"Something the matter?" Jack asked.

"Are you Eric Slater's son?" Andrea asked.

"Yes, ma'am," Danny replied sheepishly.

She suddenly looked nervous.

"Something the matter?" Jack asked, wanting to set her at ease. He knew the Slater name was tarnished, but it didn't matter to him.

"N-n-no," she stammered, sounding embarrassed. "Just curious. So sorry!"

They stood in awkwardness for a moment until Jack broke the silence.

"We'll head back now." Jack smiled and turned.

"Yes, of course," Andrea said with a sheepish chuckle.

"That was weird," Danny said under his breath once he and Jack were in the hallway beyond the door. Jack nodded in agreement, though he was sure Danny got that a lot.

The brightly lit hallway felt more like a day spa than a medical facility. Past all the doors sat a grand window that filled the end of the hallway. Through it, Jack and Danny could see the river beyond the forest—a mostly serene sight if not for the nuclear power plant spewing out clouds of steam.

Jack and Danny approached Dr. Moseley's door, which had a modest white sign with blue lettering reading, *Charles Moseley*, MD. The door was slightly ajar, and Jack tapped lightly on it.

"Come in!" Mose called.

Jack opened the door carefully and saw Dr. Moseley hunched over his computer in the far corner, tapping away on the keyboard.

"Hi Mose!" Jack was always glad to see his friend.

"Just a minute, Jack!" Mose replied.

Moseley's office was sparsely decorated—a few plainly-framed diplomas and some black and white photos of his wife and daughter, Heather, who'd both passed away years before. A modest framed landscape painting of the original Linhurst campus—before any building construction began or patient one arrived—was the centerpiece. It hung just over Mose's desk, spanning the length of it as a constant reminder of the place that perhaps never should have existed. Mose liked to remember that he had a fresh start as head of the Linhurst Care Center.

"Sorry to keep you waiting, Jack," Mose began. "Just had to get that last email sent."

Mose spun his chair and stood up from his desk, stretching his arms out. His long gray doctor's coat hung around his waist, and the top of his head shimmered from the lights above, setting his pure white hair aglow. He looked suddenly surprised to see Jack was not alone.

"Danny!" Mose blurted out.

"Hi, Mr. Moseley," Danny said quietly.

"What brings you here?" Mose replied.

"Danny is inquiring about the security work, Mose," Jack said.

"Oh, I see." Mose looked at Danny through piercing eyes, appearing to gauge his intentions. "Haven't been able to get that position going just yet, but maybe now is a good time. Come with me."

Mose passed Jack and Danny, grabbed his gray cap off a hook behind the door, then pulled it tightly over his thin white hair.

"I want to show you something," Mose said, then motioned for them to follow him as he headed out of the office.

They made their way back down the hall and out into the lobby.

"I'll be back in a few," he called to Andrea, who was checking in a visitor.

"You have a four o'clock, Dr. Moseley," she called out.

"So do I!" Jack added nervously, remembering his appointment.

"We shouldn't be long," said Mose, walking quickly for the front entrance.

Mose dashed through the automatic doors with Jack and Danny hot on his heels. They made their way around the side of the building where Mose always parked his old blue pickup truck.

"Climb in guys," he said as he hopped in and pulled the door shut. Danny and Jack jumped in the back, and Mose started up the old beater, then peeled out and drove up the road past the generating station.

Just as Jack thought they were heading toward the apartment buildings A through C, Mose took a sharp turn down an unused road Jack had only ever been down once before. He recalled one of the many abandoned buildings on campus sat at the end, strangled by the overgrown forest.

As they bumped along the crumbling pavement surrounded by dense trees, Jack could faintly see his apartment building—Building C—among the other residential buildings surrounding the fountain. Those, too, faded fast through the thick trees and brush.

They ascended a steep hill and turned onto another road, this one more uncertain than the first. Jack could hardly remember being this deep into the untamed recesses of the Linhurst campus where sat the yet-unrenovated buildings that remained. After an uncomfortably long stretch over the bumpy road, Mose came to a stop.

Jack boosted himself onto the tailgate and looked out to see they were just ten feet from the entrance to the crumbling brick building he remembered. The structure was suffocating from the sprawling arms of nature around it. He could barely make out the sign reading *Penn Hall*.

Mose shut off the engine and hopped out. "This way," he called to Danny and Jack.

Danny slung himself awkwardly over the edge of the old truck, and Jack made his way down the back bumper. They followed Dr. Moseley, racing toward the front entrance.

"Jack may have told you we've been experiencing a lot of vandalism on the property lately," Mose said to Danny as they walked at a fast clip. "If only graffiti was the least of my worries, that would be one thing. Sadly, these old buildings have been cleared out—they've stolen everything. Not that it was worth hanging onto, but we could have auctioned it off or donated it. What it tells me for certain is that there are far more people trespassing here than I imagined."

"So, there's a lot of theft?" Danny asked.

"Yes, but there's more," Mose replied uneasily. "Folks have been seeing lights again, the same unexplainable green flashes that were happening a couple of years ago. Random rumblings coming from underground. And now this."

He carefully climbed the short set of stairs onto a crippled concrete landing leading inside a pair of rusted and busted doors.

"Watch your step in here." Mose pointed down to a large patch of missing wooden planks in the porch leading inside. Danny and Jack stepped over the gaping hole and followed Mose inside the abandoned building.

Once inside, Jack saw a familiar scene he had avoided for years—peeling walls, shredded plush maroon carpeting, and remnants of life at Linhurst long ago that was now only a few pieces of overturned furniture, scattered objects, and shattered memories.

Mose led them carefully over the debris toward a long dark hallway that opened up into a wide-open room with tall, boarded-up windows through which scattered streams of light faintly illuminated the space.

Mose pulled a flashlight from his overcoat and flicked it on. He shined it around the room, chasing off unseen critters and exposing a constellation of dust floating through the air. His light intentionally landed on a long stretch of wall high above where black markings appeared clearly in front of them.

Jack squinted his eyes to see through the darkness onto the glow the light cast. Danny gasped.

"What is that?" Danny asked in a weak voice.

"I want to say vandals," Mose replied.

"Vandals did that?" Danny replied nervously.

"One can only wish," Mose replied, an air of unease lingering on his words.

Jack stared at the black marks that clearly spelled out the words: **GO AWAY.**

"But how was this done?" Danny asked.

"Not sure," Mose replied.

"You don't think it was vandals, then?" Jack asked nervously.

"I don't think so, Jack," Mose replied. "This is the work of something beyond our realm."

Jack could see that the edges of the lettering and the way they were formed was not easy to determine. It wasn't from spray paint or a marker. It wasn't even burned into the wall. It was as though the marks were coming through the wall from the outside.

"Ever since we discovered what was happening here and all that has happened since, strange occurrences like this have been cropping up almost on a daily basis," said Mose.

"Could it have something to do with the tours?" Jack asked, thinking of his recent dream where Suzanne and a man left screaming.

"Funny you should say that, Jack." Mose looked at him suspiciously. "You might remember Nurse Janice coming to me in tears this morning when you were running late? Suzanne collapsed on the lobby floor of the care center last evening."

"Suzanne?" Jack said. "That's why Hadaway was here?"

"In part, yes," Mose replied. "She had burn marks on her arms."

"From what?" Danny gulped.

"We don't know," Mose said sternly. "Captain Hadaway took down all the information to file a report just before you boys showed up today. According to Suzanne, she was wrapping up a tour when she was confronted by what she called an unexplainable force of energy down in the tunnels."

Danny shivered. Jack leaned in for more—this was too much like his dream to be a coincidence.

"She says the air grew very cold around her and a voice called out to her."

"What did it say?" Danny asked, his voice trembling.

"It told her to go away," said Mose.

"Go away? Just like the marks?" Jack asked.

"Correct," Mose said. "She doesn't remember getting them, however. Nurse Janice made the right call and had Suzanne rushed to a nearby hospital. She went into a coma in the ambulance and has been in the ICU ever since. I plan to go visit her later this evening and hope she is lucid. We need to get to the bottom of this."

"Why didn't Janice come to you last night about this?" Jack hollered.

"We've talked about that," Mose reassured him. "Janice claims she didn't want to alarm me." Mose thought for a moment. "It is curious, though. Hadaway made a note about it after interviewing her today."

Suzanne wasn't alone. Jack suddenly recalled his dream again.

"Mose, you said Suzanne was finishing a tour," Jack began. "What happened to the others?"

"That is something Captain Hadaway and I spoke about, as well," Mose said grimly. "It is disconcerting that Suzanne would leave covered in burn marks and mentally distressed beyond recognition. But when Janice asked Suzanne about those who went on the tour, she claimed they were fine and left of their own accord."

Jack continued to eye the black markings on the wall, trying to determine how they were created. His scientific mind could offer him no reasonable explanation.

"I went into the tunnel under Building A where Suzanne reportedly had the experience," said Mose. "I found nothing of consequence at first." He hesitated for a moment then reached inside his jacket for his phone. "Aside from this."

Danny swallowed hard. Jack was breathing heavily with anticipation. Mose opened the camera app then handed his phone to Jack, who took it cautiously. He looked at the image, then back to Mose, overwhelmed with the feeling of dread.

"But how? Why?" Jack said, tears beginning to form in his eyes.

"I don't know, Jack," Mose said. "But we're going to find out."

"What does it mean?" Danny asked, looking at the photo over Jack's shoulder.

Jack stared blankly at the photo. He was stunned to see the pencil drawing on a square piece of paper, lying on the dirt-covered tunnel floor. He hadn't seen the actual thing since the night at the generating station, though he remembered it well—it was the same symbol emblazoned on the amulet Jack wore around his neck after his mother passed away;

the same symbol that sat above the Linhurst Gardens sign; and the very same symbol that was etched into his mother's tombstone.

Then he remembered his dream from the night before. It was the same dream he had been having for months—only it changed. Suzanne was there. The man in the suit was there. And he swore he'd seen the symbol for a split second in the dream.

"A sun and peace symbol," Jack replied. "Eternal energy."

"Ah!" Danny exclaimed. "Isn't that the same thing on the necklace you always wore?"

Danny reached for the phone to get a closer look, but before he could slip it out of Jack's hand, a sudden thump above their heads made all three jump.

Mose shined his light up toward the ceiling. Bits of dust and debris were raining down on them.

"Let's go," Mose said quickly. "This building is not safe."

Jack handed the phone back to Mose, and they made their way out of the large room, dancing over the debris and rotting floorboards. Jack took one last look back at the black lettering before a massive piece of wall fell to the floor. He turned and quickly made for the front door and back into Mose's pickup. He and Danny watched in silence as the abandoned building slowly faded away from them, slipping back into the darkness of the overgrown forest.

Mose pulled into his spot at the side of the care center building and checked his watch.

"Just in time," he called back to Danny and Jack, who were seated on the walls of the truck bed. "My four o'clock appointment should be arriving any minute."

Jack feverishly pulled his phone out of his hoodie pocket. It was 3:57.

"I'm late!" he yelped.

"Where do you need to be?" Danny replied.

"I have an appointment in town," Jack replied.

"I can take you," Danny replied as he hopped down from the pickup. "So, Mr. Moseley…"

"Dr. Moseley, please," Mose replied, closing his pickup door.

"Sorry—Dr. Moseley—do you think I can apply for the security job?"

"Oh, right, I almost forgot what brought you here."

Mose paused and thought for a moment. He eyed Danny up and down, then looked him straight in the eye. "Are you up for it?"

"I think so," Danny replied.

"What we just witnessed is what has been happening around here."

Danny nodded.

"Whoever—or whatever—is causing it must be caught in the act and reprimanded."

Danny nodded.

"Are you up for it?" Mose asked again.

"Yes, sir!" Danny replied confidently.

"And you think you can handle it? It won't scare you off?"

"No, sir!"

"Start tomorrow?"

"Yes!"

"Right after school?"

"Yes, sir!"

"But you have to go to school first." Mose turned and subtly winked at Jack.

Danny's eyes lit up in surprise. Then he looked more responsible. "Yes, of course."

"I can start you off at $9 an hour."

"I was hoping for ten, sir."

"Nine-fifty," Mose replied.

"Deal!" Danny replied merrily.

"Dismissed!" Mose said.

"I won't let you down, sir," Danny said, then awkwardly saluted Dr. Moseley. He turned and took off for his car, then stopped halfway and faced Mose.

"Thank you so much, Dr. Moseley," Danny said quietly.

"Invite your friends," Mose replied. "I could use all the hands I can get."

Danny nodded, then took off for his car again and hopped in the driver's seat.

"Come on, Jack!" he called out.

"Oh, right!" Jack said, waking himself from the surreal conversation he just witnessed. "I gotta go!"

Jack ran to the car and hopped in, then Danny peeled out, leaving a cloud of dust in his wake.

Chapter 4

Danny slammed on the brakes as they reached Jack's destination. The red brick home with stately windows and multi-pitched roofline nestled between a new upscale butcher shop and the florist who had been on Elm Street for over twenty years.

A sign out front read, *Sandy Miller Counseling: A Better You Today*!

"Is that where your appointment is?" Danny asked, looking at the old converted house.

Jack turned red—he hated to admit that he was going to a therapist.

"Oh, it's just down the street," Jack fibbed.

Danny snorted and Jack turned to him angrily.

"Sorry," Danny replied quick. "I know a lot of people our age who do counseling, but I refuse to go. Bunch of quacks, if you ask me."

Jack grabbed his bag off the floor and jumped out of the car, then slammed the door shut.

"I didn't mean anything by it, Jack!" Danny called through the window.

Jack ignored Danny, then became distracted by his phone buzzing in his pocket. He pulled it out to see his dad was calling. He ignored the call and sent it to voicemail. Didn't help—Henry texted him immediately to say, *You're late*!

Jack quickly replied: *Wrong—I'm here.*

He turned to see that Danny was already halfway down the road, music pumping out the windows again. Jack made his way up the sidewalk to the front porch and headed straight through the screen door into the main hallway.

He was immediately hit with the familiar and nauseating scent of lavender. Sandy had only been practicing for a few years, but she did her best to create a calming atmosphere. The thing she didn't realize, in Jack's opinion, was the negative effect the scent had on him after walking in to the smell so many times a week for so long. He figured he would hate the scent of lavender for the rest of his life.

Sandy popped her head out of the first door on the left.

"Hey, Jack!" Sandy called out. "Running behind today?"

Sandy was nearly a head shorter than Jack, her hair fell like fine drapes to her shoulders. She always wore a puffy sweater and loose-fitting khakis over gray loafers.

"Come on in!" she said merrily.

The sound of her voice, pleasant as it was, grated on him as well. Jack stepped inside and dropped his bag by the door. He flopped into the overstuffed chair by the window, facing Sandy's spinning desk chair. He was trapped again, stuck inside the dreaded room where he had sweat out one long hour, several times a week, for what felt like a decade, even though it was just under two years.

Her diploma hung proudly on the wall above a very modest desk, where sat a small notepad, jar of pens, and an open laptop. Several books lined the far wall along with photos of her husband and young daughter.

Sandy came in and took a seat in the spinning chair across from Jack. She turned toward the laptop and tapped out a few things. Jack spied the clock above her head—4:11.

Thank god—under an hour today.

Sandy spun her chair around to face Jack.

"Having a busy day, I see," she began, offering a toothy smile.

"Yeah, I guess," Jack replied nonchalantly.

"I've been running behind all day, too. Good thing you're my last appointment—no worries about going over our time."

Jack growled internally.

"So, where do you want to start?" she asked.

Jack shrugged.

"All right," Sandy took in a deep breath and looked around the room. "How have you been doing with the breathing exercises?"

"Fine." Jack stared at her without expression.

"I see." She looked around the room for more ideas. "Any outbursts lately?"

Jack recalled yelling at Celia during lunch earlier and snapping at his dad that morning.

"No," he said.

"Well, that's good," Sandy said. "Strive for one percent progress each week, I always say." She patted him on the knee, and Jack pulled his leg away.

"You'd be happy to hear that I was talking with your dad the other day, and we decided to decrease the appointments to just one time per week. How would you like that?"

Jack was relieved to hear this, though he preferred to not come at all. He simply nodded.

"Well, let's get a day on the books to be consistent," she said. "Should we stick with Mondays?"

"I don't care."

"Ok, we'll keep Mondays," Sandy turned and tapped madly on the keyboard and spun around again.

"Still feeling ostracized?" Sandy asked abruptly. "Feeling like everyone still thinks of you as this so-called *Ghost Boy,*" she made air quotes with her fingers, "or that you were making things up?"

Jack stared at her irritably.

"How about the dreams?" Sandy moved one. "Have they improved?"

Jack adjusted his seat. He cleared his throat. "About the same," he replied.

She leaned in and glared at him without blinking. She looked worried.

"Jack…" she began. "I know you too well—something is bothering you. Please tell me about it."

Jack stared into Sandy's bright green eyes. He didn't truly hate her—he could tell that she meant well. It was just that he had grown very weary of rehashing the same topics over and over again, week after week, for seemingly no good reason.

Why couldn't she just let him go? Why couldn't his dad sign off on this already? Why couldn't he just be mad or sad or whatever without having to talk about his damn feelings every other day?

"I had another dream last night," Jack began reluctantly.

"Tell me about it."

"Same as all the others."

"Okay, in what way?"

"In every way," Jack snapped.

"Ok—so, you're down in the tunnels…" Sandy said.

"Yes."

"It's dark…you can't see…"

Jack nodded.

"You feel for the wall. You hear a voice or something calling down the tunnel. Then what?"

"You already know what!" Jack snapped.

"Right. Yes, I do. Sorry. Anything different? The same dream?"

Jack nodded. He didn't feel like talking about it…again!

"Just last night. What about the night before that? Did you have the dream?"

"I don't know. Don't remember. Probably."

Sandy sat quietly for a moment. He made it clear he was unwilling to say much today.

After a few moments of flicking the seam running along the arm of the chair, he broke the awkward silence.

"There was something different."

She sat upright. "Really? What was different?"

"Someone came out of the tunnels," Jack said.

"Was it the voice you had been hearing?" said Sandy.

"Not quite. I was sitting in the dirt, staring at the building. The ball of light popped out as it always does, but then two people came running out."

"That *is* different," Sandy replied with enthusiasm. She grabbed the notepad from her desk and began writing. "Who were they?"

"It was a woman," said Jack. "Actually, it was Suzanne, the tour guide. And a man. I don't know who he was. They were running from the building screaming and then ran past me. I woke up after that as usual."

"But this is not the same as usual—this is very different, Jack," Sandy said excitedly.

"I guess it is," Jack replied, less thrilled.

"Where were they going?" Sandy asked. "What were they saying?"

"I don't know where they went. I only know they left the building screaming."

"Did they say anything?" Sandy asked.

Suzanne did. She said he was the one who could stop this.

"I don't remember," Jack fibbed—he decided not to mention that part to Sandy.

"Well, this is good news," Sandy said.

"Good how?" Jack replied. He was annoyed now. "It didn't make any difference. I still awoke angry and frustrated and unable to prevent this nightmare from happening again. Every time I have it, I feel more and more like I am really there. And whatever that thing is that keeps carrying me out of the tunnels. I just can't control it."

Jack's fists were clenched, his body tense. He was sitting at the edge of his seat and breathing heavily.

"Jack, relax," Sandy said as she dropped her pad on the desk. She leaned in and touched his knee. "Try your breathing exercises."

Jack struggled with the suggestion for a moment, then closed his eyes and began breathing methodically. He could hear cars driving past. The scent of lavender filled his nose. He looked into his dark eyelids.

"Good," Sandy said softly. "Let any thoughts come to you then just brush them away with a broom."

He took a couple more breaths. Inhale. Exhale. Inhale. Exhale. Then he saw the building, saw Suzanne running toward him. He opened his eyes.

"There's something else," he said.

Sandy grabbed her pad.

"Suzanne was hurt yesterday. She's in the hospital."

"Suzanne?" Sandy asked. "The tour guide from your dream?"

"Yes, but she's real," Jack replied. "I know her. She was giving a tour yesterday and left the tunnels with burn marks on her arms."

"She was burned? Is there fire in the tunnels?"

"Of course not."

"Then how was she burned?"

"That's just it—nobody knows. And now she's in a coma."

"Oh, my!" Sandy replied. "That's terrible!"

"I can't help but wonder—" Jack stopped himself.

"What is it, Jack?" Sandy pressed.

"No, it's dumb," Jack said.

"Nothing is dumb. Go ahead—tell me."

"My dream... could it have been the same as what happened?"

"Are you suggesting, Jack, that you could have dreamed what happened yesterday before it happened?"

Jack nodded, waiting for her to tell him he was imagining things.

"Perhaps you learned about this before going to bed and dreamt it?" Sandy suggested.

"No, I learned it before coming here. Dr. Moseley…"

"Dr. Moseley—the man who saved you from the Linhurst bomb a couple of years ago?"

It wasn't a bomb—I've told you that a hundred times.

"Yes, that's him," Jack simply replied. "Dr. Moseley is the man who runs the Linhurst Care Center and the tours at Linhurst. He took me and Danny to the place where markings were left on the wall."

"Who's Danny?" Sandy asked, scribbling notes.

"He's in my class at school," Jack replied.

"Danny Slater? The Danny whose dad…"

"Yes," Jack stopped her. "That Danny. He's going to help with security at Linhurst due to all the suspicious activity."

"Now you're telling me that you think you may have dreamed what happened to Suzanne—while it happened?"

"I told you it was dumb."

"I'm just listening, Jack—trying to understand."

"I just think it's really strange that this happened yesterday, then they found…" Jack stopped.

Sandy cocked her head to the side, looking very suspicious of him all of a sudden. She caught his watchful eye and sat up straight.

"What is it?" Sandy said. "Please, go on."

Jack decided not to mention the sun and peace symbol drawing that Mose found. She would surely not believe him—or worse, think he was acting crazy.

"It's just that, well—" Jack looked for the right words to appease her. "I think the whole thing is interesting, but I don't think it has much to do with me. It is not my concern or my blame. Just a coincidence."

Sandy clapped her hands together in excitement. A huge smile formed on her face. "Yes, Jack! That's it!"

He knew that would get her off the topic.

"You see, these things are out of your control. You can't prevent these things from happening. You aren't to blame for your mother's passing just like you couldn't stop what happened to those unfortunate people at Linhurst. Just like you have nothing to do with what happened to the tour guide. These are all unrelated circumstances out of your control, Jack, and you are needlessly worrying yourself over them." She clapped her hands together in excitement again. "This is progress, Jack—you are letting go of these old ideas and theories."

She reached out a hand and rubbed his arm. Jack smiled, fraudulently, but enough for her to buy it.

"Can we talk about my college plans now?" Jack said, hoping to get her off the subject.

"Yes, we sure can!" Sandy replied and began telling him about her time studying psychology in college. Sandy loved to talk about her days in school, and Jack knew she could easily burn up a half hour going on about it.

She went on and on, and Jack was only listening enough to solicit a one word reply or facial gesture occasionally.

He began to think about the dream and what he learned from Dr. Moseley. Who had left the drawing of the sun and peace symbol there in the tunnels? What about the burn marks? Suzanne? The man with her?

Sure enough, Sandy went on and on. Eventually, she checked the clock above her desk to see that it was five minutes past five.

"Well, look at that, a whole hour gone!" Sandy smiled broadly. She opened her top desk drawer, slid the notepad inside, then closed her laptop.

She stood up and opened the door. Jack pushed himself out of the overstuffed chair and picked up his bag, slinging it over his shoulder.

"I really think you are on your way to more self-understanding and care, Jack," Sandy said as he approached the door. "You can soon begin to let go of these dreams and take action—you are the only one who can stop this."

Jack panicked for an instant—it was the same thing Suzanne said to him in his dream. Sandy looked at him in surprise, and Jack realized she knew the look on his face.

"What is it?" Sandy asked nervously.

"N-nothing," Jack replied. "It's that—I have to be home for dinner!"

He gave Sandy a short smile, then ducked out of the room and made for the screen door out onto the porch.

"See you Monday!" she called after him.

He gave her a quick wave then raced blindly toward the sidewalk.

Free at last! He no sooner felt a great sense of relief and freedom that he looked up to see his dad sitting in the PT Cruiser right in front of him.

"Figured I would give you a ride home today," Henry called through the open passenger window.

Jack growled under his breath. *Why can't he just leave me alone?!* Jack was about to say "no" when he heard a voice calling his name. He looked down the sidewalk to see Lisa Lexington and her friend Marcy leaving Collin's Stop & Shop. Jack quickly opened the car door and jumped in.

"You're welcome to walk with your friends if you would rather do that," Henry said, motioning to the girls waving to him down the street.

Jack was red in the face. After all these years, he still hadn't found the nerve to ask Lisa out—or even talk to her really. Then again, she did have a boyfriend—Dan Driver, star quarterback of the Rams football team and homecoming king—even if they were off and on. Regardless, he felt like she probably thought he was crazy these days, too.

"Let's go home, Dad," Jack said glumly, hating his life.

"You got it, bud," Henry replied.

As they drove past Lisa and Marcy, Jack gave a sheepish wave but wouldn't look at the girls. He was far too ashamed of himself.

As they pulled in through the front gate to the Linhurst campus, Jack noticed a couple of maintenance workers filling in the deep skid marks Danny had left earlier that day.

They approached the Linhurst Care Center when an older woman driving a large brown Chevy began to slowly pull out of the first handicapped spot near the front entrance. Henry slowed to a stop to wait for her.

"Good thing we aren't in a hurry," Henry scoffed.

As Jack watched the little old woman—who could barely see over the steering wheel quadruple the size of her head—his attention was diverted to the entrance doors opening. Mose left the care center hurriedly, carrying a briefcase and jacket. *Must be going to see Suzanne.*

Just then, Mayor Helowski blasted out from the lobby, chasing after Dr. Moseley.

"This will be good for the whole town, Charles," Mayor Helowski exclaimed.

"You have said this too many times before," Mose replied.

"This is different," Mayor Helowski replied. "This would free us from their grip."

"Don't think that's any of our business, Jack," Henry said. Jack just shrugged.

"The power we generate is only enough for the property," Mose said. "You just can not provide for the entire town with it!"

"Charles, listen to reason," Mayor Helowski replied pleadingly.

"I have listened," Mose said, infuriated. "But since I know you will do what you want anyway, what more can I say? Take our power! Take all you want and you'll see for yourself!"

"Charles, please," Mayor Helowski repeated, following Mose to his pickup.

"I'm done with this conversation," Mose said. "I have a sick employee I need to go see. You phone me when Spring Dale's power shuts down and we can restart this conversation."

Mayor Helowski and Dr. Moseley disappeared around the side of the building where his pickup was always parked.

"Finally!" Henry exclaimed.

Jack saw the elderly woman smiling brightly from behind the giant steering wheel as she drove past them and Henry continued up the road.

The generating station was dark inside as usual. Just inside, the fusion reactor sat unseen, humming away deep inside a brick wall facade, surrounded by iron walls that only Mose and a few others knew about. After learning about the conspiracy to store nuclear waste deep down in the tunnels of Linhurst, Mose kept a tight lid on the reactor project. He wanted to be sure the people of Linhurst were not taken advantage of ever again, but it seemed like things were suddenly heading down the wrong road.

"I wonder if we'll ever learn more about this reactor?" Henry said, responding to the conversation they overheard. "Why don't we fully understand what makes it work?"

"All I know is Mose has been working on it," said Jack.

"Well, he's a good man," Henry replied. "If anyone can make sure things are safe and sound here, it's Dr. Moseley."

* * * * *

All was eerily quiet by 9:30 that night when Jack was finishing the last of his homework under the soft glow of his desk lamp in an otherwise darkened room. He tapped out the last sentence of his AP Physics paper, saved and closed the doc, and shut down his laptop.

He stretched his arms out long over his head and took in a deep breath that was followed by an uncontrollable yawn. He ambled into the bathroom and brushed his teeth, then returned to his room and flicked off the desk lamp.

Just as he was ready to hit the bed, green light filled his room for an instant.

Jack's mind went into a tizzy. His thoughts raced back to the time he and Celia were riding their bikes fast along the cracked road entering Linhurst, wanting to learn more about the once-abandoned property in an attempt to unravel the mystery of the green flashes of light and underground rumblings. He remembered standing right in front of the darkened generating station, slipping inside an abandoned Building C. He remembered all the peeling paint and busted floorboards. He remembered Mose's daughter Heather appearing in spirit form over a wheelchair, then the flashes of green light flying around the reactor. He remembered his mother appearing from out of the sun and peace symbol in the amulet around his neck. "I will be here for you always," she said to him one last time. Then an explosion of green light.

Jack shook his head to come to. He looked around his darkened room and regained awareness of his surroundings.

"What was that?" he whispered aloud.

Another flash of green light filled his room. It was coming in through his window.

"I know I'm not imagining that."

Another flash.

"Where is that coming from?"

Jack pulled his light gray bathrobe off the hook on his door and tied the belt snugly around his waist. He slipped on his sneakers, grabbed a flashlight and was in the hall outside their apartment in seconds.

He tiptoed quickly down the hallway, dashed down the stairs to the first floor, then ran through the lobby and out onto the front porch.

The half moon overhead cast enough light to see out into the courtyard where the water trickled softly from the fountain—the only sound to be heard over the frogs croaking and the crickets singing nearby.

He stood still for a few more minutes, his sweaty palms and fingers tightly braced the flashlight in his pocket. His thumb gently circled the button on the handle, ready to pull it out and flick it on at a moment's notice.

He stood there for a few minutes, waiting for another flash of light—but none came.

This is stupid. What am I doing standing out here in the middle of the night? It's just my imagination again. No wonder they all think I'm crazy.

He let go of the flashlight inside his robe pocket and wiped his sweaty palm on the soft material. He listened to the sound of the fountain trickling and remembered his breathing exercises. Deep inhale. Slow exhale.

Just your imagination. You were working too late and got worked up about nothing.

Just then—a flash of green light. Jack opened his eyes and yanked the flashlight out of his pocket, then pointed it toward the woods. Another flash. It was far off, deep inside the overgrown forest.

He flicked on his flashlight and began to walk in the direction of the flash.

Chapter 5

Jack couldn't believe his eyes.

Am I actually seeing green flashes of light again, or am I dreaming and don't know it?

If it was true, he wished Sandy was there to witness it—surely then she wouldn't think he was just making things up.

He stepped down off the front porch and slowly began walking around the outside of the courtyard pavement. His eyes and flashlight were fixed on the deep dark woods ahead. As Jack moved forward slowly, he could suddenly feel the entirety of his surroundings at his back.

A great mass of fear instantly engulfed him like a cold wet blanket. He turned around and took in the scene—Buildings A through C surrounded him, the starry sky overhead, the dark blue ground laid out in front of him, barely illuminated by the half moon above.

He was alone, standing in a courtyard where only two years ago, the buildings were silent and dark for an altogether different reason other than that everyone was fast asleep.

Another flash of green light blast from behind him. When he turned to point his flashlight at it, he noticed a path winding through the woods like a babbling brook. He pointed his light down along the trail to see it was made of cobblestone. Leaves blew gently across the walkway toward him, almost inviting him to take the first step.

Jack cautiously put out a foot and stepped onto the path. Just then, a blast of wind hit him hard, and he closed his eyes against it. When he reopened them, it was bright outside and he squinted against the harshness of the sun shining down upon him.

Once his eyes adjusted to the light, he looked around to see Buildings A through C were much different than they had been only moments before. The brick exterior of the buildings was a much deeper red, each brick looking as though it was freshly laid that day. The sidewalks were a brighter shade of gray and in pristine condition. The trees surrounding each building were far shorter, and there was no fountain in the courtyard.

I am definitely dreaming this. But this dream was entirely new to him, that much was certain.

"Come with me, Bill," a man's voice called out. Jack looked

for the source and found a middle-aged man walking from an old green Chevrolet. The man had a kindly face and was wearing a wonderfully campy sweater. He carried an old physician's bag Jack recognized immediately, though it was in much better condition than he recalled.

"Dr. Royer," Jack whispered in awe. It was the same Dr. Royer who had been a family physician in Spring Dale for many years until his passing that summer. He had also been a doctor at Linhurst for decades, and—most importantly to Jack—his own family's doctor, who saw his mother through her final months.

"We'll go see what's going on with your medications," Dr. Royer said as he approached another man, who looked to be in his twenties, wearing mostly winter attire—even though the sun was shining brightly, and it was quite warm.

The man named Bill approached Dr. Royer and began talking up a storm as the pair made their way toward Jack.

"I ain't been feelin' right, no matter what they do," Bill told Dr. Royer.

Jack immediately realized it was a very young Bill Williams.

"Don't make no matter to me anyways," Bill continued, "I ain't got nowhere to be."

"I understand, Bill, but if things aren't set right, you just won't be yourself," said Dr. Royer. "Let's make sure we get you feeling better."

Jack couldn't understand why he would be having this dream. It was so vivid and real, everything bright and colorful. The buildings, the trees, the flowers in the field beyond were alive and flourishing. His dreams were never this realistic before. But to be dreaming about Dr. Royer and Bill Williams from long ago just didn't make sense to him.

"You look lost, young man," Dr. Royer said as he and Bill were only feet away.

Jack turned to look for the person Dr. Royer was addressing, but there was no one else around. He turned back to the pair, and they were right in front of him.

"Why don't you come with us?" Dr. Royer asked. He appeared to be staring directly at Jack.

"Who... me?" Jack replied dumbly, not expecting to be heard.

"Yes, of course you, my boy—who else would I be talking to?!" Dr. Royer laughed.

He looked Jack over then reached out his hand to him. Jack mindlessly began to reciprocate, and Dr. Royer gently pulled the flashlight from Jack's tight grip and tucked it inside his medical bag.

"Won't be needing this, now, will we?" Dr. Royer said apprehensively, while motioning toward the bright sky overhead.

Dr. Royer locked arms with Jack. "Come with us, young man, and we'll see where you are supposed to be."

Jack was confused at first but quickly realized that, with the way he was dressed in his gray bathrobe, white pajama pants, and white sneakers—and how he was standing in broad daylight in the middle of the residential buildings with a lit flashlight in hand—he must have looked rather out of place. He made no attempt to pull away and walked along with Dr. Royer and Bill, ever curious of where they were heading.

They climbed the winding cobblestone path up a short hill with a few magnolia and elm trees along either side. The campus was noticeably less dense, trees and shrubs planted with intention, a great deal of finely manicured and open lawn.

The end of the path opened up to a road where a late model black pickup truck was passing. In the bed of the truck, looking out over wooden rails, was a small crew of men in matching gray work clothes and overalls. A few gave a wave; others kept their heads down. The bed of the truck was filled with hay and tools. Jack immediately remembered the spirits at the generating station and how they were dressed the same.

They must be working residents.

Down the road, Jack could see the generating station, looking pristine and in fine condition. Every window was intact and reflecting the bright blue sky above, a nearly cloudless day. Jack watched a flock of small birds fly to the base of the smokestack that was pushing out a vertical stream of dark smoke.

Just ahead was a building like every other on the Linhurst campus—constructed of solid red brick and with many windows and arches. Only this building looked much healthier than any of the unrenovated buildings on campus. A red cross marked a sign to the right of the door.

The infirmary.

They waited for an old car to pass and crossed the road, Dr. Royer hanging on tight to his newfound stranger, Bill Williams shuffling closely behind.

Down the front sidewalk, up the short run of steps, and through the grand double doors of the infirmary, Jack found himself inside a brightly lit lobby. Dr. Royer walked him to the dark wood check-in window where there was a nurse, dressed all in white and wearing a nurse's cap. She greeted Dr. Royer with a wonderful smile.

"How are you, my lass?" Dr. Royer called to her. "I hope that husband of yours has been treating you well. Have you two any lively trips planned of late?"

"Oh, Dr. Royer—you know Larry!" she exclaimed. "Too busy down at the firm to think of doing anything fun. I'll get him thinking, you'll see!"

"You two always go to the nicest places—Rome, Paris, London, San Diego." The nurse chuckled. "Is Nancy in?"

"You can head on back." The nurse's smile faded suddenly when she caught sight of Jack. "Oh, uh… Dr. Royer… who is this?"

"That's just what I'm going to find out," Dr. Royer replied confidently.

The nurse nodded, looking Jack over nervously.

Dr. Royer pulled on Jack's arm, and they moved ahead toward a set of double wooden doors. Bill followed as they went through to a long hallway, painted a pale green and looking sterile. Jack noticed how different it was from Linhurst Care Center, with few paintings or pictures on the walls. At the far end of the hall hung a large bronze sun sculpture, staring demonically at them as they approached. The lights flickered every few seconds, some of the bulbs in need of replacement.

Jack spied inside the rooms as they passed. Each was a very outdated hospital room with a bed, chair, and the standard equipment like blood pressure checker and scales.

What was unusual about each room were the people inside—whether man or woman, young or old, Jack couldn't help but notice a shared look of listlessness. Some sat twiddling their fingers while others rocked back and forth melodically. In one room, a man was flailing his arms violently while the nurse and an orderly brute of a man attempted to restrain him.

Dr. Royer stopped at the next door. It was closed, with a window panel in the top half reading, *Nancy Maloney*, M.D. Dr. Royer tapped on the window and a woman with pitch-black flowing hair and a thin frame soon answered the door. She was dressed all in white, from her long jacket to her pants and shoes. The room was filled with cigarette smoke.

"Come in, Don," she said. "Who's this?"

"I'm taking him down the hall after we get Bill squared away," Dr. Royer replied.

They entered the room, and Nancy closed the door.

"I have to keep the smoke in here," she said. "They've been complaining, saying smoking is bad for your health. More ridiculous studies."

She went around the opposite side of her desk and pushed out a lit cigarette that was lingering in a matte black ashtray. She began to cough and, for a few seconds, hacked and hacked until she caught her breath.

"What's going on, Bill?" she asked loudly, as if he was deaf.

Then she looked at his clothing. "Aren't you warm wearing all that?"

He shook his head adamantly and she scoffed at him. Though she was accustomed to seeing him in it, she acted like he was nuts.

"Bill hasn't been feeling himself, Nancy—been making comments and acting out of sorts lately," Dr. Royer replied for Bill. "I think we need to increase a few things."

Nancy eyed up Bill then looked back to Dr. Royer. She turned to a cabinet behind her desk, pulled out a box, and placed it on her desk. The scraggly doctor gently lifted a few of the bottles from the box and set them on her desk, then popped open the tops.

"No problem. I'll take care of it." She came around to the front of her desk and pushed out a chair. "Sit," she commanded Bill. He took a seat and began to fidget in his chair.

"I'll check back in a few," Dr. Royer said.

"Don't even need that long," Nancy replied.

Dr. Royer nodded, then tugged on Jack's arm and led him out of the room. They turned and started down the hall toward the sun sculpture.

In the direction they walked, Jack began to hear screams and moaning that echoed down the hallway behind them. It sounded as if someone was being tortured. Jack tried to pull away and look around, but Dr. Royer tugged him forward.

"Keep moving please," Dr. Royer said. "Nothing you need to be concerned about, son."

They reached the last room at the end of the hall just beside the bronze sun, and Dr. Royer stopped in the doorway. Jack determined that the screams were coming from behind thick oak door.

"I told you, I've had enough of this!" a man's voice shouted.

"You've had enough, have you?!" another man hollered back.

"You can't keep doing this," said the first man.

"Oh, I can't, huh?!" replied the second. "And who's going to stop me?"

"You know it's not right."

"Maybe by your standards."

"By anyone's standards!"

"This is how you keep things under control."

"This is how you mistreat people!"

"He would have done it again!"

"You don't know that—just talk to him!"

"Once a criminal, always a criminal."

"That's how you see things. But we are not a prison. We are here to help people!"

"You fool! This was never about anything more than getting these retards off the streets and out of eyesight!"

"That's what your parents taught you. Things are different now. We need to correct that thinking."

"Nothing is different, John. These imbeciles don't belong in society with the rest of us, and you know it."

"That's just not true, Eric. Please understand that we can do better."

"That's Thomson and Slater," Jack mumbled.

"That's right, son," Dr. Royer replied. "They'll help you get to where you want to be."

"This retard is trying to court another retard," Slater bellowed. "It's happening on our watch, and I'm going to make sure this is the last of it."

"Eric, you've lost your mind! We must stop this!"

Dr. Royer, who had been nervously listening, rapped on the door.

"Who is it?" Slater bellowed.

"It's Dr. Royer," he replied. "I have someone here for you."

Jack could hear muffled conversation for a moment, then the door swung open wildly. The face on the other side immediately sent chills down Jack's spine.

"Mr. Slater, I found this boy wandering the campus by Building A," Dr. Royer began. "Perhaps you know where he belongs?"

It was Coach Eric Slater. Only he was much younger looking and not the Spring Dale High School coach. He looked very brutish and ever terrifying, his face bright red, likely from all the screaming. He was dressed in an ill-fitting brown plaid suit. Though there was a bit more hair on the top of his head, his bristly mustache was just as thick.

"John," Slater bellowed across the room behind him. "Who is this kid?"

Slater opened the door all the way to reveal a very young Principal John Thomson standing in the middle of the room. He was blotting the bloodied face of a large man in his late teens who was wrapped tightly in a straitjacket, seated on a long table covered in white paper. He had bruises on his face that looked rather fresh.

Thomson looked up from his work and spied Jack from a distance.

"Can't say I know him." The young Thomson glared at Jack as if he was sure he had seen his face but couldn't quite place it. Jack looked down at his feet quickly, averting Thomson's gaze.

"Take him to admin," Slater bellowed. "They'll know what to do with him."

Dr. Royer nodded, then hesitated. He was staring at the young man seated on the table. He took in a deep breath. "What exactly is the meaning of what we are seeing here?" the friendly physician pronounced bravely, motioning toward the beaten and bound man.

Thomson stopped blotting the bleeding bruises on the young man's face. Slater turned to Dr. Royer and grew purple as a plum.

"This is none of your business, Don," Slater growled in a low voice.

"I'm just telling you I agree with John, you cannot keep doing this," Dr. Royer said, maintaining his bravery, though his voice cracked and trembled. "People are beginning to talk."

"Let them talk!" Slater hollered. "It's none of their business either. They have no idea what this boy did."

"And what exactly did this boy…this man… do to deserve this kind of awful treatment?" Dr. Royer demanded firmly.

"This retard is trying to screw another patient!" Slater shouted back.

"What crime is this?" asked Dr. Royer. "He's an adult."

Thomson laid the wet towel on the table by the young man and raced over to address the situation. Up close, Jack couldn't believe how much different Thomson looked—his hair fuller and darker, his eyes brighter and more innocent.

"Eric, let it go," Thomson said calmly. He placed his hand on Slater's shoulder, but he shrugged it off immediately.

"This boy comes here demanding equality for himself and his friends, but he's got nothing," Slater said to Dr. Royer, ignoring Thomson's plea. "We gave him a home when his mama didn't want him. We gave him work—a purpose. What he asks for in return is to get in the sack with another of them or be freed of this place. How is any of that possible? He wouldn't make it one day outside of Linhurst even if we allowed it."

The young man looked sinister and innocent all at once. The restraints added a tinge of horror to Jack's view of things.

"He was getting a little out of hand," said Thomson to Dr. Royer. "We wouldn't ordinarily throw someone into a straitjacket if there wasn't cause for concern. You have nothing to worry about." He turned to Jack, who knew he looked rather upset. "You are safe here."

"He was asking for it," Slater interjected, pointing to the man on the table. "I'll throw him into the tunnels if he keeps it up!"

At that, the man began to throw himself around violently on the table. He rocked side to side then tossed himself off the table and came running full sprint toward them. Midway across the room in a flash, he freed himself from the jacket, his arms flailing about, the lengths of the sleeves flying all around his head and body.

"King!" Slater bellowed. "Sit down!"

"Eric, stop him!" Thomson yelped.

"*Now* you want me to do something?" Eric shouted incredulously at Thomson, then gave him a great shove, tossing him back a few feet.

Slater moved into a defensive position, squatting down and putting his arms out in preparation for the oncoming assailant, who was charging for the burly coach at full speed.

Slater leaned into the blow that was about to come, and sure enough King—who appeared twice the height of Slater—engulfed the husky man in a tight grip and began to carry him toward the doorway, full steam ahead at Jack and Dr. Royer.

Dr. Royer grabbed hold of Jack and threw him down to the floor, out of harm's way. Everything went dark all of a sudden. Jack could hear screaming and punching, and bodies wrestling on the floor around him.

"Jack!" a voice called out, echoing from far off.

Jack shook his head and began to see light again. Everything around him was a blur. A blinding light was searing into his eyes, piercing through his skull.

"Jack, it's me!" the voice called. "Wake up!"

Jack rubbed his eyes and looked around again to see that he was lying on the front steps of Building C, the half-moon gazing down at him amid a landscape of stars. He looked down to see he had gotten himself tangled up in his bathrobe, his flashlight lying next to him and still brightly lit.

He looked up to see a blurry Dr. Moseley standing over him, his hand outstretched. Jack grabbed hold of it and was pulled to his feet.

He looked around, regaining consciousness, and saw the fountain peacefully trickling water, the frogs still chirping their evening song.

"Are you all right, Jack?" Dr. Moseley asked gently.

"I suppose," Jack replied, still in a haze. "What time is it?"

"It's almost two in the morning," Mose replied.

"I've been out here for over two hours?" Jack replied.

"If you say so—I just found you," said Mose.

"How did you know I was out here?" Jack asked.

"I didn't," Mose said. "I was heading home from the hospital and saw a figure running around the woods. I tried to get your attention, but you took off toward Building C here before I was able to wake you."

Jack looked around again to get his bearings, then became suddenly dizzy. He fell to the concrete stairs with a thud.

"Are you all right?" Mose called out nervously, then knelt beside him.

"I just saw Slater and Thomson," Jack said weakly.

"Slater and Thomson? That's impossible, Jack. Where could you have seen them?"

"Not here," Jack replied, rubbing his aching head. "Well, I suppose it was here—only it was long ago."

"I'm not following you," said Mose.

Jack explained to Dr. Moseley what he had experienced—from the flashing green light to the encounter with Dr. Royer and Bill Williams to the room where Slater and Thomson held the young man captive.

"That's when you woke me, I suppose," Jack finished his tale.

"You said they called him King?" Mose asked.

"Yes, that is what I heard," Jack said. "Could it be the same King we saw in the tunnels two years ago?"

"If so, it is most troubling," Mose said glumly. "Come, let's get some rest. We'll begin tomorrow."

"Begin what?" Jack asked, confused.

"I'll tell you more after you've had rest," Mose replied.

He helped Jack to his feet and took him inside Building C.

Chapter 6

Jack awoke in a cold sweat, same as every other day lately. His nightmare returned as usual.

He was carried out of the building buried deep in the woods, and Suzanne ran past him followed by the unidentified man with the briefcase. This time, he looked for burn marks on the retreating duo but couldn't find any—at least not on quick glance just before he woke.

His blankets were thrown to the floor at his bedside. He'd had trouble clearing his mind after Mose walked him back to his apartment and said good night, but he now realized he had been in a deep sleep after all.

He looked at the clock on his bedside table—6:43. He had an entire hour to get ready for school.

Jack laid back down, his head settling into the cold wet pillow. He thought about the experience of walking with Dr. Royer and Bill Williams. *Was it a dream? Did I fall asleep outside and not realize it? Was this related to the same nightmare inside the tunnels? What does Mose want to start on today?*

He sat up, unable to bear the dampness of his sweat-soaked pillow against his neck. He made his way into the bathroom and began running a hot shower. Staring at himself in the mirror, he wondered what was happening to him. Why was he having these nightmares—these visions?

He stripped down and stepped into the shower, and pulled the curtain shut. The water running over him was immediately comforting. He closed his eyes and began the breathing exercises that Sandy encouraged him to do whenever he was feeling overwhelmed. His mind and body were so worn down he felt he hadn't slept in weeks.

His mind drifted to the drawing left behind in the tunnels. The sun and peace symbol was sketched out perfectly to his memory. *Who left it there just lying on the dirt-covered floor of the tunnels? Was it just some Linhurst fanatic who saw the symbol in a photograph?* It was, in fact, clearly emblazoned on Linhurst signs these days, but few knew what it meant. Suzanne certainly didn't mention it on her tour. As far as Jack knew, only Mose, Henry, and Celia really understood its meaning. That very symbol was on the necklace Jack had once worn every day before it disappeared inside the generating station along with the ghostly figure of his mother.

He stepped out of the shower and dried off, then checked the time—7:00. Still plenty of time to waste.

Jack dressed for school and grabbed his backpack, then started down the hall past his dad's room. Henry's door was closed. *Still fast asleep*, Jack assumed. He grabbed a breakfast bar from the kitchen cabinet and headed out.

Jack arrived at the care center and went around the side where Mose parked his truck. The parking spot was empty. He went back around to the front of the building and stood facing the generating station, then pulled out his phone. He brought up Dr. Moseley's contact info and was about to call him when a rustling in the woods caught his attention. He looked toward the sound to see a couple of squirrels chasing one another around the trees by the generating station.

That's when Jack realized he hadn't paid much attention to the generating station these days. Mose deliberately left the building looking rather dilapidated in hopes of dissuading trespassers. Shattered windows were replaced on the lower levels and upper levels, and some of the overgrowth had been cut away, but Mose allowed most of the ivy to climb the walls. He also hung a large red sign with yellow lettering on the entrance doors that read, *Employees Only: Keep Out.*

Having the care center built directly across the street was partly intentional so that Mose would have easy access to the fusion reactor that sat unsuspectingly beyond, pumping out power to the campus day in and out.

Even the contractors hired to fortify the internal structure were given the most basic details on what they were housing. And everyone from the media to local politicians to those with morbid curiosity were simply told that the structure was deemed unsafe and that vast funding and planning were needed in order to determine the future of the building. Only Jack and a handful of others really knew the great power that lie beyond the walls—or so they had hoped.

Jack's attention was diverted again when he heard a car rolling down the road. He looked to see Dr. Moseley's old blue pickup truck approaching.

"I had a feeling you'd be up early," Mose said as he pulled up. "Hop in... I want to show you something."

Jack ran around the truck and jumped into the passenger's seat and they were off.

Mose took Jack up the road and past Buildings A through C, then down a road construction vehicles had recently traveled heavily as they worked to clear out an area of old buildings on campus.

They bumped along the uneven pavement through the overgrown woods, past a series of buildings resembling the renovated buildings A, B, and C. Jack hadn't been in this section of Linhurst since he and Celia explored the campus years ago. He was aware that work was being done, thanks to the sounds of construction equipment roaring loudly. It was made clear in monthly newsletters that residents of Linhurst Gardens keep out of the area due to safety concerns, both from the large equipment being used and from health hazards caused by asbestos removal.

Piles of dirt and construction debris sat outside each building. The windows and doors were removed from each of the buildings, leaving only a shell with darkness beyond.

Mose continued past the buildings and drove to the front of the administration building, then came to a stop.

"I'm sure you remember this building," Mose said. Jack nodded. "This was the hub of the original Linhurst campus, the place where the administrative employees worked and patients were checked in. Ever since word spread about the renewal effort, folks from all around have had their eyes set on this property, and all kinds of proposals have been made to revamp the campus. A recent deal was made without my knowledge to convert this building into a Halloween attraction."

"Like a haunted house or something?" Jackasked.

"Exactly," said Mose. "Things are pretty quiet still, but I guarantee you that in no time word will spread quickly about this attraction—and people will not be happy about it."

"How did this happen?" Jack asked.

"Mayor Helowski worked with developers from a nationwide entertainment group to help bring tourism to Spring Dale," said Mose. "Helowski thought it would be a great space for it and agreed to it without hesitation. But he's been making a lot of foolish deals lately, in my opinion."

"How could he do this?" Jack said. "Why wouldn't he come to you first?"

"I've been so focused on the care center it seems he felt I didn't need to be involved," said Mose. "That's neither here nor there at this point. The bigger concern is how this will affect what's been going on recently and how to slow things down."

"Do you mean the vandalism?" Jack asked.

"The vandalism, the mysterious writing, the drawing I found," said Mose. "But these visions you've been having—I've been experiencing them, too."

"You've been having dreams?" Jack asked excitedly. For once, he didn't feel alone.

"Dreams. Visions. You name it," Mose said. "I thought maybe I was just overworked. But when you first told me about the repeated nightmare you've had and what you went through last night, I knew immediately it couldn't be a coincidence."

"What kind of dreams are you having?" Jack asked.

"Very similar to yours," Mose said. "Very disconcerting."

Mose provided Jack no details about his dreams. Jack didn't press.

"What do you think is causing this?" Jack asked.

"I'm not sure," Mose said. "My best guess is that whatever we went through the night the reactor came to life has stayed with us somehow. And I think Linhurst is reacting to all this new activity."

"I don't understand," Jack replied.

"We witnessed something truly remarkable," said Mose. "Unprecedented, perhaps. We saw spirits—ghosts—from all over this campus come to life and bring power to the reactor. It's been running without failure ever since, and I don't know how to explain that. I still don't know how it works. I just know it works—until recently."

"The reactor stopped working?" Jack panicked.

"Not quite," Mose said. "It is still providing power to the

campus, but I just learned that Mayor Helowski is pushing power from the generating station to the town. I think it's been a drag on the system."

"He did all this without you knowing?" Jack asked incredulously.

"I've been too busy to keep him honest," Mose said.

"What does this have to do with the administration building?" Jack asked.

"For every new building set up on this campus, there will be a demand for power," Mose began. "If we don't understand how the reactor is functioning, how can we determine the extent of its output? It will get to a point where we not only won't be able to power Linhurst Gardens and the care center, we also will have some explaining to do when it comes to the source of the energy to begin with."

"I thought you were applying for a patent?" Jack said.

Mose chuckled. "Another tricky situation—we can't patent something if our only explanation for how it works is that ghosts fired it up, and it's been running ever since."

"What can we do about it?" Jack asked.

"I think the dreams and visions we have been having are connected to the spiritual energy of this campus," said Mose. "It's as if those who remain here are trying to tell us something."

"Yes, they are—they want us to get out," Jack replied resolutely.

"I think you're right," said Mose. "But we can't simply abandon the work we've done. The Linhurst Care Center was established to begin righting the wrongs of those before us."

"How do we get to the bottom of these dreams?" Jack asked.

"I've hired a team of paranormal investigators to come and explore the remaining buildings on campus where we have yet to begin renovating," said Mose. "Especially where Suzanne had her experience and the building with the words burned into the wall. I fear that all the work that's being done is disrupting some underlying energy we must come to an agreement with."

Jack paused to reflect. After so many months of meeting with Sandy to come to terms with his other-worldly experiences, it was a lot to imagine that he would reverse any of his thinking and consider that he hadn't been imagining all these things.

He stared up at the administration building looming against the early morning sun. It sat quietly, undisturbed for decades. It was hard to consider that someday in the near future, it would be inviting haunted house thrill seekers from all around.

"There's one more thing," Mose said, interrupting Jack's thoughts. "I visited our tour guide, Suzanne, last night in the hospital. Her condition has improved. The burn marks have mysteriously disappeared. But her mind is still in disarray. She is trying to piece together her experience in the tunnels—it's all very overwhelming for her."

"Does she remember what happened?" Jack asked.

"Not quite," Mose replied. "She recalls starting the tour, then arriving at the care center with the burn marks on her arm, but nothing in between. And she admitted something very disturbing to me."

Jack swallowed hard and stared wide-eyed at Dr. Moseley.

"The tour she was giving was for a fellow from the nuclear power plant," said Mose. "He's from their research and development department."

Jack quickly recalled the trouble with Principal Thomson and Coach Slater working out a deal to store nuclear waste in the tunnels before their arrest.

"Are they trying to store their waste again?" Jack asked.

"Not this time," said Mose. "He wants to know what powers our campus, so he tricked her into giving a tour. I asked Suzanne for the man's name and contact information, but she couldn't recall when I spoke with her. She was still rattled. I have a call into the power plant for someone in that department to get back to me. If he had a similar experience, he must be in bad shape. We must get to the bottom of this. It's very troubling." Mose checked his wristwatch. "I'll drive you to school today."

He started up the truck and made his way around the circular drive in front of the administration building. Jack took one last long look at the building. He could almost picture the lines of visitors being spooked by people dressed as crazed and frantic mental patients, covered in fake blood and with scars and masks—a disgusting display to disgrace the memory of the tragedies at Linhurst.

Mose and Jack pulled up in front of Spring Dale High School with ten minutes to spare before the first bell.

"Are you okay hanging out for a bit?" Mose asked. "I need to get back to the center."

"No worries." Jack nodded and hopped out of the pickup with his backpack.

"Come see me after school, would you?" Mose said.

Jack nodded again and shut the door, then Mose smiled and was off.

As he made his way up the front sidewalk, Jack noticed a few other students arriving early—including Celia. She turned and made eye contact with him for a moment, then quickly looked away and continued toward the entrance.

"Celia, wait up!" Jack called to her. She stopped but didn't turn as he raced to her side. "Please don't be mad at me."

She turned slowly and he saw a mixed look of concern, anger, and confusion on her face.

"I'm sorry," he said gently. "You know I haven't been myself lately." He paused to consider his words. *Who am I anymore?*

"You didn't call or text or even wait for me yesterday," Celia replied glumly.

"I know," said Jack. "It's just that when I left school, I needed to be alone. Then Danny Slater gave me a ride."

"Slater! You got a ride from Danny Slater?"

"He offered, and I tried to refuse. He wouldn't have it. He was looking for a job at Linhurst."

"Doing what?" Celia was incredulous.

"He wants to do security for Mose."

"His dad is responsible for how those poor people were treated—he doesn't belong at Linhurst after that."

"He seems to want to make things right—or at least hold down a decent job."

"How can you trust him after all we've been through with him?" said Celia.

"I guess I just have a feeling about it," Jack replied.

"I have a feeling about it, too, and it's not good." Celia grimaced, then grinned. "Well, I guess you owe me another apology if it doesn't work out."

Jack grinned back, then sighed. "Listen, there's a lot going on at Linhurst now. Some weird things. Something's not right."

"Jack, I've been meaning to tell you something," Celia replied carefully. Jack looked her over nervously. She began twiddling her fingers and shuffling her feet.

"Celia, you can tell me, you know," Jack comforted her.

"I've been having dreams, too," she said.

"You have?" Jack replied, far too excitedly.

"You sound happy about it!" Celia exclaimed.

"No, it's not that," said Jack. "I was just with Dr. Moseley, and he says he has been having dreams. He thinks it might have something to do with that night—and this might confirm it."

"I don't know what it's about," Celia said. "I just know I don't like it."

Celia told Jack her dream; she was lost in the tunnels and found herself imprisoned by a strange unseen force.

"Then what happens?" Jack asked.

"I wake up, very suddenly."

Jack thought for a moment. He couldn't help but feel a great unease at the thought that he also had dreams of being trapped in the tunnels.

"I get carried out in my dream," said Jack. "That's the only difference maybe."

"At least you don't get stuck down there," said Celia. "It's terrifying."

"Have you told your folks about it?"

"They would think I was imagining things," Celia said.

Join the club. Jack wouldn't dare say it out loud.

"Come with me after school," said Jack. "I'm going to see Mose."

"What can he do about it? Does he have some special medication for crazy dreams?" Celia asked sarcastically.

"He's very concerned about what's happening and thinks the reactor may be part of this," Jack said. "I'm starting to think these dreams can help somehow."

"All right, I'll go," Celia said. "But I don't want to go through what we went through two years ago."

"I don't either," said Jack. "And I personally think paranormal investigators are full of crap. But what choice do we have? We can't just forget things. It won't let us."

Celia nodded glumly. The bell rang, and suddenly Jack noticed they were surrounded by students rushing past them into the school. Jack and Celia made their way inside, their thoughts riddled with anything but classroom studies.

Chapter 7

"Energy can neither be created nor destroyed—it can only change forms," Mr. Urbach proclaimed.

For once, Jack was like the rest of the class—barely present in the room as the AP Physics teacher energetically danced around the wall-to-wall white board, feverishly writing out notes.

"We won't get into quantum physics too much," Mr. Urbach said, "but consider on such a level the ideas of alternate realities that exist on parallel planes."

Even to Jack, the subject was far too advanced, whether his mind was clear or not. His fellow classmates proved as much: Andy Holcum was doodling a comic strip next to him; Linda Kinney was texting away on her phone, her AP Physics textbook hiding the device from Mr. Urbach; Phil had his head down in his textbook; and Amy was fast asleep inside the pages of hers. Poor Mr. Urbach and his enthusiasm had no willing attendees for the lesson that morning.

"Imagine a portal into another dimension, the thing of movies and other works of fiction," said Mr. Urbach. "Hit pause on reality for a moment and, through this type of thinking, once you consider the ideas that quantum physics provides in this scenario, you might actually see into other universes."

See into other universes? Despite the fact that he was following less than ten percent of Mr. Urbach's thought process, Jack's curiosity was suddenly spurred at the thought of seeing into other universes. He put his hand up.

"Yes, Jack? Question?" Mr. Urbach said.

"Can you apply quantum physics to the paranormal?" Jack asked.

"Paranormal, Jack?" Mr. Urbach asked. "Do you mean… ghosts?"

"Yes, ghosts," Jack proclaimed, ever careful to never utter the word in public.

Just the mention of the word "ghost" and the entire class perked up (aside from Amy who was still fast asleep). Hearing Ghost Boy use that word had everyone suddenly paying attention.

"Well, I haven't given it too much thought," Mr. Urbach hesitated, "but it's entirely plausible to consider the relation between quantum physics and the paranormal."

Mr. Urbach set his dry erase marker down on the ledge of the white board and approached Jack, a look of careful consideration in his eyes. Jack knew his wily science teacher was well aware of the experience he had at Linhurst, but he was hopeful Mr. Urbach would be more interested in helping him explore the realities of that night rather than question his sanity.

"When someone passes away, there's a question of where the energy from that person goes," said Mr. Urbach. "Religions teach us many things about the subject. Christians, for instance, hold that a person passes on to heaven, but where exactly is heaven? Others believe in reincarnation, where perhaps the energy is constantly returned to other beings in different forms."

Students in the class listened intently. *Is Mr. Urbach suddenly going to teach a course on religion?*

"Some people who experience something traumatic enough to die for a short period of time claim to have seen a white light and crossed over to another dimension or another world," said Mr. Urbach. "Where did they go? Was it in their mind, like a dream?"

"Or could they have seen into a parallel world?" Jack replied.

"Precisely," Mr. Urbach said. "It's possible. When you consider theories behind dark matter and quantum physics and the like, is it possible that other worlds are seeing into alternate dimensions—a quantum shift?"

Jack nodded, thinking carefully. The students were leaning in, awaiting his next words.

"Then is it possible to experience that kind of crossing over without actually dying?" Jack asked. "Like, could it happen in dreams or just, I don't know, out of nowhere?"

"Do you feel as though this type of occurrence is familiar to your experiences, Jack?" Mr. Urbach asked cautiously. "Are you, I suppose, crossing over?"

Students in the class shifted in their seats, their attention squarely, and uncomfortably, on Jack. They awaited more words with great anticipation; he could feel it.

"I… it was just…" He looked around the room. Every eye was on him. The pressure built. He could feel the sweat forming on his forehead, his palms following closely behind. "It was just something you said made me think of." Jack ended the conversation awkwardly.

Mr. Urbach could see that he'd put Jack on the spot. Frozen in place just feet from Jack's desk, he shifted his eyes around the room at the students staring coldly at Jack.

"Now!" Mr. Urbach began loudly. His holler startled everyone (except Amy, who adjusted her head on her book but didn't wake). "Quantum physics is a very thick subject." Mr. Urbach returned to the white board and picked up a marker. "Something you might consider studying down the road. Or not. It depends on your major."

A deadly silence filled the room. So deafening, in fact, that Jack could hear the clock over the door ticking second by second, matching the rhythm of his heart thumping in his ears. A pen rolled off a desk and hit the floor, bringing everyone back to reality.

Mr. Urbach jumped and turned his attention to Amy, fast asleep on her textbook.

"Miss Moyer...pay attention!" he shouted across the room. She sat up immediately and pulled a patch of hair that had gathered in her mouth.

Suddenly, the bell rang, startling the class once more.

"Read chapter four, pages 33-47 tonight!" Mr. Urbach called out over the students as they closed up their books and shoved them into their bags. "Test Friday!"

Jack slowly gathered his things. Mr. Urbach dashed over to his desk and leaned in carefully.

"Would you stay a moment?" Mr. Urbach said quietly. Jack nodded.

Once every student had gone, Jack approached Mr. Urbach standing behind his desk waiting stiffly and anxiously. He was twiddling a pen between his fingers.

"I didn't mean to call you out in front of everyone," Mr. Urbach began apologetically.

Jack didn't reply. He just stood there coldly, wondering why Urbach, who he looked up to and whose classes he enjoyed, would do so in the first place.

"I know you don't like to talk about what happened at Linhurst," Mr. Urbach said quietly, "but it certainly is curious." He ended with great enthusiasm.

Jack scrunched his face in confusion. Mr. Urbach's eyes lit up—he knew he had committed another foul.

"I mean, there are a lot of horrible things to be said about Linhurst and its past and what not. But Jack, strictly from a scientific perspective, it's really quite intriguing, don't you think?"

Mr. Urbach twiddled his pen more wildly. He took in a deep breath, shuffled his feet a bit, then began again.

Jack remained still—he was beside himself and didn't know what to make of Mr. Urbach's sudden interest.

"From what I read about the events that night, it is so fascinating to think how spirits remained alive and active all over the property after all those years. Maybe you are onto something, that there is a potentially deeper level of quantum thinking behind it. What did you experience that might point to such a theory?"

Jack hesitated. He didn't want to rehash what everyone already knew.

"I haven't really thought about it enough to have a theory," Jack said.

"It's just that I've always wanted to understand how the ghosts on campus had something to do with the explosion that ripped through that generating station tower," Mr. Urbach said. "That beam of green light could be seen from miles around!"

"I don't remember too much of it," Jack fibbed, wanting to be done with the conversation. "But it could have just been faulty equipment inside the building. That's what they determined, right? I guess that's what I saw. I was really just curious about your lesson today."

Mr. Urbach stopped playing with the pen. His shoulders dropped, and the excitement left his face.

"Listen, Jack, I know you've been through a lot after what

happened. I can't say I understand because I really don't. But I would love to talk about it if you're up for it. The scientific explanation to all this is potentially staggering and could result in substantial research funding and the like."

Jack wasn't happy with this. In fact, he felt betrayed suddenly. He couldn't prevent his face from turning into a scowl. Mr. Urbach grew nervous.

"But I understand it must be difficult," Mr. Urbach said apologetically. "I know there are lots of people who question what happened to you, but I am not one."

Jack didn't budge. He made no reply.

"Everything has an explanation, I believe," Mr. Urbach said. "You'll figure it out."

Jack nodded coldly.

"Sorry again for putting you on the spot," Mr. Urbach said, then chuckled nervously.

"It's fine, really." Jack lied, but he felt even Mr. Urbach thought Jack as something of a novelty these days. He put his head down and charged out of the classroom.

* * * * * *

Jack and Celia met up in front of the school at the end of the day. As they made their way down the sidewalk, they saw Danny Slater pull up in his old beater. He gave Jack a wave just before Tommy Thomson hopped in with him and they peeled off.

"There goes your buddy," Celia said.

Jack snorted. She was being sarcastic, but he secretly hoped his inclination to connect Danny to the security job would pan out for the best and not come back to haunt him.

They arrived at the care center to see Danny's car parked haphazardly in a space out front.

"If you were nicer, he could have offered us a ride," Jack said.

Celia groaned. "What are they doing here?"

"Danny starts the job today."

Celia groaned again.

Next to his poor park job was a large black box truck with the words *Paranormal Examiners* in block letters across the side over an airbrushed image of an apparition highlighted by a magnifying glass. Under that read *Spiritual investigation at its finest!*

"You said Mose hired a group of paranormal investigators," Celia said, "but I didn't realize they were coming today."

"It's news to me, too," Jack replied.

A tall man with a thick build and shaven head, wearing a black t-shirt over worn blue jeans, was unrolling cable from the back of the truck. Next to him was a shorter man with a thick bush of hair, wearing a gray t-shirt and baggy khakis. He was toying around with a small piece of handheld equipment.

"Your EMF is charged," he said to his larger counterpart.

"I'll get the rest of the cables out, and we can start checking everything else," the tall, bald one replied.

Jack and Celia made their way up the stairs and through the care center doors. Just inside the lobby, they spied Dr. Moseley fitting Danny with a black hat that matched a brand new gray shirt, the word *Security* embroidered across the left chest pocket.

"Good fit," Mose said.

Danny stood tall and proud. Tommy was standing next to him, eyeing up his pal's new uniform—the same one he was also wearing.

"They're both working here now?" Celia exclaimed. Jack had no reply—he was as dumbfounded by it as she was.

Jack and Celia approached the group.

Danny saluted Jack. "Ready for duty!" he said goofily.

Jack smiled awkwardly, feeling a little embarrassed.

"Thanks for letting us know about this, Jack," Tommy added sincerely. "We won't let you down."

Mose winked at Jack. Celia cleared her throat loudly, and Jack nudged her to pipe down.

"Let me have a word with Jack and Celia here, and I will get you guys set up with the rounds," said Mose.

"What's going on outside?" Jack asked hurriedly.

"That's the group I was telling you about," Mose said. "They are setting up for tonight."

"Dr. Moseley," Andrea called from behind the check-in area. "I have someone on the line for you."

"Can you take a message?" Mose called over to her.

"It's a man from the power plant," Andrea said, holding her hand over the receiver.

Mose turned to Jack and Celia. "I need to take this. Come with me."

Mose turned to Danny and Tommy and put a hand on each of their shoulders.

"Remember what I showed you," Mose told the pair, "just those areas we talked about, so you won't interfere with the investigation tonight. Stick to the property lines and watch for anyone driving or walking nearby. Check in with me every half hour. Got it?"

The pair nodded in unison, their uniforms making them look like oafish twins.

"You'll do great, I know it!" Mose told Danny and Tommy confidently, who simultaneously stood up taller and prouder at the sound of the encouraging words. Then the pair turned on their heels and promptly marched out the front doors.

Dr. Moseley turned to Andrea. "Put the call into my office please."

They followed Mose through the doors down the hallway to his office. Once inside, he closed the door tightly and offered Jack and Celia a chair. He quickly picked up the phone beeping on his desk.

"This is Dr. Moseley," he answered.

Jack and Celia looked on as Mose listened intently to the person on the other end.

"I understand what you're trying to tell me, but it doesn't explain why your guy was here. These tours are intended to be for historical purposes, a way to showcase Linhurst and help people understand the place. I'm in no position to be sharing any other information with you."

Mose listened again, his face turning redder by the second. He was clearly unsettled by what he was hearing.

"You're not understanding me," Mose began again. "I have no reason to believe that what happened yesterday was anything less than concerning and highly irregular. My tour guide is in the hospital with third-degree burns. She doesn't remember what happened to her, and I doubt your guy does either. But I feel it's important that I speak with the man who was with her."

Mose listened more. He was nodding furiously.

"Fine, send him down and I will speak with him. Yes, I will be here... very well... goodbye."

He hung up the phone then slammed his fist down.

"I don't know what they're up to," Mose said furiously, "but I don't like it."

"What did they say?" Celia asked quickly.

"They tell me the man who was here on the tour is just fine and that he called in sick today, but it's likely unrelated. They're sending his superior down to speak with me."

Dr. Moseley's phone buzzed, and Andrea came through on the speaker. "Dr. Moseley, the ghost guys are ready for you."

Mose chuckled to hear her call them "the ghost guys."

"We'll be right out," he replied. He turned back to Celia and Jack. "I feel it important that you two stick with me tonight. We have lots to uncover, and I'll need your help."

"Dr. Moseley, Celia has something to share," Jack interjected as Mose hopped up from his seat.

Celia elbowed him and shot him a look.

"Go on… it's important," Jack urged.

"What is it, Celia?" Mose asked in a comforting voice.

"I've been having dreams, too," she said quietly.

"What sort of dreams?" Mose asked.

"Getting trapped inside the tunnels… I can't get out, but then I wake up," she said.

"I see," Mose replied nervously. "I'm not surprised. But I'm glad you're here. This will be good for us all—I hope. Let's go."

They made their way back out to the lobby and Mose stopped at Andrea's desk.

"Hold my calls for the day, except for the man from the power plant," Mose said. "If he comes by, call me on my cell."

"Yes, sir," she replied.

Mose walked over to the two men from the paranormal investigation group, who were standing near the entrance to the care center.

"I want you to meet some friends of mine," Mose began. "Harrison and Morgan, this is Celia."

The tall one with the shaved head and bristly face called Harrison put out a hand to shake and Celia reciprocated. He had a strong grip, but his approach was friendly. The shorter one with the puffy hair, called Morgan, followed suit.

"And this is Jack," said Mose.

Harrison reached for Jack's hand, then paused midway. "I can sense it already," he said oddly.

Jack screwed up his face. *Sense what?*

"S-sorry... I mean... Mose told us you've been experiencing some things," Harrison apologized. "You were the one who saw your mother, correct?"

Jack nodded. *How much had Mose told them?*

"Would you come with me?" Harrison said in a polite tone, placing a firm open hand on Jack's arm. "I'd like to get more information that may help us tonight."

Jack hesitated. He was unsure of this pair of investigators and had always been suspicious of shows that followed people like them around the world in pursuit of ghosts. It was all staged. Lots of clever editing to spook the average bored homebody. Mose gave Jack a look as if to say it would be all right.

"Fine," Jack replied reluctantly.

Harrison motioned to a pair of chairs nearby, while Celia and Mose followed Morgan outside. Jack watched through the high wall of windows as Morgan began pulling equipment down from the truck.

"So, I'm Harrison, founder and lead investigator of Paranormal Examiners," the bald man said, then started fiddling inside his jeans for something until he pulled out what appeared to be a small electronic stick. "Charles found us online and gave us a shout. He said folks have been experiencing some activity here that's potentially supernatural or paranormal—uh, my words, not his. We were thrilled to hear the words Linhurst State School and

Hospital. This place has been on our radar since we first started!"

So far, Jack was unamused. In fact, he was downright irritated. And Harrison could see it all over Jack's expression.

"Listen, if it's okay with you, I just want to record our conversation, so I can go back over the answers, and I don't have to keep asking you the same questions later. Cool?" Harrison said.

Jack nodded, still cold and curt. Harrison pressed a button on the device, and a green light lit up.

"So, Jack, how long have you been having the dreams?" Harrison asked.

"A while," Jack replied.

"Could you give me more detail? Has it been days, a week... maybe longer?" Harrison asked

"Months," said Jack.

"Months?!" Harrison exclaimed. "Is it the same dream? Do you have it every night?"

"It's been basically the same," said Jack. "It changes sometimes."

"Changes how?" asked Harrison.

"I see a little bit more each time, but not every time," said Jack.

"Tell me about the dream," said Harrison.

"You already know about it, don't you?" Jack said irritably.

"Uh... yes, Charles told me about it," Harrison replied nervously. "If it's okay with you, I'd like to hear it in your own words. Good to have it on tape, you know?"

Jack stared at Harrison contemptuously. Harrison adjusted himself in the chair, attempting to seem more approachable. Jack figured he could either get up and walk away now or just give him a quick rundown and be done with it.

"Fine," Jack grunted, then cleared his throat. "I'm down in the tunnels, and it's very dark. This thing is yelling down at the other end, but I can't see it. Then I get scooped up and carried all the way out of the tunnels and dropped in front of the building. Then I wake up."

Harrison was frozen at the edge of his seat. He seemed excited and anxious, waiting for more. But Jack was done—and still perturbed.

"Are you good now?" Jack said with a tinge of disdain in his voice. "Got what you need from me?"

Harrison shook his head as if waking from a daydream. "No, wait… can you go back to the beginning for me and describe a bit more about the tunnels? You say it's pitch black. Do you think that's from your dream or is it that dark down there? Like, would you actually be able to see whatever it is that's calling you?"

"It's pitch black in my dream and in real life," Jack said. "You need a flashlight."

"But in your dream, you don't have one?" Harrison pressed.

"Are you asking me if you should bring a flashlight into the tunnels?" Jack snapped. "Are you really that dense?"

Harrison pulled back. He stopped the recording and set the device down on the table beside him, then took in a deep breath. "Look, Jack. I'm not here to make you mad. I know you've been through a lot the last few years. I get it. But Dr. Moseley said you would be the best source of information we have in figuring our way around this case. What do you say?"

Jack paused and thought for a moment. The anger inside of him was welling up, and he was tempted to explode. But considering that his breathing exercises may be inappropriate right now, he took the middle ground.

"The truth is that I don't believe in this crap you guys do," Jack explained callously. "It's just a bunch of fancy editing. I don't know why Mose would call you, but I'm not the one who did. I don't know what you want out of me that's going to make a difference after you've run around Linhurst all night shooting a bunch of night vision footage, so you can scare a bunch of your YouTube fans who have no idea what this is really about."

Harrison was obviously taken aback by Jack's harsh words. He rubbed his palms on his pants, starting to sweat from the exchange.

"Whatever you can offer here to help us figure things out," Harrison began again in a soft and rather gruff voice. "Where is this negative energy coming from? Is it just vandals sneaking in at night and ripping up the place, or is there more to it than that? We don't do fancy editing. Our name says it all: Paranormal Examiners. We examine spiritual energy and state the facts. That's it. Sometimes it helps people know how to deal with their problem; sometimes it's just good info to have down the road. Most of the time, we turn up nothing. We're not here to get anyone upset or make false claims."

Jack stared at Harrison for a moment. He had nothing to say to him, and Harrison could tell.

"Can I share a story with you?" Harrison asked.

Jack shrugged, which wasn't quite a yes and not a no.

"My dad left before I even knew him," Harrison began. "When I was young, I was really close to my mother. She was everything to me. She died in a drunk driving accident caused by another person. I was eleven years old. I went into foster care before my grandparents adopted me and eventually, we moved back to my original home. It wasn't long after that my mother came to me in a dream—only it wasn't a dream. She was really there. She didn't say anything and didn't do anything. But I swear to you, she visited me. And that was it—never saw her again."

Jack's face relaxed a bit. If he wasn't making this up, Jack was actually feeling some connection with Harrison suddenly.

"I read what happened here," Harrison continued. "I read a lot about it. And, look, I don't know you—and you don't know me, and I understand if you don't trust me—but I'm telling you that when I learned about your connection with your mother… well…" Harrison's eyes began to well up with tears. "That alone replaced all the reasons I ever cared about exploring this property to begin with."

Jack looked him over. Harrison seemed sincere, which was something, considering Jack didn't have many people he trusted these days.

"What else do you want to know?" Jack asked.

Harrison gave Jack a huge smile and excitedly picked up the recorder again, wiping the tears from his eyes. He pressed the button, and the green light was on again.

"Okay, where were we?" Harrison thought a moment.

"The tunnels," Jack replied.

"Right! The tunnels. I get that it's dark down there, but is there...?"

BAM!

A loud crash rattled the windows, and Jack jumped to his feet to see what the commotion was. He looked outside to see Harrison's partner Morgan scrambling by the back of the truck. Dr. Moseley was looking down frantically.

"What was that?" Harrison yelped, now at Jack's side.

The pair raced out through the automatic doors from the lobby. When they arrived at the back of the Paranormal Examiners' truck, they found Mose and Morgan leaning over a large black equipment case, struggling to up end it.

"Help!" Morgan cried out. "She's trapped!"

"Celia!" Jack exclaimed and rushed in to grab a corner.

The four of them pushed and pulled until the case rocked over onto its side to reveal Celia in a crouched position and covered in cables and wires. Morgan ripped the cables away, and Celia pushed herself off the ground, then brushed herself off.

"What the hell was that about?" Harrison yelled at Morgan.

"It just happened!" Morgan replied frantically.

"It honestly did. It just happened," added a stunned Dr. Moseley.

"Oh, I'm fine... just fine," Celia chimed in sarcastically. She rubbed her arm, revealing a small gash that was bleeding slightly.

"Oh, my goodness, young lady, we're so sorry." Harrison rushed to her side, but she pushed him back. He pulled a handkerchief out of his back pocket and handed it to her.

"Yeah, okay, okay… honestly, I'm fine," Celia said irritably.

"I was explaining our set up for the night and this thing just tumbled out the back of the truck," Morgan explained.

"We have to secure these things better, Morg," Harrison said as he dragged the case to the back of the truck and began picking up the cables and wires and tossing them in.

"I hear ya, Harrison, but it was out of the blue," Morgan said. "Never seen anything like it."

"These things are damn heavy, too," Harrison added. "Could have killed her!"

"Well, I hope you have insurance," Celia replied. "Did you sign a liability waiver, Dr. Moseley?"

Harrison and Morgan turned to Celia, dumbfounded.

"I'm joking!" Celia said. "I'm fine!"

Harrison finished tossing the remaining cables back in the case and put the lid on it. He checked his watch. "Let's keep an eye out for these things tonight and hope this isn't what we have in store."

Harrison checked his watch. "When are they getting here? We've got to start setting up."

Harrison barely got the words out when a modified hearse, painted purple with orange flames down the sides and showcasing giant chrome rims on oversize tires, came rolling up the road toward them. It came to a stop, and a stocky guy with a massive beard, wearing thick-rimmed glasses under a worn brown baseball cap got out of the passenger seat. He had on a black t-shirt that said *Space Ghost* in big bold letters and a pair of very baggy old carpenter's jeans.

The driver's side door opened slowly to reveal a fluorescent pink mop of hair, followed by a thin pale woman in her mid-twenties. She wore a leather vest over a neon yellow t-shirt that showed her bare stomach, and a pair of torn khakis over tall black boots. She had piercings along her ears and in her nose and bottom lip.

"Speak of the devils," Morgan chuckled.

The pair slammed the doors to the hearse simultaneously and swaggered over to greet Harrison and Morgan.

"'Sup, guys," said the bearded man.

"Harrison… Morg…" said the woman. "Are we good on time?"

"Just in time!" Harrison said excitedly. He turned to the group. "This is Garrett—" the bearded guy gave a wave "—and Sierra." She bowed then blew a kiss to the group.

"At your service," Sierra said. Jack was surprised to hear her English accent.

"They'll be helping us get set up tonight," said Morgan. "And we should get moving. We only have two hours of daylight remaining."

"On it!" Sierra exclaimed, then proceeded to gather everyone in a tight group, pushing their backs and pulling their arms. "Gotta get this for our social media." She kneeled in the middle of the group. "Smile, ya'll!" she said as she snapped a group selfie and stood back up, then hopped into the back of the truck.

"All right… let's do this!" Garrett clapped his hands loudly and pulled himself into the truck with Sierra.

Harrison turned to Dr. Moseley. "Charles, we talked basics over the phone, and I have a map of the campus, but we'll need to pinpoint some prime locations to set up. Can we do that now?"

"Jack… Celia… come with us," Mose replied.

He motioned for them to follow him around the side of the building, where they hopped in the bed of his old blue pickup followed by Harrison. Morgan took shotgun. Mose started it up and took off down the road.

Chapter 8

The sun was sitting low in the sky, casting a burnt orange hue over the landscape. Mose drove past the generating station and turned onto the road where he had taken Jack and Danny the day before.

"I guess you know every building on campus by now?" Harrison asked Jack, hollering over the noise of the wind and the old pickup engine. They were both perched on a corner at the back of the truck bed. Celia sat near Jack, looking out along the dense woods.

"Honestly, I don't," Jack hollered back. "My dad and I moved here when they opened the apartments, but I've never really gone exploring."

Jack thought about it for a moment—just two years ago, he'd wanted nothing more than to sneak into Linhurst and find the truth behind the abandoned property. He was ready to go through every building if he had to. But since the night he saw his mother join a hundred or more spirits in starting the fusion reactor, he'd had no inclination to go exploring again.

"Have you been down this way before?" Harrison asked.

"Mose took us here yesterday," Jack replied.

"You and Celia?" Harrison asked.

"No, he went with Danny, his new best friend," Celia chimed in.

Harrison looked at Jack. He rolled his eyes. Then Harrison glanced at Celia, who sneered at Jack. Harrison laughed out loud at the pair.

They came to an abrupt stop just in front of Penn Hall, the building where they'd found the burn marks on the wall. Harrison jumped down, followed by Jack then Celia.

Mose hopped out of the truck and shut the door. He stood in place, staring at the building with a concerned look in his eyes. As the sun was beginning to set, an eerie darkness was taking shape in front of them. The trees were like vast long witch's fingers stretching out over the building, as if protecting it from strangers. The broken windows and open entrance doors held a darkness beyond that sent shivers up Jack's spine and hairs standing straight up on his neck and arms.

"This must be the place," Harrison said, his voice low and dark.

Morgan climbed out of the truck and looked up at the haunting scene ahead. Jack swore he looked frightened.

"We've been seeing a lot of activity here," Mose began, "whether it's vandals or things unexplained. Just inside are the black markings on the wall from the photo I emailed you."

"The wording said *go away*?" Harrison asked.

"Correct," Mose replied.

"You can just feel the energy here," Harrison said coldly.

Jack agreed. A palpable feeling of dread hovered around the building like a demonic cloud.

"This building will take us down into the tunnels?" Harrison asked.

"Yes, every building on campus aside from the Linhurst Care Center is connected by the tunnel system," Mose replied.

"Okay, we'll begin here," said Harrison. "Anywhere else we should consider?"

Mose nodded. "Inside the administration building and Building A—where Suzanne left with burn marks and we found the drawing—and of course, the tunnels under them."

"What about the building across from the care center—the tower where all the activity occurred a couple years back?" Harrison asked.

Mose thought for a moment. Jack could see he was leery of letting just anyone inside the space.

"I can assist you in there," Mose said cautiously. "It's a tricky building, so I want to be sure no one gets injured. We'll save it for last if you feel it's necessary."

"I can assure you, Charles, that safety is our number one priority," Harrison said, "but we'll follow your lead."

Mose nodded then gave Jack a nervous look. Jack was still unsure about the investigators being at Linhurst, but here they were. Jack knew he just had to trust Mose and make the best of this in hopes they did find something.

Harrison turned to Morgan and put a hand on his shoulder. "Let's get Sierra and Garrett the layout and get them started."

Morgan nodded in confirmation, then placed a hand on Harrison's shoulder, mirroring his tall partner. They both closed their eyes and bowed their heads, then began to speak in unison.

"Tonight, we seek strength and call for defense against evil energies; may all negative thought forms, lost souls, residues, elementals, and fragments be permanently healed and freed according to the will of the universe; may we be given power and protection in every part of the examination we pursue in this place."

The pair put their foreheads together for a few seconds, pulled away, gave a high five and a hug, then turned back to the group.

"Let's do this!" Harrison boomed with excitement.

"Let's roll!" Morgan added.

The paranormal pair hopped back into the truck, followed by a bemused Celia, Jack, and Mose, and were soon heading back toward the care center.

When they returned, the sun was beginning to fall below the horizon. Garrett and Sierra had set up three tall, bright lights, illuminating the entire area at the front of the care center where few cars remained in the parking lot. Wires and cables were running amuck on the ground at the back of the truck. The inside of the truck looked like a circus attraction, with blinking colored lights and switchboards accompanying monitors and screens and all sorts of gadgetry.

Mose pulled up and everyone hopped out of the truck. Harrison and Morgan quickly proceeded to instruct Garrett and Sierra on where to set up their equipment.

Jack spotted a newer-model Mercedes parked right next to the handicap ramp. It was a shiny, spotless bronze, half overlapping a handicapped parking spot.

"Who parks like this?!" Mose exclaimed angrily. "Good thing we don't have anyone else coming tonight. I would be infuriated."

Celia and Jack chuckled. He already seemed mad. Mose dashed up the stairs and in through the doors to the front desk. Jack and Celia followed.

"Andrea, whose car is parked out front?" Mose demanded.

Andrea stood up from behind the desk and pointed to the waiting area. In one of the colorful chairs in the empty waiting room sat a scrawny bird-like man wearing a tight-fitting, pinstriped suit and obnoxiously shiny beige dress shoes. The man rose from the chair like a marionette and slowly made his way toward Mose. He had a smug look on his face, and Jack could already tell he didn't come in peace.

"You must be Dr. Charles Moseley," the man said through a deep nasally voice, his hand stretched out.

Mose turned to Jack and Celia, scoffed, and rolled his eyes, then turned back to the suit and shook his hand.

"Quite a grip you got there, Doc," the man said, grinning devilishly. "I'm Roland Allister, head of R&D at Spring Dale Nuclear."

"I see," Mose said cautiously. He motioned to the chair where Allister had been sitting. "Have a seat and we'll chat?"

"Certainly. I think we can make this brief," Allister replied.

The two men sat, and before Mose could get a word out, Allister began.

"We at Spring Dale Nuclear are looking toward the future of energy," said Allister. "When the plant was first built decades ago, nuclear was the way to go—a promising resource in a time when the future of oil was becoming problematic for a number of reasons. As we continually consider opportunities to power our society, renewable resources are more and more enticing, and we at Spring Dale Nuclear feel it's a chance for us to diversify."

Mose sat listening, his demeanor growing more agitated with each word Allister spoke. Jack and Celia stood by the nurse's station, listening intently to the conversation.

"I don't see how this has anything to do with one of my employees ending up in intensive care," Mose cut in. "Third-degree burns down her arms, and your fella supposedly just drives home and calls in sick? What is all this nonsense about renewable resources? Cut the bullshit, Allister!"

Aside from his eyebrows rising a few centimeters, the tall smarmy stiff in the suit barely fidgeted in his seat. He was clearly used to far worse language in his conference room rounds.

"Jerry was merely checking things out here at Linhurst," Allister began again. "It's no secret that you have been powering your own property since the explosion a couple of years back. I know you have proprietary means of producing your electricity, and that is good for you. But we wonder how we could work together on this movement toward sustainable and renewable energy."

Mose turned bright red, the veins in his forehead bulging and becoming very clear. "Mr. Allister, you are correct that we have our own means of powering this campus. What we have is none of your business and, quite frankly, beyond your comprehension. I suggest you stick with what you do best, and rest assured we want nothing to do with your filthy nuclear schemes!"

Allister perked up, his eyebrows raised in surprise. "Oh, Chuck," Allister said in a sinister voice.

"Dr. Moseley to you, and don't speak to me in that tone!" Mose boomed back. "Now, you have every right to come here and take a tour and understand the history of this campus. You do not, however, have the right to send spies in and try poking your nose around where people can end up getting seriously hurt."

Allister was taken aback again. He pulled his phone from inside his blazer and flicked it on, then began tapping and scrolling around. He then pointed the phone at Dr. Moseley.

"Take a look, Dr. Moseley," Allister said in a condescending voice. "Jerry is just fine."

Jack could just barely make out the photo but enough to see a man lying in bed, the sheets and blankets pulled up just under his chin. He had a broad smile on his face and was giving a thumbs up. Suddenly, the hair on Jack's neck stood up, and a shock ran up his spine. Though the face was a bit of blur from such a distance, he swore it looked familiar.

"That's the man from my dream," Jack whispered to Celia.

"How can you be sure?" Celia asked. "You can barely see him."

"I'm sure," Jack replied.

Mose noticed Jack's expression and squinted his eyes. He turned back to Allister. "Send me that photo, please."

"Gladly," Allister replied, smugly certain he had settled everything. He tapped away on his phone a bit more, then tucked it back inside his blazer. "Sent."

"Now I have a photo to share with you." Mose pulled out his phone and opened the picture of the drawing found in the tunnel. Allister got a good look and immediately began to smirk.

"This was left by your guy Jerry, wasn't it?" Mose said.

"The symbol appears to be a common occurrence here at Linhurst," Allister admitted. "What is the meaning behind it?"

"It's a sun and peace symbol," Mose replied.

"I get that much," Allister said. "Why do you use it so often? Is it something to do with your reactor?"

With that, Mose stood up abruptly.

"Where are you going?" Allister pressed, then stood up just as fast, towering over Mose and blocking him from leaving.

"Seeing that this is none of your business, and I have work to do, I won't have my time wasted any longer," Moser replied curtly, then spun on a heel.

"That is not all," Allister boomed after him.

Mose stopped dead then turned slowly back to Allister. "What more do you have to say?"

"You have quite a bit of property here, Dr. Moseley," Allister said in a suddenly professional voice that was not scathing or booming. "I would like to speak with you about subletting."

"Subletting?" Mose replied in shock. "For what purpose?"

"Solar and wind are fast becoming alternatives that we at Spring Dale Nuclear would like to provide to our customers," said Allister. He changed his entire tone and was now delivering a sales pitch. "You have the space for both. Imagine the money you could bring in to support your future endeavors."

"We have no interest in your propositions," Mose said and turned to leave.

"You can't fool us, Charles," said Allister. "We know the symbol is connected to your energy source."

Mose stopped dead and turned. Jack and Celia were looking on with bated breath.

"What makes you so certain of this?" Mose replied.

"It seems fairly obvious—the symbol of the sun… solar energy," Allister began. "We read the articles. We know the story of the boy who carried the necklace. We know it became your symbol. And now that you have this mysterious energy source on campus—and that buffoon Helowski is trying to power all of Spring Dale with it—we have every right to compete if you are unwilling to work with us."

Mose was fuming now. Jack had never seen him look angrier. He stared blankly at Allister for a moment, his face filling with rage. The tall bird-man had nothing good to say, and Mose was tired of listening.

"People like you have been coming to me for the last two years, wanting to take advantage of this place," Mose said heatedly. "Linhurst brought nothing but horror and misery to those who lived here. We had a chance to make things right decades ago, and we didn't do it. Your former bosses attempted to use this land and its abandoned buildings to store nuclear waste. And now, I get business propositions once a week that I have to turn down. Linhurst has a future that doesn't include you or the power plant, Mr. Allister. And the energy source is far beyond your comprehension. We are through here. Good day, sir."

Mose turned to walk away, but Allister, of course, had to get in a few more thoughts.

"Don't think this is over, Chuck," Allister said.

With that, Mose turned and raced back to where he was toe-to-toe with Allister, practically staring up his nostrils.

"Now you listen to me, Roland," Mose said in a surprisingly firm voice, "Linhurst became a dark place, thanks to the likes of squirmy twats like you, and I'll be damned if it's going to happen again on my watch!"

"And yet you will let an entertainment company set up a haunted house here," Allister replied. "Seems everyone has their price."

"Until we find out what is happening on this campus, nothing is coming to Linhurst other than what will benefit the people who suffered here and those willing to set things right," Mose said firmly. "I know for a fact that your guy Jerry was hurt more than you are letting on. So, if you can't get through your thick skull that this isn't about the money, you'll learn the hard way."

Suddenly, Danny and Tommy came blasting through the front doors of the care center, chatting up a storm. They stopped dead when they saw the awkward confrontation.

"Dr. Moseley," Danny chirped, "I've been trying to call and text, but you weren't answering."

Mose pulled his phone out of his pocket to see several missed messages and calls.

"Sorry, fellas," Mose replied, trying to calm himself as he backed away from Allister. "This gentleman and I were just wrapping up, and he will be on his way now."

"Hey! I'm not done with you," Allister replied.

"Yes," Mose said sternly, staring into the birdman's eyes, "you are."

Mose turned to Danny and Tommy. "Would you fellas be sure Mr. Allister finds his way to his vehicle? He's the one parked illegally in the handicapped spot out front."

Danny nodded, catching Mose's drift. He and Tommy marched over to Roland Allister and strong-armed him.

"Right this way, sir," Danny insisted, pulling him toward the door with Tommy.

"Hands off me! This is a two-thousand-dollar suit!" Allister snapped. He shook Danny's arm away, adjusted his suit, then marched scarecrow-like out the front doors. Danny and Tommy followed closely behind him to ensure he would continue on his way.

"This is not over, Charles," Allister called out.

Mose slumped down in the chair, clearly exhausted from the exchange. Jack and Celia raced over to comfort him.

"You showed him, Dr. Moseley!" Celia cheered him on.

"Yeah, well done, Mose!" Jack added.

Mose chuckled then took in a deep breath. He pulled off his gray cap, which revealed his shiny bald spot above snow-white hair. He rubbed his head, eyes closed, then took another long breath before replacing his cap.

"That was quite a conversation!" Mose exclaimed, then sat up straight as an arrow. His eyes lit up suddenly. "I almost forgot—take a look at this, Jack."

He pulled his phone out, swiped it open, then loaded the message from Allister that included the photo of Jerry. He handed the phone to Jack, who stared at it for only a moment before gasping.

"What is it, Jack?" Celia exclaimed.

"I could see by the look on your face that you saw something here," Mose said. "What is it that strikes you about this man?"

"I am positive now. He's the one from my dream," Jack replied, his eyes wide and his mouth slightly agape.

"And you never met him before?" Celia replied.

"I've never seen him in my life," said Jack. "At least not until my dream."

"I can't believe it," Celia said. Jack shot her a look. "I mean, I believe *you*—it's just scary that you saw him in a dream, and it was true."

"If this adds up," Mose began slowly, "you dreamed about Suzanne and Jerry only hours after they escaped Penn Hall with burn marks, yet you were nowhere near them at the time."

"That's like, clairvoyance, or something," Celia said.

"It tells me that there is a growing possibility all our dreams hold the truth," said Mose, his voice quivering.

Jack nodded, thinking how it was more a devastating nuisance he wished would go away. He was done with the nightmare. He wanted it to end. Then something struck him.

"Mose," Jack began anxiously, "you never told us what kind of dreams you've been having."

At that, Mose stared off into the distance, his eyes glassy, his shoulders slumped. He had a look of despair on his face. "You're right, Jack, I have not."

Jack and Celia sat patiently, ready for him to reveal his dream.

"All I can say is that they have me concerned, they are so real," Mose began. "But what's more is how did it all start? You may remember that night at the generating station." He pointed across the street at the building with the tower, sitting innocently in the fading light. "I left rather abruptly when the smoke cleared, and the crowd came in from town."

Jack thought about it. After all the commotion of the people from Spring Dale entering the campus after having seen the unbelievable sight of the fusion reactor exploding to life, thanks to the energy of a hundred spirits, Mose was nowhere to be found.

"I chose the sun and peace symbol as the emblem for Linhurst because of your mother's necklace," said Mose. "That necklace you wore so proudly, that amulet that held your mother's energy, which ultimately transferred the final shot of power that brought us this miraculous gift."

He motioned to the generating station, its silhouette rising above the setting sun visible through high glass windows of the lobby.

Just then, Danny and Tommy walked through the doors of the care center and stopped just inside, seeing the intensity of yet another conversation.

"Gentlemen!" Mose called out, suddenly very professional and normal. "Have we seen our friend off?"

"Oh, yeah, he's gone," Tommy chuckled devilishly while elbowing Danny.

"He won't be coming back," Danny laughed.

Mose shot them a suspicious look. "What did you do?"

"Oh, nothing, really," Danny started again, apologetically.

"We just acted real tough and... I dunno... adult-like," Tommy added.

"Yeah, we were just, you know, like, firm with him—told him not to come back," said Danny.

Mose smiled. "Good work, guys, and on the first day, no less! I may have to consider a raise already."

Danny and Tommy high fived one another.

"Now, what was it you two were trying to reach me about?" Mose asked.

"The lights in the town," Danny replied. "They've been browning out. I was hoping to let you know in case the same thing was happening here."

"We haven't experienced anything, but we do have a good backup system," Mose replied. "Would take something serious to bring that down. Now, do me a favor and keep an eye on the perimeter," Mose said. "We're going to be starting up the investigation soon and don't need any distractions."

"Yes, sir!" the pair said in unison, and they were out the door and running down the road in no time.

Mose looked at Jack and Celia for a reaction, and Celia just rolled her eyes. It was so comical Mose and Jack burst into laughter. When they regained composure, they shared a moment of silence, watching the paranormal investigators work feverishly in their bright spotlights just outside the lobby windows.

"You know, I feel like it was just yesterday we were standing on this very spot where we now sit," Mose said, quietly interrupting the silence. "Back then, it was just an open field." Mose sat up and leaned forward. "Jack, your mother's necklace blasted forth from your hand like it was fired from a rifle. I remember how it disappeared through those shattered windows, and a corona of green light went right through us."

Jack and Celia nodded, remembering everything as disturbingly clear as Mose recounted.

"I have a feeling it was that corona of light," Mose said quietly.

Jack and Celia turned to one another, confused and concerned at once.

"It was as if the light was loaded with spiritual energy," Mose continued, "and it became a part of us."

Jack wanted to think Mose sounded completely crazy, but somehow it all made sense. Celia even nodded her head in agreement.

"I immediately felt something different," Mose said. "That's why I had to leave. Something didn't feel quite right. I got home that night and tried to settle my nerves. Scenes from the night were racing through my head."

"Me, too," said Celia. "I couldn't sleep for days."

"Same," Jacked added.

"Did you notice that you immediately felt a strange and unexplainable connection that went beyond just remembering the events of the night?" Mose asked. "Like you could see into this place? Into its heart… its soul?"

Jack's eyes widened. He looked to Celia, who was nodding in confirmation, her eyes just as wide.

"As we got the care center up and running, my thoughts subsided a bit," said Mose. "It was like the spirits here were happy with the work we were doing. But something has changed recently. They don't like what we're doing—don't like what this place is becoming."

"But nothing has changed, Dr. Moseley," Celia said. "The care center is doing so many great things."

"It's not that, Celia," Mose replied. "It's the threat of this haunted house, the business development company, the power plant—I feel they are disturbing the energy here."

"If that's true, what can we do?" Celia asked.

"I don't know yet," Mose said. "But this is why I invited Harrison and his team, and we must work to support them in this investigation tonight."

No sooner had he finished the sentence when Harrison stepped forward from the front doors. He moved in cautiously toward the trio.

"Thank you for having confidence in us, Charles," Harrison said, blushing.

"How much of that did you hear?" asked Jack.

"Enough to know I'm in the right place at the right time," Harrison said with a smile. "Do you want to see what we have set up?"

"Absolutely!" Mose replied enthusiastically.

Mose hopped up from his chair, gave Celia and Jack a small pat on the back, then they all followed Harrison outside.

Chapter 9

"We have a camera on the front of the administration building," Harrison said, pointing to a monitor inside the back of the truck. "A camera inside the foyer, one at the top of the stairwell, then these two pointing down the tunnels."

He continued to review all the cameras, EMF sensors, EVP voice recorders, and other equipment prepared to capture any paranormal activity that night.

"What do you think?" Harrison asked Mose as he finished his overview.

"Looks good to me," Mose said, sounding impressed. "You guys know your stuff better than I do, so I trust you know how to do your thing."

"Wait, no dowsing rods?" Celia asked sarcastically.

"Dowsing rods?" Garrett asked. "That's not really a thing anymore—pretty old fashioned."

"I was totally kidding," Celia replied with a chuckle, somewhat embarrassed. Her joke fell flat. "I have no idea what half of this stuff does. Looks cool, though!"

Jack was also impressed. He was starting to feel more confident that Harrison wasn't a total knock-off and even slightly wanted to tag along for the night.

"Coming with us, Jack?" Harrison said.

"Sure, I suppose," Jack replied, trying not to sound too excited.

"Great!" Harrison said enthusiastically. "Garrett is going to monitor everything from here." Garrett spun around on his chair inside the truck and gave a wave. "Celia and Sierra are going to do some EMF and voice recordings in the administration building."

"Wait… who… me?" Celia asked nervously. "I've never done anything like this before."

"I gotcha, girlfriend," Sierra said, patting Celia on the back. "You'll catch on quick. We're gonna have some fun!" She gave Celia a quick, rough hug.

Celia gave Jack a queasy and uncomfortable look.

"Mose will take Morgan to Building A," Harrison continued. "And Jack, you and I will head straight for Penn Hall and locate the markings on the wall, then head down into the tunnels."

Jack shivered suddenly. It was becoming surreal to think that he was investigating the Linhurst campus all over again after trying so hard to remove himself from the experience of two years prior.

Garrett came to the back of the truck and held out a handful of walkie talkies. Harrison grabbed them and handed one each to Morgan and Sierra, then pocketed one.

"We'll communicate with one another as we go," Harrison said to the group. "Any questions?"

Everyone shook their heads.

"We're all ready?" he asked. The group collectively nodded but didn't say a word in reply. Jack could feel the tension as the sun was going down and they were preparing to stir up any paranormal energy.

"Let's roll!" Sierra howled. "Time to catch some ghosts!" Her pink hair and piercings shimmered from the bright light of the spotlights overhead.

Harrison clapped his hands loudly and bellowed, "We're off!"

Harrison jumped into the back of their truck, followed by Morgan, and they began a quick pow wow with Garrett.

Sierra wrapped her arm around Celia's shoulder and pulled her in close. "You're riding with the best tonight," she whispered audibly in her ear. "We're gonna have some fun."

Celia grimaced. Jack could tell by the look on her face that she was dreading the idea of spending a night with someone as energetic and wild as Sierra. She tossed Sierra a half-hearted smile, then broke away toward Jack. Sierra hopped up in the truck with Harrison.

"Save me!" she shrieked under her breath to Jack.

"I think you two will have some fun," Jack teased. "Maybe you can dye your hair before the night is through."

Celia punched him hard in the arm. He was used to this from her, but her punches were getting stronger as the years passed, and this one kind of hurt.

"I hope you both are comfortable with all this," Mose said as they huddled up.

"I'm okay with it—are you, Celia?" Jack asked.

"I've had to deal with high energy before; I can do it again," Celia said in her usual tone.

"Thanks for agreeing to this," Mose replied. "Remember, we are not looking for answers, only clues. Safety first. If this is a wash, I have other ideas. The bottom line is chipping away at restoring the balance here, and given what we've been experiencing, I think we can be of some value to Harrison and his team."

Jack and Celia nodded, though they only half understood what Mose's plan was.

"Ready, Jack?" an excited Harrison called out as he leaped down from the Paranormal Examiners' truck.

"I am!" Jack called out.

"How about you, kiddo?" Sierra yelled to Celia as she followed Harrison off the truck. "Ready for an adventure?"

Celia raised one eyebrow and held it for a few seconds, which gave Sierra pause.

"Sure, let's do it!" Celia said, letting her expression break into a feigned enthusiasm.

"Hey, Dr. Moseley," Morgan called down as he carefully climbed out of the truck. "Can you drive us up to Building A after we drop Sierra and Celia at the Administration Building?"

"Good plan," Mose said. "We'll get Harrison and Jack over to Penn Hall first."

"We'll be all right," Harrison replied. "Jack and I are going on foot. A brisk walk will do us some good… get the blood pumping!"

"Suit yourself. Let me know if you change your mind," Mose said.

The group headed off to Mose's truck parked nearby.

"Ready, Jack?" Harrison asked. "I'm feeling good about this. I think we're going to learn some things here tonight."

Jack had no reply. He wasn't entirely sure what was in store for them, but he was willing to give it a shot and see Harrison in action.

They made their way across the road toward the generating station, sitting dark and silent with its veritable monster inside. Mose passed them when they reached the opposite side of the road parallel to the station.

"Good luck, ya'll!" Sierra called out from the back of the truck. "See you on the flip side!"

Harrison and Jack watched as Dr. Moseley's truck disappeared over the ridge and beyond the trees leading to Building A. They began walking at a fast clip, turning down the side road onto the cracked asphalt road leading to Penn Hall.

The pair walked in silence for a while, taking in the sights and sounds all around them. It was cool and quiet. Comfortable, even. Maybe even eerily silent and calm. A very light breeze blew through the trees, rustling the remaining leaves that autumn was ready to take away during the winter months.

The stars above shined brightly around the half moon that faintly lit their way, slowly growing darker as the woods became thicker around them.

"I want you to know that I understand," Harrison said, breaking the silence. "I mean, I sort of know what you're going through. When my mom passed, it was so shocking to me. I just felt like nothing would ever be the same again."

Jack had no reply at first, and Harrison had nothing to add. It got him thinking about his mom and the symbol again. They walked on, only their heavy breathing and the crushing sound of dry leaves beneath their feet breaking up the silence.

"I guess what I mean to say is that I know what it's like when everyone looks at you like you are so different... so special," Harrison said after a while. "All you want to be is like everyone else, or at least a part of what everyone else is."

Jack could certainly relate now. He hadn't planned on losing his mother to cancer in fifth grade and learning how to live with his father as a single parent. And he certainly never dreamed about how fun it could be to discover that his mother was connected to a hundred spirits while trapped inside a necklace he wore around his neck every day. Now, he felt like a laughingstock or a lunatic. His only remaining friends were the people who'd experienced the unbelievable night with him.

"Yep," was all Jack could get out after thinking about Harrison's words for a bit.

"Here we are," Harrison said as he pulled out his flashlight and pointed it to the building ahead. "Penn Hall. Are you ready for this?"

Jack nodded. "Do we have a choice?"

Harrison let out a short chuckle. Jack pulled his flashlight and flicked it on, inspecting the front of the dark, eerie building.

"You're like an old pro," Harrison said. "I have to remember that you've done this before."

"I'm kind of the reason you are here," Jack replied.

Harrison laughed. "Let's head inside, my man!"

"On your lead," Jack replied confidently.

They slowly climbed the front staircase of Penn Hall and onto the porch. The wooden boards were split and creaky, with vast open spaces hither and thither. They danced their way over the boards and through the front doors that were hanging haphazardly on rusted hinges. Once inside, their flashlights showed particles of dust and debris floating all around in front of them. Harrison pointed his light down a main stretch toward a large open room.

"We have equipment in that area where the markings are," Harrison said. "Let's make our way to that space and see what's up."

Jack nodded, then took the lead. Once inside, Jack carefully stepped over debris while looking around for the equipment Harrison's team had set up. He couldn't find anything, but eventually made his way toward the wall Mose had shown him and Danny the day before. He pointed his flashlight up along the wall and from one far end to the other. Then he scanned the wall quickly again, looking for the words he saw burned into the wall just the day before.

"What are you looking for?" Harrison asked Jack in a loud whisper.

"This is where we saw the words burned into the wall," Jack replied.

"Which words?" Harrison asked.

"The words that said *go away*. They were right here!" Jack yelped.

"Are you sure it was right here? Maybe it's somewhere else in the room?" Harrison replied, shining his light all around them. Harrison couldn't find the words either. He carefully crossed to the other side of the room, shining his light all over the open space with the floor to ceiling pillars and boarded up windows running the full length of the room. His light briefly illuminated the open door leading into the tunnels, essentially a black rectangle from Jack's perspective.

"I'm telling you... it was right here," Jack called over to Harrison, who was inspecting a far corner. "They were burned into the wall right here."

Harrison made his way back to Jack and pointed his flashlight up the wall. Only dried peeling paint and water stains ran down in streams from the roof line. Harrison quickly pulled his phone from his pocket and located the photo Mose sent him. He leaned in to share it with Jack, comparing it to the wall in front of them.

"Hot damn!" Harrison exclaimed. "You're absolutely correct. The words were right here."

Harrison pulled his walkie-talkie out. "Chase, are you there?"

"Go!" Chase replied.

"Check the tape from Penn Hall and tell me if you see the words on the wall," Harrison said.

"Checking now," Chase replied. Harrison and Jack waited. "We only started filming a half hour ago. Nothing on the wall."

"Thanks," Harrison replied. His eyes were wide, his face screwed up in confusion.

Harrison pocketed his phone and walkie talkie then pulled a small handheld device from his jacket and flipped it on.

"Let's see if we get any readings here," Harrison said as he began walking around with the device stretched out in front of him. The digital monitor started off at 00.1 and bounced to 00.3 then back to 00.1 again. As he walked around slowly, the digital readout fluctuated between the two numbers.

"What are you getting?" Jack asked.

"It's very low—basically nothing yet," Harrison replied quietly. He walked the device to the wall where Jack pointed his flashlight and slowly moved it around the space.

"Anything?" Jack whispered. It was getting colder, though Jack wondered if it was the temperature or his nerves causing the sensation.

"Still low," Harrison replied. "This goes up to a reading of 5, and we're not even at .5, let alone a 1."

Jack was puzzled. He could clearly remember the words on the wall just the day before. *How could they have disappeared?* Then he remembered Mose saying that Suzanne's burn marks had also mysteriously disappeared.

"I'm not picking anything up, Jack," said Harrison, sounding disappointed. "Let's try some voice recordings and see what we get."

Harrison turned off the EMF meter and tucked it away in his jacket then pulled out a voice recorder and flipped it on. A green light appeared, and he held it up to his mouth.

"This is Harrison. I'm here with Jack in Penn Hall," Harrison said into the recorder. "We're standing in the room where Jack saw the words 'go away' etched into the wall. We aren't seeing anything now. It's just a blank wall. It's seems the words have disappeared."

Jack grimaced. He shuffled his feet, waiting impatiently between Harrison's long pauses. Harrison patted him on the shoulder, as if to say be patient.

"Is there anyone here with us?" Harrison suddenly called out, his voice echoing throughout the open space, startling Jack and sending a chill throughout his body. The reply was deadly silence. Jack could hear water dripping in a distant corner, followed by a few creaks in the floorboards but nothing else.

"We want to talk to you," Harrison called out. "Can you make your presence known?"

His voice echoed, then nothing. Silence.

"Did you write the words into the wall here?" Harrison called out a little louder. "We want to speak with whoever made the marks that said go away."

A loud thump echoed from another room beyond the great room in which they were standing.

"Was that you? Can you respond or show yourself?"

More dripping water. More floorboards creaking. Harrison turned to Jack and spotted the look of disappointment on his face.

"It's very unusual to have seen words burned into the wall and now there's nothing there," Harrison began calmly. "It's quite possible that was the work of vandals."

Jack furled his eyebrows in frustration.

"But it's even more possible that whatever left those marks covered its tracks in anticipation for our arrival," Harrison followed up. "Let's listen to the recorder and see if it picked up anything we didn't hear."

Harrison rewound the recording a bit and hit play.

"Did you write the words into the wall?" Harrison's voice played back on the recording. Only noise was heard in response. He backed it up more and hit play.

"Is there anyone here with us?" Harrison's voice played on the recording. No response, just audible noise. He backed it up more and hit play again.

"Are you really that dense?" Jack's voice came through the recorder. It was from the interview Harrison attempted when they first met. Harrison stopped the recorder.

Jack blushed. "Sorry about that."

Harrison shrugged it off.

The recording continued to play.

"Wait!" Jack yelped.

"That part is just from our interview," Harrison replied.

"No, I heard something," Jack replied. "Play it again."

Harrison rewound the recording and hit play.

"…asking if you should bring a flashlight into the tunnels. Are you really that dense?" Jack's voice played back again, only this time Harrison heard it, too.

"Sort of a low grumbling in the background?" Harrison asked.

Jack nodded.

"Could have been a car outside," Harrison said. The recording picked up again.

"Right! The tunnels," Harrison's voice came through. "I get that it's dark down there, but is there…"

"Go away!" a faint voice came through in the distance on the recording, followed by a loud crashing sound.

BAM!

"What was that?" Harrison's voice called out, then the recording stopped again and picked up with, "This is Harrison. I'm here with Jack in Penn Hall." Harrison stopped the recorder, rewound it, and played it. They listened carefully.

"There it is again," Harrison confirmed on second listen. "The voice is saying 'Go away.'"

Jack nodded, suddenly feeling terrified. He pointed his flashlight around the room to double check that they were still alone inside the dark open space inside Penn Hall.

Harrison replayed the same part.

"It's very clear," Harrison said. "What happened after that?"

"That's when the case fell on Celia," Jack replied nervously.

"Oh, man, you're right!" Harrison shoved the recorder back into his pocket and pulled out the walkie talkie. "Sierra, are you there?"

"Go ahead," Sierra responded.

"Is Celia with you?" Harrison asked.

"She's right here," Sierra replied. "We are heading for the tunnels now. Not picking anything up in the admin building."

"Stay put for a minute and wait for me," Harrison replied.

"Roger," Sierra replied. "Heading back."

"Charles, can you hear me?" Harrison called into the walkie talkie.

"We're here," Morgan replied. "Nothing to report."

"Garrett," Harrison called into the walkie. "Are you seeing anything on your end?"

"Everything is quiet so far," Garrett replied. "I am having some problems with the camera in the tunnel under Penn Hall. It's a little grainy and keeps glitching on me. I can see you and Jack, though."

"Is that unusual?" Harrison replied.

"Probably a wiring issue," Garrett called back. "Sierra, anything you can think of?"

"You set it up," Sierra replied. "Did you double check it?"

"Seemed fine to me," Garrett replied. "I tested it twice."

"Keep an eye on that camera and let me know if you see anything out of the ordinary," Harrison said.

"Will do," Garrett replied.

Harrison turned to Jack and put a hand on his shoulder. "This is when we know to proceed with caution. Could be a coincidence what happened with that case falling, but we don't want to take our chances. It could be a sign of what's causing the disturbances. And with the words gone from this wall, who knows what we're dealing with."

"Do you think Celia is in danger?" Jack replied with concern.

"I don't know," Harrison replied uneasily. "Like I said, could be a coincidence." He pulled the walkie talkie up to his mouth. "Sierra?"

"Yes, Harrison?" Sierra replied.

"I want you and Celia to stay near the front of the administration building where the cameras are set up and do some recordings. Getting anything on EMF?"

"Nothing on EMF. We'll try to get some EVP responses," Sierra replied.

"Good idea. Jack and I are heading into the tunnel here in Penn Hall. Will report back shortly. Let me know if you get anything."

"Got it," Sierra replied.

"We're going to head back up to the first floor," Morgan replied. "It's quiet down here."

"Thanks, Morg," Harrison replied. "Keep us posted."

Harrison tucked the walkie talkie back into his pocket. "Let's get down into the tunnel and see if we can figure out what's going on with that camera," he said to Jack.

"All right," Jack replied nervously, feeling the chill throughout his body.

Harrison took the lead, and the pair made their way across the great room toward the dark expanse leading to the tunnel entrance. They shined their lights all around the space, devoid of life and filled with rusted metal beams, broken glass, and peeling walls.

They arrived at the far end adjacent the main entrance to Penn Hall, where they were met with a large rusted metal door fully ajar. Harrison moved inside the stairwell and carefully onto the first step, his boot crunching on the debris that blanketed the staircase. He slowly made his way to the bottom, holding gently to the rusty railing, Jack closely behind.

They reached the bottom, and Harrison shined his flashlight one direction, Jack the other. As far as their light would travel, they saw only a long dark hallway with concrete block walls covered in peeling green paint, dark water stains, and graffiti. The ground was covered in a fine layer of dirt with bits of debris and large pieces of broken concrete scattered all about. Jack spied boot prints left behind by Sierra and Garrett.

They stood still for a moment, listening intently. It was like a dark cave buried inside a mountain. Even the slightest sound echoed forever. Droplets of water sounded like a spoon handle tapping a pot.

"The camera should be down this way if they followed my map," Harrison whispered. His words blew out clouds of cold air and lingered for a moment.

Jack pointed his flashlight in the opposite direction of where Harrison suggested they go. He wanted to check his back before moving ahead.

"You go first," Harrison said, noticing Jack's hesitation. "I got your back."

Jack obliged. It had been two years since he had been in the tunnels, and that was when he had a head full of steam and adrenaline to match. Now, he was only following the crazy notion to be down there in the first place.

Jack passed Harrison and began walking slowly down the tunnel toward the camera. It wasn't long before he spotted it, seated on a tripod at waist level. Jack approached it carefully, not wanting to bump anything.

Harrison walked to the camera and leaned over it. He turned it on and off then on again.

"Are you doing that?" Garrett called through the walkie.

"Yeah, that's me," Harrison replied. "Are you getting anything?"

"Seems to be working now," Garrett said. "What percentage is the battery reading?"

Harrison checked the reading on the monitor. "It's full."

"Okay, good," Garrett replied. "Could have been interference from anywhere. I'm getting a good picture now."

Harrison stood up and pointed his light at the ground, then knelt and ran his fingers around the dirt. He pointed his flashlight in either direction down the tunnel.

"Let's go that way and see what we can find," Harrison said, pointing his light beyond the camera. He pulled the EMF meter out again and flipped it on. Jack could see it was reading 00.1. Harrison began walking with the device held out in front of him, passing the camera with Jack in tow.

They walked along slowly, the tunnel stretched out far in front of them. It looked like it went on forever, though Jack knew it didn't. They could continue for ten minutes or less and eventually make it to Building A.

"What are we looking for?" Jack asked quietly, breaking the silence.

"Any shift in energy," Harrison replied. "Voices. Maybe a cold spot."

"It's pretty cold down here already," Jack replied with a shiver.

"Oh, you would know if it got cold suddenly," Harrison replied. "Wait! I'm getting something. Check it out."

Harrison showed Jack the EMF meter. It was dancing around .6 and .8 on the digital display.

"Is that good?" Jack asked.

"It's something," Harrison said excitedly.

Harrison continued, walking slowly and cautiously, his eyes wide and glued to the meter reading. It spiked suddenly, jumping to 1.3.

"Whoa! Did you see that?" Harrison called out in a loud whisper. Jack nodded anxiously. They continued. The meter jumped to 2.2 then back to 1.8 then 2.0 and down to 1.8 again.

"Is that normal?" Jack asked.

"We're picking up on something." Harrison looked up in front of them then pointed his light behind and back in front again.

"Is there someone here with us?" Harrison called out, his voice echoing loudly. The hairs on Jack's neck couldn't have stood up any straighter. *Is it getting colder?*

"Do you feel that?" Harrison said in a shrill whisper. "Can you feel it got colder?"

Jack shivered a nod.

"Who are you?" Harrison called out ahead of them. The EMF was reading a 3.3 now. "Can you show yourself?"

"Do you really want to do that?" Jack suddenly remembered the first time he saw Dr. Moseley's daughter, Heather, in Building C. The small ghost came to them in an unexplainable shape of glowing bright light at first until she wanted to be fully seen. Jack wasn't so sure he was ready for that again.

"What's your name?" Harrison yelled. "What do you want here?" Harrison tried to get a response, but none came. The EMF jumped to 3.7 on the meter.

"That seems pretty high, right?" Jack said, pointing to the meter. "You said it only goes to five?"

Harrison nodded. He looked terrified and ecstatic at the same time. "This is one of the higher readings I've gotten. But there appears to be nothing here."

No sooner had the words left his mouth when a colder blast of air filled in around them. Jack wrapped his arms around his body. Harrison pulled the walkie talkie out and fumbled it a bit before pressing the call button.

"Garrett, are you getting this?" Harrison said.

"Everything seems normal," Garrett replied. "I just see you and Jack way down in the distance. Just your flashlights, really."

"Something is down here," Harrison replied frantically. "I'm getting almost a four on the EMF."

"Wow, that's big." Garrett's voice came through with static interference.

"Did you say four?" Morgan chimed in on the walkie, static accompanying his voice, too. "Where are you?"

"We're in the tunnel under Penn Hall," Harrison replied. He looked down at the EMF again. "It's at 4.5 now!"

"That's crazy!" Sierra called through static.

Just then, Jack could see a bright green light appear down the far end of the tunnel in front of them. It was small at first, then grew twice the size in an instant.

"Look!" Jack hollered.

Harrison turned to see the light had grown ten times the size and appeared to be racing for them.

"Go!" Harrison yelled at Jack.

They took off down the tunnel, heading for the stairwell.

"Holy shit!" Harrison hollered as they ran like mad. "EMF is at a solid five!"

They passed the camera and picked up the pace. *We're not far from the staircase.*

"I still don't see anything, Harrison!" Garrett called through the walkie talkie.

"Oh, it's here!" Harrison called back, then shoved the walkie talkie into his pocket.

The green light was beating them to the stairwell, shining brightly all around them. Harrison grabbed the railing first, then grabbed hold of Jack and gave him a shove up the first step.

"Hurry!" Harrison yelled.

Jack turned his head to see the entire opening of the tunnel filled with a blinding bright green light. He looked away and raced madly up the stairwell, two steps at a time, with Harrison close behind.

They blasted through the doorway at the top of the landing and flew through the great open room, hurdling over the debris several feet at a time. The room was soon filled with the green light as they reached the entrance to Penn Hall and leaped out the doors, completely dismissing the front porch and flying beyond the staircase, landing hard on the ground outside.

Jack's ankle gave out, and he tumbled a few yards. He scrambled to his feet and turned around to find that the green light had vanished. Everything was calm and dark, as if they had imagined the entire thing.

"Harrison?" Garrett called through the walkie.

"What's going on there, guys?" Morgan added.

Harrison dug in his pocket and pulled out the walkie talkie. "Garrett, did you get any of that?"

"Where are you?" Garrett replied frantically.

"What did you see?" Morgan added.

"We were just chased out of the tunnel by a giant green light. EMF was at a full five!" Harrison hollered. He was breathing heavily.

"Wait!" Garrett cried out. "I see it! I see it!"

"What are you getting?" Harrison replied.

"It's a bright light, just like you said," replied Garrett. "It's going down the tunnel away from the camera." Static. "It's fast!" Static. "It's gone!"

"Amazing," Harrison said to Jack. "That was intense!"

Jack was distracted, catching his breath and rubbing his ankle, but could think of other words aside from amazing.

"See anything else?" Harrison asked.

"It's dark again," Garrett said. "Wait…" Static. "I'm picking up something under Building A." Static. "It's the light again. It's the same light! It's coming down the tunnel to the camera." Static. "Oh, shit! It just knocked out the camera!"

"The camera's down?" Morgan replied.

"Yeah, we lost the camera under you guys," Garrett called out.

"What is going on?" Jack replied with concern.

"I have no idea," Harrison said dumbfounded. "I've never seen anything like this."

"Wait… there it is again." Garrett came back on the walkie talkie. "It's coming down the tunnel under the admin building." Static. "Fast! Real fast!" Static. "Lost another camera!"

"Celia!" Harrison shrieked. He pulled the walkie talkie right up to his mouth. "Sierra!" he yelled into the walkie. "Sierra, pick up!"

"We're here, Harrison," Sierra replied.

"Where are you?" Harrison screamed frantically.

"We're in the admin building, out by the entrance," Sierra replied.

"Are you listening to this?" Harrison shouted.

"Yeah, just trying to follow along," Sierra replied, a tinge of nervousness in her voice. "You said the light is in the tunnel below us now, Garrett?"

"It was! We lost the feed," Garrett shouted back.

"Sierra, get out of there now!" Harrison screamed. He grabbed Jack's arm and pulled him into a run down the road. "Sierra, get out of there now!" he called into the walkie talkie.

"What's going on?" Sierra hollered back.

"You gotta get Celia out of there now!" Harrison screamed in panic. He ran even faster, and Jack struggled to keep up with Harrison's tall strides.

"What is it?" Jack cried out.

"They're in danger," Harrison replied. "I can feel it!"

"The door is locked!" Sierra cried out through the walkie talkie.

"What do you mean it's locked?" Harrison replied. "Ram it down!"

"The front door to the admin building just slammed shut," Garrett called out. "I saw it on the feed."

"Get it open!" said Harrison. "Kick it down if you have to!"

"They're trying!" Garrett added. "They're trapped!"

Harrison and Jack were nearly at the turn to the generating station.

"I lost the feed!" Garrett hollered.

"Sierra?" Harrison called.

"We can't get out," Sierra yelled back, following by a blood curdling, "NO!"

"Sierra?" Harrison cried out.

"Harrison! What is going on?" Morgan pressed.

"It has her!" Sierra said in a shrill cry.

"What has her?" Mose came through suddenly on the walkie talkie.

"The light… it took her!" Sierra replied in desperation.

"Took her?" Mose called out. "Where?" he demanded.

"She's gone!" Sierra cried out. "Down into the tunnels. It happened too fast—there was nothing I could do to stop it."

Harrison and Jack reached the road to see Garrett jump out of the back of the Paranormal Examiners' truck. All the spotlights that surrounded the truck were dark. The emergency lights were on inside the care center.

Captain Hadaway's cruiser was parked in front of the building, his lights flashing blue and red. He stepped out of the car and began walking toward Harrison and Jack.

Harrison turned and looked up the road in the direction of the admin building. Jack was desperately longing to be with Celia and Sierra, and he could sense the same was true for Harrison.

"What is the meaning of this?" Captain Hadaway said to Jack, motioning to the Paranormal Examiners' truck.

Jack didn't reply. Harrison didn't even pay attention to the police captain questioning them.

"This is serious," Harrison said to no one in particular.

Just then the ground beneath the generating station rumbled like a magnitude 7.0 earthquake, and a flash of green light shot out of the tower.

"Not again," Captain Hadaway grumbled.

Chapter 10

Danny and Tommy jogged up the road, flashlights in hand and pointing them at Harrison, Jack, and Captain Hadaway, who were staring up at the generating station tower.

"Point those lights down!" Hadaway yelled, shielding his eyes.

"Sorry, Captain Hadaway!" Danny apologized as he approached.

"Where are you two coming from?" Hadaway asked, checking out their new security uniforms.

"Walking the perimeter," Danny replied, respectfully nervous. "We were just coming to check in with Dr. Moseley when we felt the ground rumble. Did you see the light shoot out of the tower?"

Hadaway nodded, then turned to Harrison. "What is all this?"

Harrison ignored the captain and ran to Garrett, who was hanging out the back of the Paranormal Examiners' truck with a worried look on his face.

"Show me the tape from the Administration Building," Harrison said to Garrett as he pulled himself into the truck filled with equipment. Jack dashed over and hopped up inside, eagerly looking for answers.

Harrison followed Garrett to the console with the screens above keyboards, all displaying noise.

"All cameras are offline now," Garrett said. "But we can roll back the recordings."

Harrison pulled his walkie talkie from his jacket. "Charles? Morgan? Where are you now?"

"We're heading for you now," Morgan replied.

Garrett was toying with the equipment as Harrison hovered over him. Jack was standing byhis side as Captain Hadaway, Tommy, and Danny approached the back of the truck.

"Sierra!" Harrison called into the walkie talkie. "Where are you now? What do you see?"

"I'm going into the tunnel," Sierra called back, breathless and frantic, sounding as if she was running.

"Stop!" Harrison replied. "Turn back and wait for us!"

Silence on the walkie talkie from the other end.

"Sierra, did you hear me? Wait for us!" Harrison demanded.

"Okay, I'm heading back," Sierra replied solemnly. "I'll meet you out front of the administration building." She paused. "But please hurry."

"Charles, Morgan," Harrison called, "When you arrive, we're going to hop in your truck, so you can take us to the admin building."

"Got it," Morgan replied, the rumble of Dr. Moseley's truck engine in the background. "We'll be there in a minute."

Harrison turned back to focus on the footage Garrett was scanning. Every video monitor in front of them was displaying noise with the exception of the techie's computer screen, which showed footage from the administration building.

"Stop!" Harrison called out. "There! Did you see that?"

Garrett shook his head.

"Go back!" Harrison called out. Garrett took the footage back a few seconds. "There!"

"Oh, yeah, good eye, Harrison," Garrett said, awestruck. "But that's from right after we set up the cameras."

"What is it?" Jack asked.

"A glowing orb of some sort," Harrison replied. "It comes in from the great room where the tunnel entrance is. Then the camera is adjusted."

Harrison rubbed his smooth head, thinking.

"What could it be?" Jack asked.

"It looks as though a body of energy enters the area and toys with our equipment," Harrison replied, perplexed. Then his eyes lit up. "Garrett, go back to the other camera footage and check around similar timestamps."

Garrett opened more windows on the screen and began rewinding footage. First, he reviewed the inside of Building A. Nothing of note. Then he opened the footage from the tunnel under Building A and quickly scanned it. They saw the same white light glitching the camera. Next, he pulled up the footage from Penn Hall tunnel and backed it up to a place where he could see Sierra standing in front of the camera.

"Okay, that's where we left the camera," Garrett said.

"Move ahead," Harrison replied.

Garrett fast forwarded the footage quickly.

"There!" Harrison said.

"I see it!" Garrett replied.

Jack was so taken by the image on the screen, his eyes opened wide and his body felt suddenly weak.

"That's King," Jack said soberly.

"King?" Harrison replied.

The trio stared at the image on the screen that only appeared to be a stretched wisp of glowing light. Jack leaned in and outlined the shape he could make out, and they could clearly see the outline of a man.

"Sam King, He was a resident here," Jack said.

"How do you know this?" Garrett asked.

"He was here the night my daughter left us for the last time," Dr. Moseley answered from the back of the truck.

Harrison, Garrett, and Jack turned to see Mose climbing up into the truck, assisted by Captain Hadaway. His blue pickup was parked nearby, engine humming. Morgan followed him, and they walked up to the monitor and leaned in to see the outline of the man on screen.

"Though he was filled with rage, Heather appeared to have become friendly with this spirit," Mose said. "I think she may have had a calming effect on him—she was like that." Mose stared at the image, rubbing his long chin. "But it doesn't add up. He left with Heather that night, sucked into the vortex that blasted from inside the generating station. We saw it."

Jack nodded. "We did. King carried Coach Slater out of the generating station and tossed him out a window."

"Then he disappeared into the light with all the other spirits," another voice called from the truck.

Jack turned to see Henry standing with Captain Hadaway, Danny, and Tommy—the latter two looking terrified.

"Dad?" Jack yelped, perturbed and surprised. "What are *you* doing here?"

"This is like déjà vu, Jack," Henry said in a concerned tone. "You didn't come home for dinner, didn't call or text, and now I see Dr. Moseley's truck barreling toward the generating station that just let out a blast of light and is rumbling like mad."

"Yeah, what is going on?" Tommy asked nervously, his voice trembling.

"I don't know," Mose replied. "But this was my worst fear."

"What, exactly, was your worst fear, Charles?" Henry asked in a suspicious tone.

Mose didn't answer Henry but turned to Jack and whispered to him, "I dreamed this was going to happen, Jack. I dreamed that someone would be taken into the tunnels—a girl. I never saw her face, though. I simply wrote it off that I was dreaming of Heather, because of how much I still miss her." He paused, his eyes looking glassy. "But I've grown to care for Celia so much that I wouldn't let myself see it was actually her in my dream. I knew this and could have prevented it."

Harrison put a hand on Dr. Moseley's shoulder. "Charles, this isn't your fault," he said calmly. "But we must take action. We have to find out where he has taken her, this King character."

Mose wiped the tears away with his sleeve, then straightened. "What do we need to do?"

"Get us to the admin building," Harrison said confidently.

"Right, let's go!" Dr. Moseley said eagerly.

"Now wait a minute," Henry said. "Jack, I want you home—you're sitting this one out."

"No!" Jack replied firmly.

"Jack, please! I've had enough of this. You especially have had enough of this," Henry pleaded.

"Dad, he took Celia," Jack replied firmly. "I can't just let this play out. This thing has been following us. All of us."

"Jack, please…" Henry pleaded again. "You've been making so much progress with Sandy ever since—"

"That's just it—I haven't!" Jack interrupted. "Look, I know you're worried about me and you wish I would feel better, but these dreams aren't going away. They've only gotten worse. And all Sandy wants me to do is deep breathing exercises and tell myself this isn't my fault. But I'm not blaming myself for anything. I can help here."

Henry sighed, his shoulders dropping in despair.

"Dad, you have to trust me," Jack pleaded. "You have to understand that why this is all happening again is beyond anyone's comprehension. But I've been having dreams and experiences, Dr. Moseley is having dreams, and now Celia, too. And now she's trapped, and we've got to save her. She's my best friend."

Henry looked on in silence, his face showing the distress of indecision and heartbreak. "Fine, son. I trust you. Go do what you need to do." He swallowed hard as he teared up slightly. "Your mom would be proud all over again."

Harrison clapped his hands to break the moment. "Garrett, you're coming with us." Harrison turned to his bearded partner seated behind the console. "Bring a camera, extra batteries… I have an EVP and a voice recorder. What else?"

"Some guns?" Tommy called out.

"Guns?" Garrett replied. "Are you going to shoot a ghost?"

"Ghost?" Hadaway replied with a long sigh. "It is happening again." He pulled his phone from his pocket and began dialing a number.

"What are you doing?" Dr. Moseley asked Captain Hadaway as he hopped down from the truck.

"Calling for backup," Hadaway replied, his aging strong features illuminated by the screen.

Moseley put his hand over the face of the phone and pressed gently down to stop Hadaway from making the call. Hadaway looked at Dr. Moseley in confusion.

"Please, Captain, let us handle this," Mose pleaded quietly.

Hadaway stood frozen, thinking intently before disconnecting the call and tucking his phone away. "Charles, I hope you know what you're doing here."

"I have no idea what I'm doing," Mose said.

He paused then pointed up at Harrison, Garrett, and Morgan, all gathered at the back of the open truck, finalizing their equipment prep.

"But they do."

Hadaway looked up at the paranormal investigators, sighed, then looked back at Mose. "If this gets out of hand, I'm calling in reinforcements."

"Fine," Mose replied. "Just give them some time."

"You've got an hour," Hadaway said, looking at his watch, then walked back toward his cruiser.

Jack checked his phone for the time—7:58. We have till 9:00.

"What should we do, Dr. Moseley?" Danny asked.

"You two stay with the captain," Mose replied. "We need to be sure no one enters the campus after seeing what just happened at the generating station."

The pair nodded and followed Captain Hadaway.

"That's exactly what I'm going to do now," Hadaway called out from his cruiser as he pulled his door shut and started up the engine. "I'm going to keep that entrance off limits. Hop in, guys."

Danny and Tommy climbed into the police vehicle, and Hadaway spun around and sped toward the Linhurst entrance, his red and blue lights flashing across the wall of trees on either side of the road.

"I'm not just going to go home and sit on my hands hoping everything will work out all right," Henry announced.

The entire group turned to see him standing aloof at the back of the Paranormal Examiners' truck.

"Will you stay here and keep an eye on things?" Mose replied.

Harrison tossed a walkie talkie to Henry. "You can let us know if you witness any strange activity."

"It would be my pleasure," Henry said, proudly hooking the walkie talkie to his belt. Jack could see his dad was enamored to be part of the team.

Mose made for his truck, the engine still running, and climbed into the driver's seat. "Let's go!"

Harrison and Jack jumped up into the back of the truck. Garrett tossed a duffle bag filled with equipment off his shoulder and heaved it over the side of the bed and set it down, then stepped onto the back bumper and began to pull himself up. Harrison leaned over and grabbed hold of his friend and assisted him over the side. Garrett took a seat in the far back corner, his weight making the bed sink for a moment.

Harrison pounded his palm on the side of the pickup. "All set!"

Mose sped off, heading up the road toward the administration building to hunt for King and their friend Celia.

They raced on in silence past Buildings A through C. Many of the apartments were lit with the nighttime glow of TVs and e-readers. Mose sped around the fountain in the courtyard and onward toward the construction site. The road was rough and bumpy, but Mose didn't slow down. Jack, Harrison, and Morgan bounced around in the bed of the truck.

"Hold on back there!" Mose called out.

They were soon under a canopy of darkened trees and forest surrounding them, passing construction equipment saddled on the side of the road by piles of dirt and trash.

They made their way out into a clearing and Mose swung a hard left, everyone hanging on. Garrett's arm was hanging out the back of the truck, and he suddenly lifted himself and nearly toppled out. Harrison quickly grabbed the back of his sweatshirt and pulled him upright.

"Going somewhere?" Harrison hollered at him.

"Dropped my damn flashlight!" Garrett replied loudly over the noise of the engine.

"At this speed, you'd have taken a pretty good tumble yourself," Harrison told him. "Hang on tight, man!"

Mose raced up the straightaway leading to the administration building, then into the circular driveway. He stopped abruptly at the end of the walkway leading up to the massive double doors atop the grand wooden staircase to the front of the building.

Mose got out quickly and slammed his door, wasting no time as he started up the walkway. Jack and Harrison hopped down from the sides of the truck as Morgan jumped out of the passenger side. Garrett clumsily pushed himself up off the floor of the bed, then grabbed hold of the duffle bag and handed it down to Harrison.

"I got ya, Garrett," Harrison said as he reached out a hand to his friend and helped him down, with a bit of a struggle.

"I'll carry this up to the building," said Harrison, noticing Garrett was out of breath from the fast pace already.

"Thanks, man," Garrett replied. "You know I'm always behind the console in the truck. Haven't done field work in, like, a year."

He followed Harrison and Jack as they caught up with Mose and Morgan, making their way to the entrance of the administration building at a fast clip.

The moon overhead cast the face of the already hollowed out interior in an ominous shadow. A pink mop of hair appeared from the darkness at the top of the porch, a few bits of jewelry sparkling in the faint light. Sierra was pacing the busted wooden floorboards Jack could clearly recall in his mind from the night he and Celia outran Tommy and Danny from the tunnels.

"Are you all right?" Harrison called up to Sierra.

"Harrison, Morgan, dudes!" she began frantically, dashing halfway down the stairs and coming into the light. "I've never seen anything like it! It was so intense!"

She was waving her hands all about, her body electrified with emotion.

"Was she hurt?" Mose asked.

"It happened so fast," Sierra replied quickly. "We were trying to get out through the doors. The light was growing brightly behind us. We were both pushing on the door and then in an instant, the light was so blinding I had to look away. When it dimmed, I turned to reach for Celia, but she wasn't there. All I saw was this massive body glowing from inside the orb of light. Then it disappeared through the door into the tunnels, and they were gone. She was yelling for help the whole way, then her voice faded."

"We must find her quickly!" Mose yelled to the group, then he ran up the stairs, past Sierra, and through the open doors with Morgan on his heels. Harrison met Sierra halfway, and she glued herself to his side.

"You know how we're only capturing little orbs or mumblings or whatever?" Sierra asked Harrison in a clearly upset tone of voice. "This was a giant, full-bodied apparition glowing bright as the sun!"

"We saw it, too!" Garrett said to Sierra, breathing heavily as he climbed the steps.

"So, we have it on film?" Sierra asked, eyes wide.

"Yes, we captured it," Garrett confirmed.

Sierra's expression went from shock to awe to a humongous smile in an instant. "Holy shit!" She began laughing. "That's amazing! Dude!"

Garrett put out his hand and she high fived him, then jumped on him, wrapping her tiny frame around his large torso and hugging him wildly, practically making him lose his balance on the stairs.

"Whoa! Easy!" Garrett yelped.

She hopped down and patted him on the back, regaining composure.

"My friend is down there," Jack snapped, "and you're celebrating?"

The pair turned to Jack, their excitement vanished, and they began to apologize before they were interrupted.

"Jack's right," Harrison called from the top of the porch. "What's the matter with you two? Celia is somewhere down in those tunnels, taken by an unexplained force the likes of which we've never seen, and you are excited about capturing it?"

Sierra and Garrett looked up at Harrison in embarrassment.

"You should be ashamed," Harrison continued. "Lives are at stake here—this isn't like every other time."

The pair nodded and regained composure.

"Now get up here!" Harrison demanded. "We've got work to do."

Sierra put her head down in shame and grabbed Garrett by the arm, practically dragging him up the rest of the stairs and inside the administration building. Harrison watched their every step, then came down to Jack, who was still standing in place, fuming.

"Hey, Jack," he began, "I know how that must have felt, and I apologize. We normally do get excited when we find something unique, but this is different, and they don't feel this the way you and I do."

Jack was breathing heavily, his body filled with anger and fear. He'd nearly stopped trusting Harrison because of how Sierra and Garrett had celebrated, but he was over it again and ready to focus.

"Okay, what do we need to do?" Jack asked, looking up at Harrison, standing tall on the staircase with the moonlight shining down on his head.

"We're going to track down that ghost and get Celia out of the tunnels," Harrison said confidently.

Jack nodded, and he and Harrison dashed up the stairs, danced around the busted boards of the porch, and walked through the giant double wooden doors.

Inside, Jack had a quick look around. Things hadn't changed much since he and Celia were in there last. The only thing different was that it was a bit emptier. The grand staircase leading to the second level was still intact, the walls still peeling of paint. *How can they think to put a haunted house in here?*

Garrett was emptying the duffle bag of its equipment, Sierra picking up devices and getting things set up. Morgan was walking about the room with an EMF meter.

"Picking up anything?" Harrison asked.

"Nothing yet," Morgan replied.

"Jack and Charles, come with me to the tunnel entrance," Harrison said, then turned to Morgan. "We're going to do some readings."

They walked across the expansive lobby of the administration building to a set of double doors. They went through to find a great room with high windows lining the walls on the left and right and floor-to-ceiling pillars reaching high into the void above their heads, running the length of the room, just like other buildings on campus.

Harrison jogged to the far end of the room, shining his flashlight into the darkness until he located the door that opened into the tunnels.

"Jack, your light?" Harrison said without stopping. "Keep it fixed on the tunnel door."

Jack nodded as Harrison tucked his light away and pulled out the EMF meter then flicked it on.

"What's it reading?" Jack asked.

"It's low. Just 0.2 right now," Harrison replied.

They reached the door and Mose, Jack, and Harrison squeezed through quickly, undeterred by the threat of the spectral giant that had swept Celia away.

"Still reading low," Harrison said as the trio stood at the top of the landing. He leaned over the railing and tipped his ear toward the black abyss below. Jack and Mose silenced themselves and steadied their breathing. Deafening silence. No drips of water. Not even the slightest brush of air to disturb their ears. Harrison stood up.

"I'm going to call for her and see what we get," Harrison whispered. Mose and Jack nodded in confirmation, and he leaned back over the railing.

"Celia!" Harrison called down into the abyss below. His voice echoed for what felt like an eternity.

"Wow, that was louder than I wanted it to be. Sorry," Harrison said, turning his head to look up from the railing while still leaning over it. Once the echo stopped, there was no reply. "Let me try again," he warned Jack and Mose.

"Celia!" Harrison called out again.

It echoed on forever. Nothing in return.

Harrison stood up and turned to Mose and Jack with a look of frustration on his face. The trio stared at one another for a few moments, and Jack sensed they had run out of ideas. *What can we do now?* They couldn't simply go down into the tunnels and wander aimlessly, hoping Celia would be at the first turn. The network of tunnels below them weaved and wound for miles among the thirty-plus buildings on the Linhurst campus. It could take them all night—and then some—to explore every turn and empty room down below.

Jack walked over by Harrison's side. He leaned over the railing and cupped his hands. "We want Celia! Bring her back now!" he bellowed down the twisting stairwell.

His voice echoed for a few seconds when suddenly a great gust of wind blasted right out of the abyss, causing Jack and Harrison to stand up and stumble back a few steps.

"Whoa! Did you feel that—" Harrison barely got the words out when he was struck by an equally booming "GO AWAY!" that knocked him back a few more steps.

Jack ran down the stairs into the abyss, feeling suddenly fearless through his great anger.

"Jack, stop!" Harrison called to him.

"Jack!" Mose added. "You won't find her that way."

Jack knew this, but he was angry and desperate.

"You bring her back!" Jack screamed as he raced down the steps. "Now! Bring her back, you monster!" His voice echoed, his anger rising inside him with each yell.

Harrison grabbed hold of the back of Jack's sweatshirt and tugged him as he began down the tunnel. Jack turned around and looked at Harrison.

"Come on, Jack," Harrison said. "We must find another way."

Jack shoved Harrison away. He marched farther down the tunnel and screamed at the top of his lungs, "Bring her back here, NOW!"

His voice echoed loudly throughout the caverns when suddenly a green light glowed faintly ahead of him and grew brighter by the second.

"Jack!" Harrison yelled from behind.

Jack could feel Harrison's fist grip the back of his sweatshirt again, then tug on him, this time so hard Jack fell backward. He was going to land hard on the ground...

Chapter 11

J ack found himself sitting in a chair in the middle of the great room inside the administration building.

It was suddenly bright, the sun pouring in through the windows, the glass panes completely intact. The walls were freshly painted, and the pillars holding up the ceiling showed the same high-gloss white. The great open space was sterile and clean, with a handful of people at wooden desks and chairs tapping away at typewriters and filing paperwork.

His vision was slightly blurry, and he tried to rub his eyes but realized his arms wouldn't move. A hand touched his.

"Relax, son," a voice said softly to his side.

A blurry Dr. Royer stood by his side, leaning down to his level. Then Jack realized he was restrained, his wrists and ankles tied tightly to a wooden wheelchair.

"You don't need to say anything. You'll be all right soon enough," Dr. Royer said, then he stood up and walked toward the entrance of the tunnels where a man was standing.

"Now that we have him sedated, what will you do about Sam?" Dr. Royer asked the man.

Jack tried blinking to remove the haze in front of him. His head felt dizzy, as though he was floating in a cloud. Suddenly, behind him, screaming echoed throughout the room. Jack tried to turn around to face the commotion, but the restraints prevented him. Several people in the room rushed behind Jack toward the screaming voice.

"Bring him over here!" the man by the tunnels yelled. Slater. Jack would recognize that voice anywhere.

Soon, the screaming voice—a man yelling "Let me go!" and "Get me out of here!"—was standing right in front of Slater. He was bound in a straitjacket. It took five people to hold him.

"You see what you've done, Sam?" Slater demanded of the man. "You've gone and hurt another resident. I warned you about this."

King!

Slater paused, and the large man in front of him struggled against the restraints. Jack tried but couldn't make out his face.

"He's got bruises, a bloody lip, and a missing tooth, all thanks to you," Slater growled. "Have anything to say for yourself?"

"He got in the way!" Sam replied in a low grumble.

"Who were you going for today that you had to mow down so many people in your path?" Slater asked.

Sam only growled.

"I'll keep sending you back down to the lower wards and putting you to work for every time you lash out."

"Go ahead, I'll just keep coming back," Sam replied.

"You're just going to keep fighting me, are you?" Slater chuckled. "Always causing trouble and thinking you're going to get away with it. And all over that hussy in Mayflower. That's the last thing we need here is retards having kids with other retards!"

Sam growled at Slater and pulled on the men and women holding onto his straitjacket. They appeared to lose their footing, and Slater pulled back, nervous that King might actually reach him. When he realized the people tugging on him were able to restrain him, Slater regained his composure and let out a hearty laugh.

"Your mama put you in here when you were just a little boy—best decision she ever made," Slater said in a downright mean and nasty tone. "You have no control here. We own you now. And there ain't no way you're getting out. You're mine."

Sam growled again. "I'm leaving here when I turn 18, and you'll never see me again!"

Slater turned a brilliant red and began breathing heavily. "Get him out of here!"

King was taken from the room, through the door into the tunnels, screaming the entire way down the stairwell. His voice was loud and echoed throughout the great room where Jack sat restrained. The handful of people who remained in the room were frozen in place, their attention on the open door where King was led.

Jack could hear King struggling down in the tunnel, then the sound of a large metal door slammed shut, and King's voice was muffled. The men and women who took Sam down returned through the tunnel door.

"How long this time?" one of the men asked.

"I'll take care of it personally," Slater replied. "He won't be seeing the sun for a few days."

Slater slammed the door tight, and the others returned to their work. Then Slater walked over to Jack and stopped in front of his wheelchair.

"You'll feel better in no time, boy," Slater said to Jack. "Sam King thinks he can one-up me, but he ain't going anywhere. He's a menace to society. You have nothing to fear."

Slater turned to Dr. Royer. "Good to go, Doc?"

"I'll take it from here," Dr. Royer replied, sounding displeased and frustrated. He walked behind Jack and started wheeling him out of the room away from the tunnel. The room slowly fell dark.

Jack looked up to see a green light glowing above him. He looked around and focused his eyes to see he was staring up into the ceiling at the top of the stairwell. A wide beam of brilliant green light poured out from below, then it blasted into many vibrant streams of light in every direction and a giant form of a man appeared above him.

"GO AWAY!" a voice called out from above, echoing down upon them.

"It's King!" Jack called out.

"She's mine now!" the voice bellowed.

Jack was suddenly scooped up off his feet. He turned to see Harrison, who had a tight grip on the back of his sweatshirt.

"Run!"

Jack and Mose hastily made their way back inside the great room. Harrison pushed the metal door to the tunnel and turned the rusted lock on the door, then ran toward them. They made it to the other end of the great room and stopped inside the lobby doors when they heard a maddening quake behind them.

A great force of energy charged the tunnel door from the opposite side, causing it to shake and the entire framework of the door rattled on its hinges. Pieces of plaster shook from the walls all around the door, then a fissure split through the corner of the doorframe, followed by a crackled web breaking the wall apart in every direction.

"Run!" Mose yelled.

The trio took off from the great room door and out into the administration building lobby with Morgan, Sierra, and Garrett looking on in horror.

"Come on!" Sierra yelled, hand outstretched. Jack grabbed her open palm and she pulled him toward the entrance doors of the admin building just as the floor under them quaked. Jack turned to look.

The door to the tunnel was outlined by bright green light as it continued to rattle and shake. Then the door blasted off its hinges and flew out into the middle of the great room, slamming the floor hard and skidding to a stop just yards away from them. A great blast of wind was followed by the unmistakable voice of Sam King, who yelled, "GO AWAY... NOW!"

The light vanished back down the stairwell as if it was sucked in by a giant vacuum, and suddenly all was calm and dark beyond the broken doorframe. The group stood helplessly inside the darkened and quiet administration building entrance.

"Now what?" Sierra broke the silence, sounding helpless.

Suddenly, the building began to rumble greater than ever beneath their feet. The rafters above them followed suit, raining down bits of dust and debris. The tremors grew into a constant and violent quake, until boards began to fall inside the great room and inside the lobby around them.

"Everyone out!" Mose belted out.

Sierra scooped up the duffle bag and ran for the door, with Garrett close behind. Morgan swept up a camera sitting on a tripod and was right on their heels.

In a matter of moments, everyone in the group dashed out onto the porch and down the stairs, stopping just before the circular drive. They turned in time to see the front pillars of the administration building porch crack amid the rumbling quake, snapping like toothpicks. The porch roof caved in, leaving a cloud of dust and a pile of rubble around the entrance.

A piece of rock came tumbling down the stairs and stopped right at Jack's feet. He picked it up and held it tightly in his fist, feeling the small jagged edges pressing into his palm. He looked up the stairs to the entrance then heaved the rock at the building.

"Give her back!" Jack shouted.

A blast of green light shined brightly from the windows of the admin building for only a moment, as if in response to Jack.

"What do we do?" Sierra said quietly.

"This is new territory for us all," Morgan replied, nervously running his fingers through the puffy mop of hair on his head.

"Did you see that?" Henry called over on the walkie talkie.

Mose pulled his walkie talkie from inside his deep jacket pocket. "We did. A blast of light from the administration building—we're standing in front of it."

"Not that," Henry answered. "A light coming from the generating station. Lots of rumbling."

"We're on our way back," Mose replied, sounding nervous.

"Everyone in the truck," Morgan declared.

"You can't give up!" Jack pleaded.

Harrison turned to Jack with a look of determination on his face. "Not giving up, Jack. I know someone who can help us."

"So do I," Jack replied.

"Who?" Dr. Moseley asked.

"Slater," Jack replied.

"He's locked up. What good will he do us now?" Mose asked.

"I had another vision of Sam King," Jack began. "Slater had him taken into the tunnel under the administration building in a straitjacket. There must be a confinement cell down there somewhere."

"We're going to try and reach him," said Harrison.

"You already tried. Look how he reacted," Jack replied.

"We're going to have a séance," Harrison said. "Come on. Get in the truck. We don't have much time. I'll explain more later."

With that, everyone followed Harrison's lead and piled into Dr. Moseley's small blue pickup truck.

"Sorry!" Garrett called out.

"That's not on you, buddy," Harrison said, pulling his friend into the bed of the truck with all his equipment.

Mose started up the engine and they were off. Jack stared at the front of the administration building, looking innocent and purely evil at once. His mind was racing with thoughts of where King could have taken Celia deep inside the recesses under Linhurst. And why? Did it have something to do with Slater? Why was King's spirit still lingering there, even after he swore he'd seen it join all the other spirits at the generating station two years ago on Halloween?

The little blue pickup loaded with people raced past the construction area, through the courtyard at Buildings A through C, then through the short run of woods that opened to the generating station and Linhurst Care Center.

All was eerily quiet, as if everyone else on campus but theywere completely unaware of what was happening, or didn't want to admit it was happening. For a moment, Jack wondered if he was possibly dreaming all of this, too.

Dr. Moseley pulled to a stop behind the Paranormal Examiners' black truck, the doors still slightly ajar from when they had left. Beyond the truck sat the Linhurst Care Center, completely dark inside with the exception of the emergency lights lit in the lobby where Henry was seated. He saw the crew pulling up and ran outside.

"I'm going to make a quick call," Harrison said as he hopped down from the pickup, Mose and Morgan hot on his trail. "I only hope she's available."

"Who's available?" Jack asked.

"He must be calling Allyson Cardec," Sierra said, her voice rising with excitement as she leaped down off the truck. She turned to grab equipment from Garrett.

"Who's that?" Jack said.

"A psychic medium," Garrett said.

"She's, like, the best!" Sierra said as she reached up a hand to help Garrett down.

"I guess anything is worth a try at this point," said Jack.

"We haven't seen anything like this before," Garrett said.

"We've gotten pushed and felt stuff, but nobody was ever injured," Sierra said.

"Well, except that one time," Garrett said as he lifted his sleeve to show a small raised scar on his forearm.

"What's that from?" Jack asked.

"He slipped and fell going down a set of stairs while recording," Sierra replied. "It was his own fault."

"We caught something on camera in that room!" Garrett squeaked.

"But the fall was your fault, not the apparition's. It was nowhere near you," Sierra said.

"Jury's still out," Garrett replied, grabbing his stuff from Sierra and walking away.

"The jury decided!" Sierra called after him, then turned back to Jack. "I am kind of scared about Celia. Dude, I was in the room when she was taken. I've never seen anything like this. But Harrison is the best, and Allyson is awesome. We're going to find her, and we're going to find that bastard who took her."

"And then what?" Jack demanded.

"Then what? What do you mean?" Sierra asked dumbly.

"You said it yourself—you've never seen anything like this. How do you stop him?" Jack said.

Sierra had no answer. She was moving her mouth, but nothing came out. Suddenly, Jack knew she, for one, didn't have a clue what to do to get Celia back.

"She's on her way!" Harrison called out from the back of the truck.

"You got her?" Garrett called up to him. "When will she be here?"

"Going to take her a little over an hour," Harrison replied. "We need to find the best spot to set up, and I think it's Penn Hall."

"Wait a minute." Henry stopped everything. "Who's coming? What are we doing? Do we have a plan to find Celia? What is with all the flashing lights and rumbling?"

"Allyson Cardec," Harrison said. "She's the best psychic medium around. She's our next best hope and will find us some answers, I'm certain."

"Yes!" Sierra called out, then turned and gave Jack a look to say, "Sorry for being excited."

"What do we need, Harrison?" asked Garrett.

"Bring the board," Harrison instructed. "Pack up some small equipment."

"The Ouija board, some lights, a camera, audio… right… on it." Garrett climbed into the truck and got straight to work.

"What do you want me to do?" Henry asked.

"I think we all could use a rest and reset," Dr. Moseley said. "Come inside the care center, and I will dig up some drinks and snacks."

Jack raced over to Dr. Moseley and grabbed hold of his sleeve, fighting his growing desperation.

"Drinks and snacks? Dr. Moseley, what are you saying? We need to go find Celia!"

"Easy, Jack!" Henry protested.

"Yes, Jack, we need to find Celia," Mose said in a calming voice. "But you see what great energy is stopping us from getting to her. What resources do you and I have? We have to trust Harrison and his team. And we need to give ourselves a moment to process this and refuel."

Jack felt terribly let down. He couldn't believe what he was hearing. He felt as though Mose didn't even care about Celia.

"Henry, would you do me a favor and go into the kitchen just past the check-in?" Mose said to Jack's father. "There should be some things in there we can put out to help us reenergize."

Henry nodded and walked away. Jack knew Mose was trying to get a moment alone with him.

"What's gotten into you, Mose?" Jack said.

"Jack?" Mose replied, stunned. "What are you accusing me of?"

"You may not care, but I'm going after her," Jack said. "There must be another way into the tunnels to get past that monster."

"Jack, of course, I care about Celia, but it's just too dangerous," Mose pleaded. "We have to learn more about what we're dealing with first. Look what happened to Suzanne and the man from the power plant. I had a dream this would happen to Celia. We can't risk this happening to us all." He turned for the care center. "I'm going to phone Celia's parents to come here so I can explain what is happening."

Jack kicked the ground in anger when he saw a set of headlights coming up the road. It was Captain Hadaway in his police cruiser. Suddenly, he had an idea. He ran toward the captain.

"Where are you going, Jack?" Sierra called after him, but Jack didn't reply.

He approached Hadaway's car, throwing his arms around wildly in the headlights to get him to stop. It worked, and Jack ran straight up to the captain's window.

"Your hour is up, Jack," Hadaway said. "And I've got a slew of angry Spring Dalers demanding to know why they are without power and what the flashes of light are. Where do we stand?"

Jack noticed that Captain Hadaway was alone—Tommy and Danny were not in the car with him.

"I need you to do me a favor, sir," Jack said.

"Have you found the girl?" Hadaway asked firmly.

"No, not yet, but—" Jack began breathlessly.

"Then I'm calling this in," Hadaway interrupted, then pulled out his cell phone. "We need a search team here."

"Wait!" Jack pleaded. He put a hand out on Hadaway's arm to stop him.

Hadaway looked appalled. "You haven't found the girl yet, and we are having power outages. I've given you and that team enough time."

"Sir, please…" Jack pleaded.

Hadaway let out a low growl. "What do you want from me?"

"Sir, they have an idea," Jack began more calmly. "They have someone coming to help track Celia in the tunnels."

Jack wasn't entirely sure that was the plan, but that didn't matter to him now. He just wanted to convince Hadaway of his idea.

"So, you want me to wait? How much longer? How many more people will go missing?" Hadaway demanded.

"Sir, please, I have a different favor to ask," Jack said slowly. Hadaway grimaced at Jack, then nodded for him to continue. "I need to talk to Coach Slater."

Hadaway's face lit up with a mix of shock and confusion. "He's locked away in a federal prison!"

"But I think he can help us," Jack said.

"You'll never get to him, not without jumping through some hoops," Hadaway said. "And especially not at this hour of the night."

Jack thought quickly. "What about Thomson?"

"John Thomson?" Hadaway asked, dumbfounded. Then his face relaxed a bit more as he considered it. "Him we might be able to get." Hadaway thought a bit more, then screwed up his face and looked sternly at Jack. "Whatever for?"

"I think he knows the man behind this and can help us find answers to what's going on here," Jack said.

Hadaway thought a few moments. Jack could tell that, while Hadaway could be fair and lenient, this request was really tearing him apart inside. Then Hadaway tucked his cell phone into his pocket and unlocked the cruiser doors.

"Get in," Hadaway said soberly. "I will take you over."

"Thank you, sir!" Jack gushed, then raced around the back of the car. He opened the passenger door and slid into the leather seat. He could see Captain Hadaway's laptop, anchored to the center console, with a photo of Celia on screen.

"If we don't find her soon, I'll need to submit a missing person's report," Hadaway said.

Jack had no reply but suddenly realized the weight of the situation was more pressing than he personally felt. Hadaway spun the car around and made for the front entrance.

"Can't believe I'm entertaining this," Hadaway mumbled. Jack wanted to thank him again but figured he'd be better off not pushing his luck.

Jack's phone vibrated in his pocket. He pulled it out to see a message from Dr. Moseley that read, *Where are you going?*

Jack hesitated. He didn't want Mose to talk him out of it or, worse, come along and ruin Jack's plan. He felt he had to confront Thomson on his own.

Jack typed back: *Be back soon. Trust me, please.*

They arrived at the front entrance to see Danny and Tommy standing shoulder to shoulder under the massive, curved Linhurst sign. They were doing their best to hold back the group of Spring Dalers gathered. As Hadaway approached, he slowed to a crawl to pass carefully by Danny and Tommy, and hopefully, slip past the townspeople, as well.

"The green light?" Tommy said to one person. "Yeah, just some electrical work going on."

"Is that why my power is out?" demanded a grumpy old man.

"Rumbling?" Danny said to a woman. "We have been known to get earthquakes here, you know. Could been what you were feeling."

"We don't want a repeat of what happened here two years ago!" another woman shouted at Danny, pointing her finger in his face.

"No, Ma'am," Danny replied politely, his face turning red.

"It's bad enough what they did to all those people who lived there before the place went under!" a man yelled out. "Torture and drugging them. Terrible! We don't need the same treatment because of some electrical work! I have a job to get to in the morning!"

"And my kids have school!" a woman added.

Another woman came up to Captain Hadaway's open window and leaned in. "Captain Hadaway, you must know what's going on here?"

"Electrical work, Mrs. Hendricks," Hadaway replied coolly. "These boys are just doing their job."

"Why are we to trust these two, anyhow?" the woman asked. "Their dads caused all that trouble here to begin with."

"Why don't you head on home and get some sleep?" Hadaway said, clearly uninterested in addressing the woman's complaints.

He pressed his foot on the gas and maneuvered the car carefully through the crowd and out onto Main Street.

"Captain Hadaway, wait!" Mrs. Hendricks called after him.

"That woman," Hadaway said grumpily. "She calls down to the station with the most trivial reports nearly every day of the week."

Jack chuckled, then the pair rode in silence as they passed

by the stores, businesses, and homes along Main Street, all without power. They drove through darkened neighborhood streets and out onto the main township road.

"What exactly do you need to ask Thomson?" Hadaway asked after nearly ten minutes in silence, with only the police radio interrupting their thoughts.

"There was a man who lived at Linhurst," Jack said.

Hadaway waited for more, but Jack couldn't think of how to tell him.

"And?" Hadaway replied. "What about him?"

"I know his name is Sam King," Jack replied.

"Never heard of him," Hadaway said.

"He was taken there when he was a boy," Jack continued. "He wanted to get out when he was eighteen, but I don't know if he ever did. I think he has something to do with what's going on tonight."

"Well, this Sam King, he lived there well before your time," Hadaway said. "Linhurst has been closed for decades."

"I think he must have died in there," replied Jack.

"Now hold on," Captain Hadaway said, perplexed. "I figured he was a vandal or trespasser. Now you're telling me he's dead?"

"Yes, sir, I believe he is," Jack said.

"How would you know that?" Hadaway demanded. Jack grimaced. "Oh, I see, more of these Linhurst ghost stories."

Hadaway sighed and said nothing more for a few more minutes. Hadaway pulled through the main gates and up to the booth where he was given a wave by the facility attendant.

"Good evening, Captain," the officer in the booth called out.

Hadaway nodded and they continued down the winding road and pulled up in front of the main building. He hopped out and put on his police cap—looking immediately more official—then walked up to the front door of the visitor's entrance. Jack followed closely behind.

They entered the orange brick-walled lobby area to see a waiting area to their left, adorned with three rows of hard metal chairs and a twenty-inch television playing a local news station. A guard sat just ahead of them, in a small room with minimal light behind thick glass with a small round area for them to speak into.

"Captain Hadaway," the guard called through the small opening. "What brings you here?"

The guard looked Jack up and down, appearing rather confused.

"Mike, I have a favor to ask," Hadaway stated. "I need to see John Thomson."

"Thomson?" the guard asked, then picked up a binder on the long metal desk in front of him and started flipping through the pages. "He's in work release. What exactly is this for?"

"I need to ask him a few questions about an incident this evening," Hadaway replied.

"This is really unusual, sir," Mike replied.

"We have a missing person on our hands," Hadaway added.

"I don't know, Captain," Mike said.

"Mike, I'm asking as a favor," Hadaway said.

"Who's the kid?" Mike asked, pointing to Jack.

"He's with me," Hadaway said. "He knows more about the incident than I do."

Mike hesitated. He pushed a different binder under the window and placed a pen on top. "Sign in."

Hadaway nodded to Jack, who filled in his info and slid the book back.

Mike pressed a button on the wall and a door to their left buzzed. "Go on back. We'll bring him up soon."

"I owe you one," Hadaway said, then he and Jack walked through the door into a plain, dimly lit windowless hallway.

A guard appeared from around the corner ahead, and they followed him down the hall past closed and locked doors, then entered a room with small round tables with four seats to each. The room smelled like the boys' locker room at Spring Dale High.

"Sit anywhere," the guard said, then closed the door tightly behind him.

Jack and Captain Hadaway took a seat at a table near the door and waited. As they waited, Jack recalled the last time he saw Principal Thomson was in the generating station where he confessed to all that he and Coach Slater had done wrong at Linhurst. Though Slater's ten-year sentence was far worse, they were both serving time for involuntary manslaughter due to the deaths of those found buried inside the tunnels.

As Jack looked around at the plain concrete walls and shiny linoleum floor, he couldn't help but immediately realize the irony in the fate of Thomson and Slater, who had worked so many years to keep people locked away in Linhurst.

The door opened, and Thomson passed the guard and entered the room. He was dressed in a plain white t-shirt, dark gray pants, and filthy white sneakers. His hair had more gray in it than Jack recalled. His glasses looked slightly misshapen compared to how well-groomed Thomson would normally keep himself.

The guard called over to Captain Hadaway, "Ten minutes enough?"

"That should be plenty," Hadaway answered.

Thomson pulled out a chair and took a seat across from Jack, with Hadaway on his right. He looked at Captain Hadaway, then to Jack, then back to Hadaway.

"I imagine you aren't the one who wants to talk?" Thomson asked the police captain.

"No, I am," Jack said, staring at Thomson.

Thomson turned to Jack, a weary look in his eyes. "You know, it's been weeks since Tommy has visited me? He's ashamed of me. I get it. I deserve it." He paused and sighed, then placed his hands on the table and leaned in slightly. "How is he?"

"He's fine, I guess," Jack answered quickly. "Look, Mr. Thomson—"

"Call me John," Thomson said. "You can't call me Principal Thomson any longer, and you certainly don't need to call me mister anything. I don't deserve that either."

Jack was surprised. The last time they were face to face was in the principal's office at Spring Dale High School. He was grilling Jack about investigating the Linhurst property. The shell of that man in front of him was hard for Jack to take in, but he pressed on.

"There's something going on at Linhurst again," Jack said, refusing to call him John. "A lot of strange happenings lately like what we saw that night. Flashes of light and rumblings."

"It's happening again?" Thomson asked, sounding frightened.

"*Something* is happening," Jack replied.

"From where I sit, I'm sure there's nothing I can do to help," Thomson asked.

"I think there is," Jack said. "It's about Slater."

"Eric?" Thomson shouted. "I want nothing to do with that man. He brought this on us."

"I understand that," Jack said, trying to calm the former principal and one-time leader of Linhurst. It didn't help.

Thomson slammed his fists down on the table and leaned in toward Jack. "I am counting the months to when I get out of here," he growled. "I want to go home and try to repair what is left of my family and my life. And you come here to talk about Eric Slater?"

"Just hear him out," Hadaway said firmly to Thomson.

Thomson withdrew, settled back into his chair, and folded his arms, attempting to appear calm. "Go on."

Jack took in a deep breath and leaned in. "I have been

seeing things. Ever since that night, I've been in counseling. I have these… dreams… these visions." Thomson sat up straight, listening more intently. "I have been dreaming about something—someone—down in the tunnels. And now, I think whatever that thing is—it has Celia."

"I still don't see what any of this has to do with me," Thomson interrupted Jack's story. "It's been years since I worked there and almost as long since the place has been closed."

"I had a vision of you," Jack said.

"Of me?" Thomson replied.

"I see Linhurst how it used to be," Jack tells Thomson. "I see it how it once was. I am going to a room with Dr. Royer. We look inside to see you and Slater with a man on a table and he's in a straitjacket. The man breaks free and charges for Slater. His name is Sam King."

Thomson's eyes lit up, and he unfolded his arms. "Sam King?"

"Yes, you remember him," Jack replied.

"He was in the generating station that night—as a ghost," Thomson said.

"Correct!" Jack said.

"So, you had a dream about him?" Thomson replied.

"I had another vision of Slater ordering people to take Sam King down into the tunnels," Jack continued. "He was confined to a straitjacket again."

"This is crazy—where are you going with this?" Thomson interrupted.

"Just shut up and listen to him, would you?" Captain Hadaway barked.

Thomson pulled back.

"They were arguing, Slater and King," Jack continued. "He told King he owned him after his mother brought him there when he was a boy."

"Sam did come to us early," Thomson said. "He was maybe four years old when he arrived. His mom didn't want him at all. A sad but common story. We admitted him and realized early on that he was actually quite gifted. But by then, we were so overcrowded and understaffed, and certainly had no education program in place." Thomson sighed. "Sam simply became a helper."

Thomson leaned in and removed his glasses, wiping his weary eyes and fixing his hair as though he was taken back to the time he was an administrative leader.

"As Sam got older, he wanted nothing more than to leave Linhurst. Without a place to go and no family to support him, he was stuck. We could have done more. What I witnessed was a young man with great talent and potentially a high IQ, but with no way to harness it."

"So, what happened to him that made him so angry?" Jack asked.

"Eric Slater happened," Thomson grumbled. "You saw it, Jack. Eric wanted nothing to do with helping the people who lived at Linhurst."

Jack nodded. Slater had obviously thought of the residents at Linhurst as subhuman, and he made his opinion well known.

"As Sam grew older and more restless, Slater became increasingly violent toward the young man," Thomson said. "I should have done more to stop it, but Eric was a force. I watched as the two of them became warring factions. It grew to become accepted—Slater and King always going at it. I suppose I just hoped that Sam would go, or Slater would go, and things would get better."

"But neither of them left, did they, John?" Hadaway interrupted, looking sickened by the story.

"It had come to a point that Sam insisted on leaving and Slater punished him for considering it," said Thomson. "I swear he just wanted someone to torture."

"I heard Slater say something about a woman," Jack said. "Something about them having kids?"

Thomson sighed, then his head dropped to his chest. "It's true." Thomson looked up at Jack. "They had a kid."

"Who had a kid?" Hadaway asked in shock.

"Sam found a girl he really liked," Thomson began slowly. "She lived in the Mayflower building. It was one of the lower wards Sam was sent down to as punishment. Only thing was that she was also sent there, but because she worked well with the younger ones, they made her a bed there."

"So, she didn't belong there either?" Jack asked.

"She didn't," Thomson said. "So many of them didn't belong there."

Suddenly, without warning, Thomson's eyes welled with tears. He removed his glasses, closed his eyes, covered his face, and began to sob.

Jack looked at Captain Hadaway. They were both surprised by Thomson's sudden outburst.

"Sir, please," Jack said quietly to Thomson. "We don't have much time. Celia is trapped down there."

Just then, the door to the room opened.

"One more minute, Captain," the guard called over to them.

Hadaway gave him a wave and the guard pulled the door shut again.

"Please, John, can you give us any more information?" Hadaway urged. "We need to get Celia out of there."

Thomson looked up, wiped his eyes, and put his glasses back on, then patted his already disheveled hair. "Forgive me. I kept this bottled up all these years. Now it is just too much for me."

"What else can you tell us about Sam and the girl?" Jack asked calmly, though he was growing more desperate and anxious by the second.

"Her name was Maria," Thomson began. "She came from the city, also quite young. The pair met at a summer event and immediately connected. They must have been nine and eleven years old at the time. They were inseparable when they were together, whether he was helping her pick flowers, or she was helping him move loads. Didn't matter what they were doing, they were always together.

"When Slater found out, he wanted nothing more than to break them apart. He thought it was deplorable for two people of Linhurst to be together like any couple you would see on the streets of Spring Dale. In his mind, they were in this institution for a reason, and it was because they were deemed unfit for society. I knew better. These two children were not violent. They were intelligent, capable, and certainly weren't in need of medical attention.

"I tried subtly to move them both into positions that would give them a sense of humanity. I found them work that would keep them occupied while we tried to establish an educational program. But it was not meant to be.

"The two became teenagers at Linhurst. Times were changing, and we had plans for improvements that would benefit residents like Sam and Maria, but we couldn't keep up with the overcrowding and drop in funding.

"One late spring evening, Eric found the two of them fooling around in the laundry building. She was half dressed and lying in a pile of freshly washed sheets with Sam on top of her. It so enraged Eric to see two delinquents fornicating, he lost his mind.

"Sam spent five days in solitary confinement under the administration building. After that, Eric made it more difficult for the pair to see one another, changing their routines so that there was never a chance their timing would let them be together.

"After several weeks passed, Sam began acting out. He was injuring himself and others. All he wanted was to see Maria. Then he learned the horrible truth. A nurse told Sam that Maria was with child—"

Jack gasped. Captain Hadaway shook his head furiously. "—but the leadership decided to abort."

"My word," Captain Hadaway said.

"I had nothing to do with the decision," Thomson continued. "I only found out after Sam tore apart an entire floor with his bare hands. We found overturned beds, chairs, and equipment everywhere. Broken glass, shattered picture frames—the ward was demolished. Several residents were injured along with the few staff we had on hand. No one could stop him from the rage.

"Eric put Sam in solitary for an entire week, but I pleaded with him every day to let him out and try another way. He wouldn't hear it.

"Before the end of that week, someone found Maria down in the tunnels. Some said she lost her way and simply starved to death. But I know she wasn't down there long enough for that. I believe she took her own life."

Captain Hadaway groaned sorrowfully.

"What about King?" Jack asked.

"He just disappeared one day not long after that," Thomson said. "Slater told me he ran away, and I was so relieved he got out of there, I never questioned it any further. We were faced with energy problems, money problems. You name it. Linhurst closed not long after that."

"Time's up!" the guard hollered as he opened the door.

"Just another few minutes," Hadaway said.

"It's almost lights out, Captain," the guard insisted. "We need him back in his cell."

Captain Hadaway nodded and stood up.

"Wait!" Jacked yelped. "How do we stop him?"

"Stop him?" Thomson asked as he stood up.

"What can we do to stop King?" Jack replied.

"Time's up, John," the guard said and pulled Thomson toward the door.

"He took Celia!" Jack hollered. "King took Celia down into the tunnels!"

"Are you certain it's him?" Thomson replied.

"Yes, we are certain, and he won't let us near him!" Jack pleaded. "We need a way in."

Thomson stopped at the doorway and turned to Jack. The guard tugged on him, but Thomson held his ground.

"Jack, I am sorry for what happened," Thomson said longingly. "I wish I'd done more, but I was stupid. Scared. Please tell Tommy I said hello?"

Jack was furious for answers as the guard pulled Thomson through the door and they disappeared around the corner.

The first guard entered the room. "Follow me, gentlemen."

As Jack quickly got into Captain Hadaway's car, he desperately searched his mind for ideas on how to get to King, but he was coming up empty.

His phone vibrated in his jacket. He pulled it out to see a message from Mose:

Hurry back. Allyson has arrived.

Chapter 12

The crowd at the front entrance to Linhurst had grown to over fifty people. This would be an unusual sight any given day but especially at 10:15 on a cool Tuesday evening in October with every light in town gone dark.

Hadaway pulled the cruiser up slowly and hit his siren a few times, warning the residents to move out of his way. The angry mob moved enough to allow him to squeeze through, their bodies brushing up against the sides of the car.

"We demand answers!" a man yelled.

"What is going on here, Captain Hadaway?" a woman followed. "Why don't we have power?"

"What are the flashing lights?" someone else screamed.

Another police vehicle was parked on the far side of the group¬¬, its red and blue lights flashing. A work truck was set up near the cruiser, and a handful of workers were setting up safety cones, preparing to inspect the power outage.

Hadaway pulled up beyond the angry Spring Dalers and just inside the entrance under the curved iron Linhurst sign between the stone pillars and stopped.

"We're doing our best, sir," Danny said, standing beside Hadaway's open window.

"Should I call for more hands here?" asked a fellow police officer as he approached Hadaway.

"Yes, Jones, let's get these boys back on the campus," Hadaway replied. "They aren't equipped for this."

"Yes, sir," Officer Jones replied and walked away from the car, calling into his radio for backup.

"Once additional officers arrive, you two head up to the care center and wait for my instructions," Hadaway commanded.

Danny and Tommy nodded, and Hadaway started down the road into Linhurst. Jack looked into his sideview mirror to see the crowd quickly fill in where Hadaway's cruiser just sat—Danny, Tommy, and Officer Jones filled in to keep the frustrated crowd at bay.

They arrived at the Linhurst Care Center to see all sorts of activity. Through the tall windows inside the lobby, Jack could see his dad sitting with Celia's parents. The couple appeared frantic from afar while Henry tried to comfort them.

The back of the Paranormal Examiners' truck was blinking all sorts of colored lights while Garrett, Sierra, and Morgan appeared to be gathering equipment and cables. Harrison was standing with Dr. Moseley and a woman with a thick mane of curly red hair.

The door to the generating station was open with a few dim lights on inside. Jack couldn't remember the last time he had seen the lights on in the old building housing the secret reactor.

"Dr. Moseley!" Jack called as Hadaway came to a stop near the Paranormal Examiners' truck. He hopped out of the cruiser and dashed up to Mose and Harrison.

"Dr. Moseley, I have some new information," Jack began excitedly.

"Jack, please, manners?" Mose replied, showing unusual authority. "Would you introduce yourself first?"

"No apologies necessary," said the woman with the red hair. Her eyes narrowed as she inspected Jack from head to toe. "You have such energy about you, Jack."

He immediately screwed up his face and leaned away. *How did she know who he was?*

"You have a hot red aura right now when you really want to be a bright and smart yellow. Very curious. Why so much energy?" She paused. "Your friend? Yes! Your friend Celia concerns you greatly. But she is safe. I can see her, and she is safe and sound. We will find her, I can feel it."

"Jack," Harrison interrupted. "This is Allyson Cardec,

an old friend of mine. She is a medium who will try to connect us with the spirits here and help us locate Celia and, hopefully, King. Celia first, of course."

Allyson put out a hand, and Jack reciprocated. She grasped his hand firmly but kindly, then held onto it, closing her eyes.

"I can see that you've been venturing deep into this place," she said, then inhaled a long, deep breath. "Yes, you have seen some interesting things here. Looked into the past. Quite far, I see!"

Jack pulled his hand away.

Allyson reopened her eyes suddenly. "Who is that man we seek? Is he the one I see in your vision?"

"What man?" Jack asked irritably.

"The one with the mustache," Allyson replied.

"No, that's Slater," Jack replied.

"Ah, so, it's the tall one?" Allyson replied. "He, too, had a fiery red aura, but much more intentional than yours, Jack."

Jack didn't know what to make of Allyson. She had come on rather strong, but she didn't appear to be rude or unfriendly. He looked her over, noting the long black trench coat that draped over her small frame like a silo. She wore a black blouse, black jeans, and thick black boots. All the black made her face look quite pale in the shadow of her full red curls.

"I think we have everything," Garrett said to Harrison, interrupting the group as he hung out from the truck.

"Excellent," Harrison replied. "Mose, can you take Morgan, Sierra, and Garrett in your truck?"

"No problem," Mose replied.

"I will ride with Allyson," Harrison said. "Jack, will you come with us?"

Jack hesitated.

Mose put a hand on his shoulder. "It's all right, Jack."

"Wait just a minute," Captain Hadaway interrupted, listening from afar until that moment. "This has gone too far. What exactly do you plan to do now?"

"We are going to connect with the other side," Allyson said whimsically.

"The other side?" Hadaway replied.

Harrison cleared his throat. "What Allyson means is that we are going to perform a séance to try and get answers from the spirits here."

Hadaway screwed up his face. This answer clearly didn't play much better with the police captain. He was a man of the law, meant to serve and protect his community every day. He wasn't buying into the ghost business very easily.

"Look, Mose, I have a crowd of Spring Dale residents ready to rip through the front entrance of this campus," Hadaway said. "I have a lost girl somewhere down in those tunnels who you all swear was taken by a ghost. How do I go along with this?"

"Taken by a ghost?" a small voice called out from behind them. "Our Celia?"

They turned to see Celia's mother and father embracing one another, standing just feet from them with Henry looking on from behind. Celia's parents looked terrified and disheveled, shaken to their core. Celia's mother had been crying. Her eyes and cheeks were red, lines from tears streaming her caramel-colored face. Celia's father looked mad as hell.

Hadaway turned to Mose and leaned in. "Charles, I have always trusted you, but I'm not so sure this time. After everything I have seen and heard tonight, I think it's time to shut this down and find a more practical way. We need to get a search party into those tunnels."

"You won't make it down there," Mose replied calmly. "He won't let you down there."

"Who is he? This King guy?" Hadaway demanded.

"You got it," Mose replied.

Hadaway growled. "If I hadn't seen what I had seen two years ago, well… I just—I don't know." Hadaway struggled for the words.

"She is safe," Allyson interjected. "We will find her."

"Give us more time, Captain," Mose softly pleaded.

Hadaway placed his police cap on his head and nodded to Mose, then turned with intention and walked over to Celia's parents. He huddled with them for a moment, then began to walk them back toward the care center entrance along with Henry. Just before they reached the staircase, Celia's father pulled away and pointed a stiff finger at Dr. Moseley.

"You better find my daughter safe!" Celia's father exclaimed.

"We are doing everything we can," Mose answered, as calmly and coolly as possible.

Hadaway put his hands gently on their backs and walked them inside.

"We must go now," Allyson said impatiently. "Our window is closing."

"Everyone load up!" Harrison called out.

The teams split up and headed to different vehicles.

Jack ran to catch up with Mose. "Dr. Moseley, wait a minute."

"Jack, you must go with Harrison and Allyson," Mose said, stopping Jack in his path. "Time is short."

"But, Mose, I talked to Thomson," Jack interjected desperately.

"John Thomson? How? When?"

"Captain Hadaway took me to see him, and I pressed him for answers about Sam King," Jack replied.

Mose looked surprised and impressed at once.

"What an idea, Jack!" Mose replied. "You must share what you learned with Harrison and Allyson. Please work with them."

Jack nodded, though he was longing for his old friend to give him a hand. Mose walked off quickly.

"Mose, why is the generating station door open?" Jack called after him.

Mose stopped and turned. "You must have missed it while you were gone—more rumblings and more flashes of light.

We're trying to find the source."

Mose hopped into his truck, started it up, and leaned out the window. "Go, Jack!" he called out, then took off with Morgan, Sierra, and Garrett hanging on in the back.

Jack turned to see Harrison directly by his side, hanging out the passenger window of Allyson's old black Honda Accord.

"Come on, Jack!" Harrison said.

Jack ran to the back door and hopped in, then they took off up the road past the generating station.

"Turn left here," Harrison said, pointing up the road toward Penn Hall.

"No!" Jack called out as Allyson swung a hard left onto the bumpy, busted pavement. "Not this way!"

"We're going back to Penn Hall to set up the seance," Harrison replied as they bumped along, Mose's truck kicking dust into the car headlights ahead. "It's where we found the most activity tonight aside from the administration building, and that entrance is impassible now."

"We need to go to the Mayflower," Jack replied urgently.

"The Mayflower?" Harrison asked. "Is that another building on campus?"

"Yes, we must go there!" Jack pleaded.

Allyson stopped the car and turned to Harrison. Mose's truck continued on ahead of them. "You have a feeling about this Mayflower building," she said with certainty.

"More than a feeling," Jack said.

Jack quickly told them the tale that Thomson shared with him and Hadaway at the prison.

"Seems to me that the Mayflower building makes sense," Harrison declared at the end of Jack's story.

"Indeed," Allyson said.

Harrison pulled out his walkie talkie. "Mose, turn back. We need to go to the Mayflower."

"The Mayflower?" Mose replied. "I haven't been over there in a long time. That building is in bad shape, though. Why there?"

"I'll tell you when we get there," Harrison replied. "Can you lead the way?"

"Turning around now."

"Jack, this may have helped us get closer to Celia," Harrison told him proudly. "Going to see Thomson was a brave and intelligent decision on your part."

Jack blushed. He wasn't thinking about what accolades it would get him; he just needed answers. Allyson spun the car around just in time for Mose to arrive. He pulled up to a stop on Harrison's side of the car.

"The road to the Mayflower is rough. Can your car handle a few bumps?" Mose asked.

"Show me the way!" Allyson replied confidently.

Mose nodded and sped off, kicking up stones and dust, tossing Morgan, Sierra, and Garrett around in the back.

They drove to the end of the road and made their way past the care center. Jack quickly looked inside the dimly lit lobby to see Captain Hadaway talking to Danny and

Tommy while Henry was sitting with Celia's mom. Celia's dad was pacing the floor, throwing his arms around and hollering, looking terribly upset.

The door to the generating station was still open. It made him nervous to think that just anyone could wander right into the building with all the commotion going on tonight.

Mose took a sharp right turn past the generating station and began up a long road that was paved for the first few hundred feet before becoming cracked and rough. The sides of the road were met abruptly by overgrown forest, the outgrowth of unplanned trees suffocating in a twisted macabre of vines and branches that stretched into the darkness beyond.

Mose suddenly slowed just ahead of them, then threw his arm out the window and pointed toward the wall of trees. Just off the road, parked carelessly in the grass, was a bronze Mercedes.

"Allister," Jack scowled.

"Who is Allister?" Harrison asked.

"A man from the power plant who's been snooping around Linhurst," said Jack.

"Looks like he still is," Harrison replied. Jack could only imagine what the smarmy executive was up to as they feverishly worked to rescue Celia from the depths of the tunnels.

As Allyson drove onward up the bumpy hill, the road soon turned to rocks and gravel. The car was bouncing them around considerably. Harrison hit his head a few times on the roof.

"Ouch!" Harrison yelped. "Maybe a bit slower, Al?"

"Sorry, Harrison," Allyson replied. "Getting anxious. How much farther is it?"

Allyson no sooner said this than Mose veered off the road and drove between two massive tree trunks, disappearing into the darkened woods beyond with only his rear headlights visible through the wall of dust ahead. Allyson followed, causing Harrison to practically spill into her lap. He apologized and quickly reset himself in his seat. Jack was holding on to the grab handle for dear life. The thrill of the ride was beating back his nerves a bit.

They rode down a dirt and rock-covered path through the woods, all along wondering if it had ever served as an actual road. They were so engulfed by the canopy of the forest, the headlights of Mose's truck barely lit the road ahead of him, which was the same for Allyson's car.

Finally, they entered into a slight clearing with overgrown weeds and brush, and a structure appeared. At first, it looked to be a giant block of tangled vines and ivy. As they drew nearer, Jack could see the outline of a building with brick facing. Then he could make out a porch-like structure that matched the other buildings on campus he had become familiar with. As they came to within yards of the building's entrance, Jack saw a dilapidated red sign with peeling white lettering that was still barely readable.

"The Mayflower," Harrison said, also spotting the sign. "We've arrived."

Harrison opened the door of the car and hopped out before Allyson could even get it in park. Jack was right there with him. Jack followed Harrison toward the front of the building, and then his tall friend hastily sprinted up the crumbling concrete stairs and onto the porch. Before he could walk another step, the ground rumbled, and the building let out a small groan.

"Might want to take this slow," Allyson called up from behind him.

Harrison turned to see Allyson standing at ground level, Mose, Morgan, Sierra, and Garrett gathered around her in a circle. The car headlights shined a dusty spotlight on the group.

"I was just looking for a way in," Harrison said as he came back down off the porch.

"I hear ya, honey, but this thing doesn't want us here to begin with," Allyson said. "May be best to take our time and think it through."

She stood in place, closed her eyes, and stretched her hands out in front of her chest. "I am calling on all spirits of this place," she began, causing everyone to stop what they were doing and observe her.

The car headlights shined on her back, giving her a long dark shadow that stretched across the ground toward the Mayflower building.

"All good spirits, come to us, be present with us now," Allyson said aloud in a monotone and soothing voice. "Join us as we attempt to reach the angry lost soul here. Surround us with good energy, positive energy, and light, and protect us as we invite you into our world. We ask you to invite us into yours and promise we will not take what belongs to you. We only want to hear from you and hope you will hear from us."

Allyson then brought her hands together in front of her and, palms touching, raised her arms high over her head and reached toward the sky. She held the pose for a moment.

"This is silly," Jack said, accidentally out loud.

"Seriously?" Sierra shrieked through a loud whisper just behind him, startling Jack. "She's the best!"

"If you say so," Jack replied impartially. "Harrison and Morgan did something similar tonight and look how far that got us."

He watched as Allyson brought her hands down into a prayer position in front of her chest, opened her eyes, took a deep breath, then turned to Harrison with a relaxed smile.

"Now try," she said to Harrison.

Harrison nodded, then turned and—slowly this time— made his way up the concrete stairs and onto the porch strangled in twisted and dying vines and ivy. He paused, turned to give a quick thumbs up, then walked across the porch to the door. He reached out for the handle, grabbed it firmly with both hands, and gave it a tug. Nothing. Didn't even budge.

"It's locked," Harrison called down. He tried a few more times but the doors were stuck shut.

Dr. Moseley immediately responded by racing up the stairs and carefully crossing the darkened porch to the door. Jack followed, noticing how decayed this building was compared to the rest. The bricks were crumbling in many places, the mortar between the lines missing in long lines between the rows of masonry. The wood around the door frame was barely intact, and what was left was broken beyond repair.

The doors entering the building appeared to be held down by the weight of the building itself. Mose noticed it as well.

"This entrance may be impassable," Mose said.

"We have to find a way in, Charles," Harrison replied.

"I understand that," Mose said. "I'm afraid this building is in some of the poorest conditions on campus."

"We can try a window," Sierra said, pointing to the boarded up framework barely noticeable through the twisted vines.

Harrison came down off the porch and made his way to a window, pulling and kicking at the overgrowth to clear himself a path as he went. When he arrived at the boarded up window, he could see that even he was too short to reach it.

"Do you have a ladder in your truck, Charles?" Harrison asked Mose, who was standing on the porch watching.

"Would you believe I do?" Mose said, then went to his truck and returned with a small stepladder and leaned it against the crumbling brick exterior just below the window.

Harrison climbed to the top, braced the board covering the window at one edge, then started pulling at it. The sound immediately put everyone on edge. If Allyson's little spell didn't work, whatever caused the rumbling and moaning when they first arrived wouldn't like this at all.

Luckily for the group, Harrison muscled the board off the window in no time. He pulled his flashlight and pointed it in through the glassless window frame and looked around.

"I'll be right back—I hope," Harrison said, then pulled himself up over the windowsill and inside the building with the grace of a gymnast.

Harrison's light beamed rays all around the space beyond, and Jack could see the destruction from where he stood. The building was in far greater disrepair than anything he had ever seen. The ceiling appeared to be burned like logs in a fireplace. The old paint on the walls hung in great masses like curtains on high windows. Before long, Harrison's light disappeared, and they could see only darkness through the window.

"Harrison?" Morgan called out nervously. "What are you doing?"

"Shhh," Garrett hushed him. "Not so loud!"

"We are safe now," Allyson said confidently.

Jack eyed her for a moment to see if she meant it or was trying to encourage bravery. She seemed sincere from what he could tell.

Suddenly, a loud bang came from the main doors at the top of the porch. It was only one bang at first, but it was loud and caused pieces of the framework around the doorway to fall to the porch. Another loud bang came, and more framework fell. Another bang and the door on the right began to give way, bending outward from the crumbling frame. One more loud bang and the entire door fell open, swinging wildly from the top hinge and scraping across the porch. The remaining framework of the doorway split into hundreds of pieces and flew out from the walls, along with a couple of bricks and bits of mortar. Then out flew Harrison, stopping himself from taking a spill down the stairs from the force by which he slammed the doors.

"We're in!" he said breathlessly, brushing himself off. The group stood in awe of his antics. "Well, don't just stare at me, let's move!"

Jack was the first to respond, heading up the steps and onto the porch. He continued past Harrison and inside the building, then pulled his flashlight out and flicked it on.

Jack began immediately surveying the room. A surprising amount of old furniture and decor had been left in the Mayflower building—beds, wheelchairs, medical equipment, old picture frames, and more. Everything was rusted, rotten, or otherwise had an aged and horrid appearance, but it was clear that vandals hadn't found their way here yet.

"He is waiting for us," Allyson said as she entered the room, taking in a full breath of air and walking around with her arms outstretched by her sides.

"Who's waiting?" Jack asked.

"I feel the presence of a male in this room," Allyson replied.

"Quickly, get me a table to set the board on," Harrison said.

Sierra entered the room and made her way to a far corner where she spied an old wooden table and chairs. She grabbed the table and started dragging it across the rotted floorboards, the legs screaming out a terrible scraping sound.

"Someone please grab the other end and carry it?" Harrison yelled out.

Morgan raced over to grab an end.

"Garrett, you have the Ouija board?" Harrison asked his portly friend, who had set the duffle bag down and begun to unload equipment.

"Yeah, Harrison, it's in here," Garrett replied.

"Where do you want the table?" Sierra asked Harrison and Allyson, who were standing in the middle of the demolished room.

"Right here," Allyson replied, walking in a small circle.

Morgan and Sierra walked the table to where she paced and set it down, then raced back for the chairs.

"Here you go, Harrison," said Garrett, pulling the Ouija board from the bag.

"Take it to the table, please," Harrison replied.

"I'll do it," Jack interjected, then grabbed the board from Garrett's outstretched arm and walked it toward the table.

Morgan and Sierra returned with two disintegrating wooden chairs and set them down at the table, then ran back again for more.

As Jack approached the table, Allyson pulled a stout white candle and black lighter from her long black trench coat. She set the candle on the edge of the table and lit it.

"Right there is fine," she said to Jack, motioning for the middle of the table.

Jack opened the board and laid it out on the table, displaying the board's numbers, letters, and the large YES and NO parallel to one another. He placed the planchette in the middle of the board, and there it sat quietly, awaiting questioning.

Sierra and Morgan ran back with the two remaining chairs. Just before they made it to the middle of the room, the chair Sierra was carrying completely fell to pieces in her hands, the legs and spindles of the chair back hitting the floor and rolling everywhere.

"What the hell?" Sierra yelped.

"Leave it!" Harrison replied. "Three is enough."

Morgan carried the third chair quickly to the table and set it down.

"Jack, have a seat, please," Allyson said quietly.

"Me?" Jack asked.

Allyson nodded. Jack pulled up a chair, took a seat, then pulled himself in close to the table overlooking the board. Harrison joined them and took another seat, then Allyson opened her long coat and sat in the last open chair. They pulled in close, their faces dimly lit by the candle that helped them see the board more clearly.

"Guys, give me just a minute," Garrett called from near the entrance where he was rifling through the duffle bag, his voice echoed throughout the room. "I can't find the battery for the camera."

"No time, bud," Harrison replied, his voice echoing back. "Start filming when you can."

Sierra walked around the table with an EMF meter. "Dude, Harrison," she whispered excitedly, "I'm getting a 3.2 reading already!"

Harrison simply nodded. With that, she put away the device and pulled out the EVP recorder and began walking around the room with it.

Allyson placed her fingers on the planchette, the curved plastic piece on wheels sitting innocently in the middle of the Ouija board. Harrison stretched his arms out long to loosen his sleeves from his wrists, then gently placed his fingertips on the disc.

"Now, Jack, place your fingertips on the planchette, please," Allyson said gently.

Jack hesitated. He turned to see Mose standing by his side, just a few feet away. Mose offered no advice, audible or physical.

"It's okay, Jack," Harrison encouraged. "Go ahead and place your fingers."

Though Jack had heard several horror stories his fellow classmates had experienced when using one, he had never seen an Ouija board in person. He remembered a girl in the tenth grade swore the Ouija said she would die on her fifteenth birthday, but she hadn't. Anthony Cappelli once claimed the Ouija told him of a ghost that haunted his bedroom and only wanted to be given jelly beans in return for not haunting him, but he gave up the practice after a few days when his mother found a pile of melted candy by the radiator and told him he was being ridiculous.

Jack hesitantly stretched his arms out and placed his fingers on the small disc, expecting something to happen. To his relief, nothing did.

The trio sat around the table, the Ouija board resting gently in the center, all six of their arms outstretched, with fingertips placed on an edge of the planchette.

"Do we have someone here with us tonight?" Allyson began.

The planchette didn't move.

She waited a moment. "Would you speak to us this evening?"

No reply.

"We would like to talk to you."

Nothing in response. The planchette remained in the center of the board.

"This is a waste of time," Jack groaned. "We have to get to Celia."

"Give it time, Jack," Harrison said.

"Can you please talk to us if you are here?"

The planchette suddenly raced across the board to the word YES.

"Did you do that?" Jack asked Allyson.

She didn't look at Jack, so he turned to Harrison, who was shaking his head.

"Would you tell us your name?" Allyson continued.

The planchette sat still for a moment before racing across the board to the word NO.

"Won't tell us his name," Allyson whispered.

She thought a moment. "How old are you?" she called out.

The planchette moved to the 1 then to the 9.

"You're nineteen years old?" Allyson asked.

The planchette moved to the word YES.

"Were you a resident here at Linhurst?" Allyson asked.

The planchette rolled to the center of the board slowly then rolled back to the word YES.

"Did you live in the Mayflower?" Allyson asked.

The disc raced to the word NO.

"Curious," Allyson said as she turned to Mose, her fingers still on the planchette. "Was this a residential building, Dr. Moseley?"

"I believe it was," Mose confirmed.

"This spirit didn't live here," Allyson said, pondering this in her mind.

"What are you thinking?" Harrison asked.

"Just thinking," Allyson said.

Meanwhile, the planchette rolled back to the center of the board, their fingers still resting gently on the plastic piece. Garrett appeared in the candlelight over Allyson's shoulder, camera in hand, filming them sitting around the board. Sierra continued to walk around with the EVP, while Morgan held an EMF meter nearby.

"How long did you live here?" Allyson asked.

The planchette moved over the seven and stopped.

"Seven years you lived at Linhurst?" she asked.

YES.

"Did you move away from Linhurst?" she asked.

The disc raced to the word NO.

"You didn't move away, but you only lived here seven years?" she whispered to herself, thinking aloud. Then her eyes widened. "Were you murdered?"

Jack gasped.

The planchette raced to the word NO. Jack sighed in relief.

"Did you become ill?" Allyson asked.

YES.

"Did illness kill you?" Allyson asked.

The planchette rolled from the word slightly then returned to YES.

"Why would this spirit have come to Mayflower if it didn't live here?" Mose asked.

"I don't know," Allyson said. "Why did you come here?" she said quietly to herself.

The planchette raced to the letter H, followed by the I, followed by the M.

"HIM," Allyson said. "He brought you here?"

YES.

"Who brought you here?" Allyson asked.

The planchette moved to the S, then the H, then back to center.

"S-H?" Allyson said aloud. "Is that it?"

"Shh," Jack said. "It's telling us to be quiet, I think."

"Ah, good one, Jack," Harrison added.

"Is it King?" Jack asked.

"We can ask—" Harrison began, but he was interrupted by the planchette.

It raced to YES.

"King brought this person here," Allyson said in a low whisper. The air suddenly turned colder.

"I'm getting a 4.3 on the EMF, guys," Sierra said, her voice shaking.

The planchette started moving again—first to the M, then to the O, then to the R, then to the E.

"More?" Jack whispered.

"There are more of you?" Allyson asked quietly.

YES.

"How many?" Allyson asked.

The planchette moved to the center of the board then rolled slowly to the 1 and stopped.

"One?" Allyson asked.

2.

"Twelve?" Harrison asked.

7.

"127?" Jack exclaimed.

The floor rumbled beneath them. Sierra let out a quick shush at Jack. He apologetically leaned in over the board.

"It's at 4.8 now," Sierra called out.

"There are so many of you," Allyson said.

YES.

"Are you all here with us?" Allyson asked.

NO.

"Are you in this building?"

NO.

"Are you *under* this building?" Harrison asked.

YES.

"Buried?" Jack added.

NO.

"Are you trapped in the tunnels?" Allyson asked.

YES.

"Are you trapped by Sam King?" Harrison asked.

The planchette moved to the center of the board and rested. It stayed for a few moments, then moved to S, then to H.

"Shhh," Jack said quietly.

"What is it, friend?" Allyson asked. "Are you afraid?"

The planchette moved to the center of the board, then very quickly spelled:

H-E-H-E-R-E.

"He-here?" Jack puzzled.

"It's spiking past five," Sierra cried out. The room was frigid, the energy palpable and unnerving.

"He's here," Allyson said grimly. "*He* is in the room with us."

They waited for the planchette to answer Allyson, but it sat still for a moment, then suddenly Allyson's hands flew off the small plastic disc and into the air as if she were possessed. Harrison's chair broke under his weight, and he hit the floor.

"What the—!" Harrison yelped.

Jack still had his fingers on the planchette. He was suddenly horrified and began to struggle.

"Jack, what is it?" Harrison yelled, pulling himself up.

"I... can't... take my hands off!" Jack hollered, struggling against the small plastic disc on top of the board.

Harrison grabbed hold of Jack's arms and tried to pry them away from the board, but they wouldn't budge. Allyson grabbed hold and tried prying him away but she couldn't move him. Just then, she ripped her hands away madly.

"Ouch!" Allyson shouted. "It shocked me!"

The planchette began to move rapidly under Jack's fingertips. It went to S, then to H, then to E, then S-M-I-N-E.

"She's mine!" Allyson yelped.

Before they could do anything else, the planchette raced across the board. Jack's fingers released from the possessed disc in a fury over his head. The planchette soared across the room and smashed into the wall, shattering into pieces.

The Ouija board lifted off the table in front of them and hovered for a moment, then shot up into the darkened ceiling, ricocheting back down to the floor behind Dr. Moseley.

Suddenly, Jack was pulled to his feet, his chair tossed several yards behind him.

Then, before he could make sense of what was happening around him, Jack was lifted several inches off the floor and flying across the room into the darkness at the other end, the group fading away behind him.

"Jack!" Dr. Moseley yelled behind him in unison with the others. Their voices faded rapidly.

Chapter 13

Total blackness.

Jack put his hands out in front of him. He couldn't see or hear anything. A putrid odor filled his nose. Then the faint sound of someone breathing. It was quiet, low, and shallow.

Is that me breathing?

It couldn't have been—it was too far off. Or was it? It could have been only a few feet from him.

A door slammed like a sledgehammer hitting an anvil, and echoed on forever. It may not even have slammed; it could have been clicked shut and the echo made it sound that much louder.

Suddenly, a light appeared. It was razor thin and floor level. Jack began to walk toward it, the ground under his feet noticeably solid and slick. But that smell—it was like urine and feces and vomit had dried and been rewet.

He stepped slowly and carefully toward the sliver of light. He didn't want to make any sudden movements or sounds until he could understand where he was.

He heard footsteps. Very distant and faint—solid against concrete. He stopped to listen. The footsteps were growing louder, drawing nearer. Just then the footsteps stopped, and the razor-thin light was interrupted by two long shadows. Suddenly, there was a rapping sound on a metal door and a new light appeared at eye level. It was searingly bright and wider than the light at floor level. Jack shielded his eyes.

"You ready to behave?" a voice called from the light.

He knew this voice. It was all too familiar. He looked out toward the light and saw a shadowy figure on the other side.

"Slater," he whispered.

"Yeah, it's me, boy," Slater replied, staring through a peephole in the door. "Where are you hiding?"

No reply. Jack calmed his breathing, so Slater couldn't hear him. *Wait, I'm standing right in front of him, and he can't see me?*

"Been two days. You wanna be nice, I'll let you out."

Is he talking to me? Where am I?

Just then, a voice came from behind him.

"I've got nothing to say to you," Sam King whispered gruffly from a corner.

"So, you are giving up?" Slater called out.

"You took her away from me," Sam growled, sounding weakened from rabid rage.

"She brought it on herself," Slater yelled back. "You brought it on her."

"You gave her no other choice!" Sam replied. "You took our child from us—and you kept us apart—what else is there to live for?"

"I told you we ain't having retarded babies around here, let alone retarded boyfriends and girlfriends," Slater bellowed. "You seem to forget your mama left you here because she knew you didn't belong in society with the rest of us."

"We are not retarded!" Sam hollered back. "Half the people in this hellhole aren't! We don't belong here. Maria wanted to help you make things better here—I wanted to help you. But you are too foolish to see what can really be done to improve quality of life."

"Don't give me this quality of life bullshit," Slater roared. "Did you read that on the back of a book?"

"You can keep me down here long as you like," King said more quietly. "I've got nothing left in this world."

Slater began to chuckle, quietly at first, then quite mad. "You just don't know when to give up," Slater bellowed through his laugh. "So be it. One more day."

Slater shut the peephole and the room fell dark, aside from the sliver of light near the base of the door. Jack could hear Slater walking down the hall away from them, then the remaining light left the space.

We're in solitary confinement. It was a terrible vision to be stuck in. *Why am I seeing this?*

A rush of air blasted through his body, and a dizzying sensation, as if he was being spun like a top.

The peephole opened again, bringing the searing light back into the pitch-black space around him. Jack turned around and could faintly see King balled up in the corner of the small concrete cell. The smell was more rancid, the air inside thick and lacking oxygen.

"Three days, Sam," Slater announced from the other side. "Ready to come out?"

No reply from King.

"I'm talking to you, boy!" Slater yelled.

Sam didn't say anything. *Had King perished in the back of the room in the darkness?* Jack couldn't even hear breathing, King was so quiet.

Suddenly, King arose from the dank floor like a marionette. He stood in the corner for a moment, swaying from side to side like a drunk. Then King clenched his fists and dashed past Jack, knocking him back a few steps. King reached the door, and Jack could see the silhouette of his sharp face from the slit of the open peephole.

"You have nothing left to take from me," King growled, his voice sounding ethereal, maddening and distant.

"I've heard enough! You don't talk to me this way!" Slater yelled, then turned away from the peephole. "Get him out!" he called down the hallway.

Slater slammed the peephole shut, returning the room to darkness. A small herd of footsteps came marching down the tunnel hallway and stopped at the door. A turn of the lock and a twist of the knob, and the door was opened so quickly—and King's limp body yanked out of the cell even faster—it was all a blur to Jack.

Jack stepped cautiously to the edge of the cell door and slowly leaned out to see three large men in neat white shirts and matching pants dragging King down the hall of the tunnels and into a room. King, who was at least a head taller than the tallest one, didn't even struggle.

Jack stepped out into the hallway quietly. He crept down the hall toward the room, hanging close to the concrete walls. When he arrived at the doorway, he heard a lot of indefinable sounds mixed with grunts and Slater barking one-word instructions every so often.

Jack leaned in to look around the doorframe, then everything went dark, and he felt the spinning sensation again.

"Wake him up already!" Slater bellowed. His voice was far off, like it was coming out of a tin can.

Jack looked around and tried to adjust his eyes, but everything in the space around him was blurry and hard to make out. A single bulb swung chaotically overhead.

"We've tried!" a voice cried out. "We've given him too much!"

The room faded into darkness for a moment, then the light returned.

"Nonsense. We've administered far more than this to men his size before," Slater bellowed.

"But he was already weak," another man said.

Finally, Jack could make out his surroundings a little better. Though everything was blurry, he seemed to be standing in the cell with King and two orderlies. The walls were painted a dark green, the floor damp. He could see Slater standing over King, who was strapped to a chair, his arms and legs bound by tight leather belts. His head was slumped over on his chest, and his body was limp.

The room faded into darkness then returned again.

"I don't care what you have to do, I'm not letting him die on my watch!" Slater screamed.

"We've tried everything," one orderly replied.

"Maybe we just need to give him more time?" said the other.

"Fine!" Slater hollered. "We'll come back in an hour."

The men left the room, followed by Slater, who slammed and bolted the door shut. Jack was stuck, standing in the middle of a small square cell with Sam King—the man who had taken his best friend Celia—visibly impaired beyond humanity.

King didn't move. Didn't even twitch. Wasn't even blinking. Jack stood there, trying to figure out what to do next. He usually left a vision by now.

Why am I still here?

He looked around for a way out. There were no windows and only the one locked door. He raced to the door and tried opening it, but it was no use. He turned back around for more ideas.

"Wake up, Jack!" he told himself. "You're just imagining this!"

The only thing in the room aside from King and the chair was a squat metal end table a few feet in front of King. Jack wandered over to inspect it and found a few long syringes sitting on top of the table beside several empty bottles.

He turned back to Sam and looked him over. He still wasn't moving.

Is he dead this time? The idea sent chills up and down his spine.

Jack began to shake from the nerves. He stepped closer to Sam, inspecting him more as he drew nearer. He could make everything out clearly now—nothing was blurry. It was amazingly crisp and vivid.

He got to within just a foot of Sam and stared at his plain white t-shirt covered in stains and rips. Jack looked at the center of King's shirt, watching for the rise and fall of his chest, but he saw no movement whatsoever.

"He's dead," Jack said aloud. Then panic overtook him.

I need to wake him! I need answers—only he can tell me why he haunts this place.

Jack moved in to where he was hovering over King's limp body. He looked straight down at him, then slowly began to reach out his hand to try and shake him or push him awake.

Before Jack's hand reached King's body, he was suddenly transported again, this time surrounded by pure white light. A spinning motion engulfed him—slowly and nonstop.

Jack tried to get his bearings. Everything was simply pure white light.

"Why do you seek me out?" a voice echoed through the blinding light.

It was King. He sounded more human than Jack had ever heard him. His voice was crisp, firm, and eerily monotone. There was no rage and no hollowness to it.

"Why do you come for me?" King asked.

"I want my friend back," Jack replied, his voice sounding like he was in a very small room.

"The girl?" King replied.

"Yes, I know you have her," Jack said. "I want you to let her go."

"You're right, I do have her," King replied. "But what makes you think I'm willing to give her up? I want *my* girl back, too."

"Why did you take her?" Jack said, his voice rising with anger. He tried to remain calm, but it wasn't working.

"You should be asking why did *they* take her from me?" King replied just as angrily.

"I had nothing to do with that," Jack replied more quietly, trying to encourage King to do the same.

"Are you not of the living? Are you not one of them?" King asked.

"Yes, of course, I am one of the living," Jack replied.

"Then are you not one of those who lives his entire life without boundaries, without confinement?" King's voice echoed throughout the blinding white space that surrounded Jack. "You live without walls, or locks, or gates. You have every freedom you desire and make your own choices. Go where you want, when you want. Do you fall in love as you please? Are you not one of them?"

"I don't have all that you say—I am not that free!" Jack hollered back. "And I didn't choose for it to be that way for you. I wasn't even alive then!"

"It was your forefathers who witnessed and allowed these things," King said.

"Things are different now," said Jack. "Linhurst is changing… for the better."

"It is not!" King's voice bellowed. "And now you are only making this harder on yourselves!"

"What do you want from me? What do you want from us?" Jack asked.

"What I want, you cannot give me," King replied, his voice low and angry. "So, I will take from you instead. I am taking back this place—taking back the machine, taking back the land… and taking your friends with me."

"You can't do that!" Jack yelled. "She belongs with us!"

"They belong to me now," King replied demonically. "It is your final sacrifice for all the things your forefathers wrought on us. They will help me take back the energy from that machine and with it, all of Linhurst. And from it, they will learn—they will all learn—to never come back here again… starting with you!"

There was a sudden clap of thunder and a great wind like from a hurricane. The bright light faded, and Jack found himself spinning very fast into darkness.

Then a face. A girl. No—a young woman. She had a face like an angel. Her long black hair was blowing gently in the wind, the sun shining down upon her. A hand stretched out in front of Jack, but it wasn't his. The woman reached up and entwined her fingers with the hand. She had a blissfulness and worry-free look. They spun around as if they were dancing. Behind her, the Linhurst campus fields rested peacefully against a clear blue sky. The woman fell backward into a black hole. Her face became twisted and blurred, as if it was smudged. Then her face came back from the blackness, and she looked altogether different. The woman became Celia.

"Celia?" Jack called out.

She was falling, as if in slow motion, into the black hole. The lush green field and blue sky were gone. Celia reached out a hand, looking at him in terror.

"Jack!" she called up to him. "Only you can stop this!"

Then a blinding light—and something else. The sun and peace symbol flashed before his eyes but just for an instant. Then darkness.

Complete silence surrounded him.

He could hear a scream—faint at first, then it grew louder. Full-throated and roaring.

Jack stared down into the darkness, the scream barreling toward him as he stood frozen in place. His feet were swallowed up by the darkness that surrounded him, as if they were set in black quicksand.

He knew he would have to try and move out of the way of this thing—he already knew it wasn't planning to stop. He reached out a hand to feel for the wall, his arm stretched to full length. It was farther than he recalled. He yanked his feet from the black quicksand, like pulling out of an oily mud, and moved a few inches to get closer to the wall. His open palm met the damp, brittle face of the tunnel. It felt real, as always—like it was really there, like *he* was really there.

But he had seen this before. He had been here before, far too many times. It was the dream again. Only this time— for the very first time—he was absolutely certain it was actually real.

Jack pulled his mind, and feet, out of the oily quicksand he knew was never there. It was only his mind that made him feel stuck in that moment. He struggled at first to move them, his feet felt like giant lead weights.

The scream was growing down the tunnel behind him— he had to move before King got hold of him. Jack pulled himself away from the spot and could feel the hard surface of the tunnel floor with great relief. He began running, fast as he could, in the opposite direction of the scream, keeping his hand on the wall for guidance.

The voice seemed to be outpacing him. Finally, he saw a light in front of him. Faint at first but growing enough that he could make out the edges of a railing glowing from the moonlight.

"The stairwell!" he said aloud. He ran faster. It was only feet away. Jack reached out and grabbed the railing, pulled himself up onto the first step, then ran fast as he could, skipping a step at a time.

The scream sounded like it was right behind him.

He reached the top of the landing and raced madly through the doorway leading into the great room when he heard something through the scream.

A voice yelled, "Jack, I'm down here!"

It could have been the scream playing tricks on his mind, or King toying with him. He ignored it and continued across the room. Everything seemed so familiar suddenly.

As he ran across the room, leaping and bounding over debris, he spied a new sight—a table in the middle of the room holding a lit candle.

"The séance!" Jack said aloud. He was back in the Mayflower building, where they had called on the spirits what felt like hours ago.

Where is everyone? They abandoned me!

The voice was right behind him. He turned to try and outmaneuver it, but before he could react, he was swept off his feet, held tightly by something. Jack looked in front of him to get a good look at the thing racing him backward out of the great room but there was nothing there.

It carried him all the way through the room, out the front doors, onto the porch, down the stairs, and tossed him out onto the dirt road in front of the Mayflower building, causing him to skid several yards. A great gust of wind arose and pulled on him like a vacuum, then a glowing orb of hot red-orange took shape amid the dust and burst into a ball of light. The orb dashed back to just inside the portico in front of the entrance to the abandoned building fifty yards away. It hovered several feet above the busted wooden planks of the porch for a moment, looking innocent, heavenly, and terrifying all at once. Above it, the broken windows stared down at Jack like a great skull wishing to swallow him whole.

Jack was now certain this was real—King had been the one who carried him out.

"I know what you want from me now!" Jack yelled at the orb of light. "But you're not going to get it."

With that, the red ball of light blasted back inside the Mayflower and disappeared. Everything was quiet for a moment, and Jack thought King had gone back into hiding inside the tunnels.

He pushed himself to his feet and brushed off his pants. At once, the ground began to rumble and shake like never before. A great white light blasted forth from the building, lighting every opening from within, illuminating the trees and branches of the surrounding woods.

A crack split down the face of the Mayflower building, reaching the porch and splitting it in two. The crack continued and busted the concrete staircase in two. Then the rupture hit the ground and made for Jack.

He broke into a full sprint down the road away from the Mayflower, looking back every so often to see the fissure following him, tearing the road in two and uprooting trees and shooting rocks in every direction.

Jack ran hard down the road until he was out on the main stretch leading to the generating station. He turned to see the gap widening and still following him. He kept running, trying to speed up, but his legs were starting to give out on him. Exhaustion overwhelmed him.

The events of the evening raced through his mind, starting with meeting the paranormal investigators, to seeing the man from the power plant, to Celia disappearing, and now running from a building, being chased by her ghostly captor after discovering him through a séance.

It was almost more than Jack could handle, but he had to find a way to stop King and get Celia back.

He turned again to see if the fault line was catching up to him. To his immediate relief, it had stopped. The road behind him was divided in half but the fissure no longer followed him. This suddenly made him nervous. *Why did King stop and turn back?*

A large explosion erupted behind Jack. He turned to see green light blasting out the top of the generating station tower in the distance. Jack gasped, took in a deep breath, and started running again. His legs were tired and weak.

As he neared the end of the road leading from the Mayflower building, Jack could see a small crowd gathered in front of the care center. The lights were still down, and the investigator's truck was wide open, with three new police cruisers sitting nearby. Mose was in the forefront, surrounded by the paranormal group, his dad, Celia's parents, Danny, and Tommy, along with Captain Hadaway and several police officers.

Then he saw Roland Allister's Mercedes.

As Jack drew closer to the crowd, he could make out Allister standing with an officer, his hands in cuffs.

Everyone was staring in awe at the generating station, and when Jack turned toward the front of the building to see what all the commotion was, he couldn't believe his eyes.

Inside the generating station, glowing green spirits flew all around.

He fell to his knees, overwhelmed by exhaustion.

"Jack!" Mose and Henry called out in unison.

They ran side by side across the road and grabbed one of Jack's arms, pulled him to his feet, and helped him back to the group gathered in front of the care center.

"Where have you been?" Harrison asked.

"I should ask you the same thing!" Jack raged. "Why did you leave me there?"

"I can explain—" Harrison began.

"And why are the police here now?" Jack asked frantically.

"We had to get help, Jack," Mose said.

"We have search and rescue teams down in the tunnels now," Captain Hadaway said.

"It's not safe!" Jack hollered.

"It's not safe!" Allister shouted suddenly, the officer next to him pulling him back. "You've created a monster here."

"Calm down, you," Captain Hadaway called out to the smarmy executive, still wearing his pinstripe suit, only he was covered in dirt and looking rather disheveled.

"What happened to him?" Jack asked, exasperated.

"He was snooping around in the tunnels and seems to have had a run-in with Sam King," Mose replied.

"I know what's powering this place," Allister said madly. "*Ghosts!* They are everywhere!"

"They'll never believe him," said Mose, grinning devilishly. Jack understood the look on Mose's face—he had what he needed to keep the power plant executives in line.

"Get him out of here," Hadaway called to the officer, and he dragged Allister to a cruiser and stuffed him in the back. "Already have him on trespassing and breaking and entering. Let's see what else he's been up to."

"They got Garrett," Sierra interrupted desperately. She looked like she had been crying.

"Where is he?" Jack asked.

"King took him just like he took Celia," Sierra replied. "Just like he took you."

"How did you escape?" Harrison asked.

"He confronted me," Jack said weakly. "I saw him die, then he brought me into a bright light and said he was taking this place back. Next thing I knew, I was stuck in the darkness of the tunnel—it was my dream all over again, only it was the real thing. I was able to break away. He chased me for a while but gave up. I don't know why he didn't follow me all the way here, but it makes me very nervous."

"This is a great energy the likes of which I have never seen," Allyson said in a mystified voice.

"Why did you all come back here?" Jack asked breathlessly.

"We got a lot on EVP," Harrison said frantically. "Listen!"

Sierra quickly stepped forward and pulled out her voice recorder and played it.

"Do we have someone here with us tonight?" Jack could here Allyson on the recording.

"Should we talk to her?" a voice answered. It sounded like a female.

"What would we say?" said a male voice.

"Would you speak to us this evening?" Allyson asked.

"We need to communicate with them," said the female voice.

"We would like to talk to you," said Allyson.

"Please, Frederick, talk to her!" said the female voice.

"I can't, Dorothy. What if he hears us?" Frederick replied.

"We have to try!" Dorothy replied.

"This is a waste of time," Jack's voice groaned from the recording. "We have to get to Celia."

"Give it time, Jack," Harrison replied.

"Can you please talk to us if you are here?" Allyson said again.

"Yes," Frederick replied finally.

"Did you do that?" Jack asked Allyson.

"Would you tell us your name?" Allyson continued.

"No, I can't," Frederick said.

"Won't tell us his name," Allyson whispered. "How old are you?" she called out.

"I am nineteen years old," he said.

"You're nineteen years old?" Allyson asked.

"Yes, that's right," said Dorothy. "Go on, Frederick. We haven't much time."

"She's asking the questions!" Frederick bit back.

"Were you a resident here at Linhurst?" Allyson asked.

"No," Frederick said. "Oh, please, lady, hurry!"

Sierra fast forwarded the recording and hit play.

"He's coming, we must hurry," said a new voice.

"We're getting there, Gerald, please be patient," Dorothy snapped.

"Did illness kill you?" Allyson asked.

"Yes, I was very sick," Frederick said.

"We all were that winter," Dorothy replied. "The lack of heat didn't help!"

"Why would this spirit have come to Mayflower if it didn't live here?" Mose asked.

"Tell them he brought us here!" Gerald yelped.

"HIM," Allyson said. "He brought you here?"

"Yes, against our will!" Gerald added.

"Be quiet," Frederick insisted.

"Who brought you here?" Allyson asked.

"Don't say his name," Dorothy cringed.

"Is it King?" Jack asked.

"Yes!" said another voice.

"Tell them it was Sam who did this!" added another.

"Tell them it's King!" came another.

"They can help us be free!" said yet another voice.

"Shhhh," Frederick replied nervously.

"King brought this person here," Allyson said in an audible whisper.

"Tell them there are more of us," said the first voice.

"I'm getting a 4.3 on the EMF, guys," Sierra called through the recording.

"He's coming!" Dorothy yelled.

"We must go now!" Gerald added.

"How many?" Allyson asked.

"There are 127 of us, right?" said Dorothy.

"I think so," Frederick replied.

"We don't want to leave anyone behind," said Dorothy.

"127?" Jack exclaimed.

"Are you under this building?" Harrison asked.

"Tell them we are in the tunnels!" said Gerald.

"Tell them we are going to the generating station—we must find the machine and stop him," Dorothy exclaimed.

"Buried?" Jack added.

"We are trapped by King!" Gerald yelled grumpily.

"Stop yelling! He will hear us!" groaned a voice.

"He already hears us," said Frederick. "Dorothy's right. This may be our last chance to get away from him."

"Are you trapped in the tunnels?" Allyson asked.

"Yes! Say yes!"

"Are you trapped by Sam King?" Harrison asked.

"Say yes!" said Dorothy excitedly. "Quickly, he's coming. Everyone, come this way!"

"What is it, friend?" Allyson asked. "Are you afraid?"

"He's here!" yelled a new voice from a distance.

More voices repeated anxiously, "He's here! He's here!"

"He's here?" Jack puzzled aloud, repeating himself on the recording.

Sierra stopped the voice recorder.

"That's when King came into the room," Sierra said.

"You were taken down into the tunnels," Harrison said, "along with Garrett."

"We were taken at the same time?" Jack gasped, then thought quickly. "Slater took away his love, and now he wants revenge. He said he's going to take back this campus—the machine and all."

"The machine!" Mose exclaimed. "That's what the spirits said on the recorder. But what does he want with the reactor?"

"To control its power," said Allyson grimly. "King has managed to find a way to reside in two worlds—both his and ours. We see his as a spirit realm, which is much like he may see ours. He insists on staying here until he has gotten his revenge—and the woman he loves."

"Which is how he managed to remain here that night we thought he departed with all the other spirits," Jack said in awe.

"Precisely," said Harrison.

"But how do we stop him and get Celia and Garrett back?" Jack asked.

"The only way to stop this menace now is to set a trap," Allyson replied. "He doesn't want to live in our world, only control a part of it. We need to push him on to the next place where he belongs. Only then can we free Celia and Garrett."

"Along with all the others," Jack added, referring to the spirits on the recorder.

"How do you intend to do that?" Mose asked.

"We start by talking to them," Allyson said, pointing across the street to the spirits flying chaotically throughout the generating station in a vibrant green whirlwind.

Chapter 14

"What equipment will we need?" Sierra asked.

"For this? Nothing," Allyson replied.

Sierra screwed up her face. "How do you intend to speak with them?"

Allyson turned to Mose and Jack. "I read about what happened here years ago. It's mind blowing. People everywhere are still talking about it, weighing the possibilities of what paranormal experts like Harrison and I have been exploring our whole lives."

Jack had never considered the broader ramifications of that night two years ago. It was already a lot to process all he had witnessed, but to deal with the fallout it had in his own life only added to the pain of feeling like an outcast. People in Spring Dale, especially his fellow classmates, thought he was crazy and had made most of it up.

"What was most incredible from what I read by the experts you spoke with shortly afterward is that you openly talked to the spirits," said Allyson.

"That's right, we did," Jack confirmed.

"That is simply remarkable!" Allyson replied with joy.

Jack didn't know how to respond to her enthusiasm. The feeling of having his words taken at face value was strange and unfamiliar. Could there really be an entire following who yearned to understand the paranormal just as Jack had witnessed firsthand?

"Wait, you're thinking we can just go in there and talk to these apparitions?" Sierra asked, incredulous.

"We can certainly try," Allyson replied. "But just Jack and me." She turned to Harrison. "Is that all right with you?"

"If you think you can get us answers, by all means," Harrison replied.

Allyson turned to Jack and put her hand out to him. He hesitated at first, joined her, and they crossed the street.

"Son!" Henry called out from behind the group. "Be careful!"

Jack stopped and looked back at his dad.

"You got this, Jack," Henry added with a confident smile. "I believe in you."

The rest of the group nodded at Jack, confirming their support, and Harrison gave him a hearty pat on the back. Jack felt a sense of kinship, like he finally belonged somewhere after years of being ostracized by those around him.

Jack and Allyson made their way toward the open door of the generating station, looking up through the wall of windows that stretched four stories toward the roof where the tower shot out into the sky. The crowded mass of glowing green apparitions drifted aimlessly around the reactor.

They stepped in through the large open metal door past the sign reading *Employees Only: Keep Out* and took in their surroundings. Jack remembered being inside the building years earlier with its shattered windows, rusted metal equipment, long overhead beams, and labyrinth of staircases.

It seemed that Mose hadn't changed much. The most notable addition was a large room rising out of the middle of the space. Its walls were at least 10 feet tall and stretched nearly the length of the station in either direction. All 127 apparitions were flying around the room, like massive glowing moths drawn to a flame.

"They're trying to get inside that space," Jack said.

"What could they want in there?" Allyson asked.

"That's where the reactor is."

"Reactor? I don't remember reading about that. Does it have a different name?"

Jack hesitated. Mose wanted as few people as possible to know about the energy source that powered their campus, but Jack knew this was important information for her to have.

"The night they said the generating station exploded…" Jack paused. "The thing is, it didn't explode at all. The spirits we found here were working to get a fusion reactor up and running."

"A fusion reactor… like a nuclear generator of some kind?" Allyson replied.

"It's a safe, clean, alternative form of nuclear power. With it, we don't need Spring Dale Nuclear Power Plant's energy," Jack said.

"They once tried to use this place for nuclear waste, correct?" Allyson said, fascinated by the new details.

"And they've been trying to get their hands on the reactor technology ever since," Jack said.

"And so, the machine is inside there?"

Jack could see Allyson sifting through this new information in hopes of finding some answers. He walked a few more steps into the room and looked up.

"Can someone help us?" Jack called to the spirits. "We need to bring our friends back."

"Is it that simple?" Allyson puzzled.

Jack nodded and smiled just as one of the apparitions broke from the twister of spirits and flew down toward them.

Allyson looked on, mesmerized. "It appears so…" she whispered to herself, awe-struck.

The ghost inspected Jack for a moment, its wispy green shape translucent and unsteady.

"You must be the boy he is after," said the spirit, whose shape and face were that of a young man.

"Yes, I believe King is after me," Jack said. "I've been seeing into his past."

"We want to help," said the ghost. "We tried to get to it, but we cannot."

"Get to what?" Allyson asked, fascinated to be speaking directly with a ghost.

The spirit pointed to the wall.

"The reactor," Allyson said quietly.

Another spirit broke away from the crowd and joined the first one. She looked like a middle-aged woman.

"Is it him, Frederick?" the spirit woman said to her ghostly friend in an audible whisper.

"It is him, Dorothy," Frederick replied.

"What's your name?" Dorothy asked.

"Jack," he replied. "And this is Allyson… you were talking to her tonight in the Mayflower."

"Yes, we remember," said Frederick. "Listen, we don't have much time before he gets to us again."

"Are you talking about King?" Allyson asked.

"Yes, he is preparing to take over the machine in hopes of controlling all of Linhurst," Frederick said.

"Controlling what?" Jack asked. "There's nothing left for him here."

"We know—we just want to be freed from this place," Dorothy despaired. "We are ready to move on—have been forever!"

"Ever since the machine began working, we have been trapped in the sub-tunnels by King," Frederick said.

"Sub-tunnels?" Jack blurted.

"They don't exist on your plane," Frederick explained. "He imprisoned us deep in the recesses of Linhurst, waiting for his moment to use our energy. We've been trying to escape but it's no use. At first, he only had a few of us, then he rounded up more and more as time went on."

"We were only able to slip away tonight because he has been preoccupied with how to harness the energy of his human captors," Dorothy added.

"What does he want with us?" Jack asked.

"He believes he can use our combined energies to bring his Maria back to his plane of existence," Frederick replied.

"He couldn't possibly control who stays in what realm," Allyson protested. "The worlds are chosen by forces we don't understand."

"I believe you are correct!" Frederick concurred. "What he doesn't understand is that Maria has long since passed on to the next world and she is likely unreachable—but he won't listen to reason."

"Sam King was stubborn and fanatical in life, just as he is in death," said Dorothy sadly.

"I still don't understand what you're all doing here," Allyson said.

"The reactor," Jack replied. "They are here for the reactor."

"Yes, I realize that, Jack—but why?" Allyson asked.

"Two years ago, we were standing here in this very spot," Jack began. "Those men who died in the tunnels were working with Professor Vidar to make the reactor fire, but it wasn't until more spirits from all around the campus came together that they truly got it working. Once their work was done, they moved on to the next world."

"And we want to do the same," said Dorothy. "It's our only hope of escaping him."

"Wait," Allyson interjected. "You're telling me that spiritual energy made the machine work to power a reactor that provides energy to the campus?"

"Correct!" Dorothy said gleefully.

Allyson shook her head in awe.

"Simply amazing," Harrison's voice came from over her shoulder.

Allyson and Jack turned to see him standing a few feet behind, accompanied by Mose, Morgan, and Sierra.

"This is insane!" Sierra yelped.

"Sorry to bust in on you, Allyson, but we had to see this," Harrison apologized.

"Please, don't apologize. I'm glad you're here," Allyson said. "I've spent my career trying to connect us with the spirit realm. I thought this was going to be more challenging and focused. Yet here I stand talking to them as simply as I would talk to you. I suppose my work is done here tonight."

A new spirit broke from the flying circus and joined them. "What are you doing?" he said hurriedly. "We have to go!"

"Yes, Gerald, we know," Dorothy replied, annoyed.

"We have to find a way past these walls," Frederick said. "We cannot penetrate them for some reason."

The ground beneath them suddenly began to rumble and quake.

"Please, Frederick," Dorothy pleaded. "He's coming!"

"Dr. Moseley," Jack said breathlessly, "They can't get past the walls."

"It must be the metal we used to surround the reactor," Mose replied. "No problem—we just need to open things up."

Mose turned and ran along the space to a far corner and approached a panel on the station wall. He opened the door of the panel, flipped a few switches, then pulled down a lever. The wall began to move, slowly unfolding one panel at a time like an accordion. The group watched as the massive wall glided seamlessly along a track, revealing the reactor beyond.

The spirits hurriedly surrounded the hulking metal beast with missile-like arms and a large round body. All hundred-plus spirits filled the space inside and began soaring around it like a turbulent tidal wave, slamming into the reactor as if trying to find a way in. Their motion created so much wind and sound, it was like a tornado had formed inside the station.

"Now what?" Jack called out.

"We have to find a way inside the machine, I guess," Dorothy said.

"How did the spirits leave here before?" Frederick asked Jack.

"I don't know," Jack said. "They were soaring around it, continuously picking up speed."

"Maybe they have to go faster!" Gerald called to the spirits, then flew up to join them.

"I don't think that's it, though," Jack told Dorothy and Frederick. "I remember that night, as the spirits surrounded the machine, the reactor sparked but nothing really happened. We escaped the building because we thought it was about to explode. We were outside when everything lit up and a beacon of energy just kind of blasted out of the tower above. But what set it off?"

Just then, a rumbling erupted under their feet. The floor began to crack and split, small fissures opening in the concrete base of the station. A bright green glow shot from the tunnel door and a massive body of light flew out, racing above the spirits over the reactor and diving down inside their twister, scattering them in a rush of green flashes all throughout the station, some flying out through the walls and windows.

The new body of light took on a human shape and flew down toward Jack and the others. It shot through Frederick and Dorothy, causing their spectral bodies to dissipate right in front of Jack.

The glowing body spun in an angry vortex, doubling in size and stretching out into the form of Sam King as it took shape in front of them.

"I SAID…" King's voice boomed throughout the station, "GO AWAY!"

King's lower jaw appeared to unhinge from his face as he bellowed, the monstrous scream. It was accompanied by a wind so powerful that it blew Jack and the others back a few steps.

Jack regained his footing and leaned in toward King. "Stop this!" Jack yelled up at the monster.

"Jack!" Mose hollered. "Get back!"

"You're mine!" King howled at Jack, racing down toward him.

In an instant, Jack was swept up into a twister of bright green light that had been King's spiritual body only a moment before.

They spun toward the ceiling and all around the generating station, flying past Allyson, Frederick, and Dorothy before speeding toward the open door of the building and out into the night sky. Jack saw the care center disappear below him, followed by the generating station, as they flew high into the sky above Linhurst. He saw a group of Spring Dalers walking along the road entering the campus with flashlights and cell phones lit.

With lightning speed, King carried him along the road leading to the apartment buildings, zipping past the fountain in the courtyard between Buildings A, B, and C. They flew through the darkened woods past the construction zones and out into the clearing in front of the administration building, up the staircase toward the entrance that had crumbled earlier. King took a sudden turn up the front face of the building and raced along the rooftop, where

Jack could see the surrounding brick buildings nestled among a network of interconnected raised walkways down below. King dropped suddenly, and Jack's stomach flew up as if he was on a roller coaster. King picked up speed as he raced toward the boarded-up doorway to a building. Jack clamped his eyes shut as they broke through the doors, zoomed across the expanse of the great room beyond, then dashed down the stairwell into the pitch black tunnels.

Suddenly, Jack realized he could just make out King's face in the glowing body that absorbed him—like a light projection amidst the spectral glow. His sharp jawline and hollow eyes were horrifying, an expression of determination and pure rage.

Jack shifted his gaze and that's when he saw it: around King's glowing neck was his mother's necklace. The sun and peace symbol he once wore around his neck every day—the amulet his mother had given him before she passed on to the other side that night two years before—was somehow hanging around the monster's neck. Just as Jack reached out to grab it and take it from King's neck, the demon released him into the darkness.

Jack hit the ground hard, skidding on his back several feet. He sat up and shook his head, feeling dizzy and aching. He looked up to the apparition hovering over him, the glowing green body shaking with madness. Jack stared at the amulet.

"That doesn't belong to you!" Jack screamed.

King looked down at the amulet then gently brushed it with his long ethereal fingers.

"Give it back!"

King simply smiled. Then he began to chuckle, soft and low at first, then more madly. "Give it back? This is the key! You will never have it."

Then he violently turned and darted down the tunnel at an incomprehensible speed, his green light leaving a thin trail behind.

Complete darkness and silence overwhelmed the space around Jack once more. He got to his feet then reached out and braced himself against the brittle concrete wall of the tunnel.

How do I get out of here now?

"Jack?" said a small voice in the darkness. "Is that you?"

Jack's heart skipped a beat and a lump formed in his throat. "Celia?"

"Jack! I can hear you!" Celia's voice sounded weak but excited.

"Where are you?" he asked.

"I'm right here," she replied.

"It's dark, Celia—I don't know where right here is."

"Just feel around," she replied sarcastically.

He did just that. His hand waved through the air helplessly. He couldn't see a thing. He couldn't even recall which direction was the way out now.

"Jack," Celia said. "I'm right here."

Finally, Jack's hand met with something. He felt hair, then skin, then an arm. He locked hands with Celia. Then suddenly he could feel the space around him squeeze in tightly all around him. He felt as though he was being sucked through a straw, into some vortex to another realm. Light filled the darkness and flooded in all around him.

He could see he was no longer in the tunnels. He was surrounded by warm sunlight pouring in through open windows. A breeze gently blew the curtains in what appeared to be a living room with comfortable furniture, a television, and family pictures hanging from bright yellow walls.

"That's your cousin Amelia," said a voice.

Jack turned to see the familiar face of a woman seated on the edge of the sofa, leaning over a small child on an equally small chair at a coffee table.

The woman's features were angelic, framed by long, soft strands of black hair. The child turned a page in her book— it looked like a scrapbook—and the woman placed a finger on the open page.

"This is your great uncle Hector," said the woman. "He was a farmer."

The little girl pointed to a picture on the opposite page.

"That's your great aunt Rosa," the woman said.

The child smiled grandly, repeating the name Rosa.

The girl flipped the next few pages quickly, then stopped and pointed at a specific photo. The woman sighed, her expression taking on a mixture of sadness and joy.

"*Tusabuelos,*" the woman said.

The child touched the photo. Jack moved in closer to see a black and white picture of a couple sitting outside on a bench in front of the Linhurst Administration Building.

"Your grandparents, *hija*," she said. "Samuel y Maria."

Sam and Maria!

"They died before I knew them," said the woman sadly. "Mama died while giving birth to me, so I was raised by Aunt Rosa and Uncle Hector." She turned to the child and gently brushed her hair with her hand. "Now I have you."

Jack looked on in awe. He knew who this was. *Sam and Maria's daughter! There was no abortion after all! Another one of Slater's vicious lies just to get the better of King!*

The woman scooped her daughter off her chair and embraced her warmly, then began giving her little kisses all over her face. The child let out a wonderful laugh.

"I love you so much, Maria," the woman said to the little girl.

"I love you, too, Mama!"

The scene suddenly faded and Jack was transported and suddenly in the dark again. He felt dizzy and nauseous.

"Jack?" Celia said. "Jack, grab my hand."

Jack squeezed Celia's hand tightly.

"Guys?" said another voice weakly.

"Garrett, is that you?" Jack asked, looking around in the pitch blackness.

"Yes, Garrett is here, too," Celia said. "We need to get out of here quickly!"

Jack reached into his jacket pocket and found his flashlight. He still had it! He flicked it on and, though it was dim, the light was just bright enough to see a foot in front of him.

He aimed the light toward Garrett's voice. He was curled up in a ball on the floor against the wall. Jack reached out a hand and helped him up.

"Which way?" Jack said.

"I don't know, Jack," Celia said, her voice weak and frail. "I've been down here so long, I don't even know which way is up or down."

Jack tried to think, tried to remember how he landed and which way King had left the tunnel.

"Come. This way. Let's get out of here," Jack said confidently.

Garrett grabbed hold of his sweatshirt as he took Celia's hand and they started walking. Celia kept losing her footing, and Jack put his arm around her to help her along. As they moved along slowly, one step at a time, Jack kept one hand against the wall. He wouldn't let her get taken again. A rumbling shook the floor beneath their feet and dirt rained down on them. They pressed on.

They walked and walked, a little faster now. His light stayed lit, but it was fading with each step.

I hope this is the right way.

Garrett began to wheeze and his breathing grew heavier with each step.

Finally, a dull light appeared ahead. Jack picked up the pace, struggling to pull Celia and Garrett along with him.

They began to pass rooms with open doors spilling into greater darkness on either side, and Jack soon realized they were not where he had thought. He finally made out the railing of a stairwell leading up to the main floor.

"We're almost there!" Jack called. He pulled his companions on as he reached out for the railing and started up the staircase. Celia struggled with each step, Garrett, though weak, kept an iron-tight grip on the back of Jack's hoodie, and Jack had to use every remaining ounce of his energy to get all three of them up the steps.

As they reached the half-landing, light poured in from the top floor. They could hear voices. One in particular was very clear—it was Allyson, who was yelling as if she was possessed.

"All spirits come together now," she called in a deep, monotone sort of drone. "Create a shield around the machine."

Jack tugged harder on Celia and Garrett, finally pulling them to the top of the stairwell. Garrett fell to the floor against the railing, breathing heavily. Celia collapsed to her knees, pale and exhausted. Jack noticed burn marks on her arms. He looked at Garrett and saw that he, too, had the marks. Then Jack looked at his own arms—they were free of wounds.

"How did you get those?" Jack asked, bewildered.

Celia looked down at her arms, seeing the marks for what seemed to be the first time.

"When he pulled me into the tunnel, it felt hot all around me," Celia replied weakly. "I wondered why my arms were stinging so badly."

"I think it's from all the energy he is emitting," said Garrett weakly. "He is putting out so much negative energy."

Garrett was right. King was spewing red-hot energy, and Jack had to do something to reverse course.

"Stay here," Jack whispered to them.

"Like I have a choice," Celia croaked sarcastically, slumping back against the stairwell railing. She closed her eyes, breathing heavily, and Garrett fell to a half-seated position next to her.

Jack peered around the corner of the doorframe into the station to see Allyson standing just in front of the reactor, looking up at the spirits flying overhead. Her arms were stretched out wide and high above her head.

"Faster now," Allyson called out to them. "Protect one another. You are almost ready to leave this place!"

Jack looked around for King, but there was no sign of him. *Where is he now?* He broke from the tunnel door across the station toward Mose, Harrison, Morgan, and Sierra, who were watching from a far corner.

"What is she doing?" Jack whispered loudly, startling the group on his approach.

They turned, and Mose gave Jack a huge hug.

"My boy!" Mose exclaimed. "You're back!"

"Yes, I'm all right," Jack said. "And I have Celia and Garrett, too."

He turned and pointed to the open tunnel door, where they could see the pair catching their breath by the railing at the top of the landing.

Sierra immediately took off and ran to check on them.

"I thought I had lost you," Mose said.

"Lost me?" Jack replied, bewildered.

"My dream, Jack," Mose began. "I keep dreaming that King takes you to the other side with him. He has tried twice now, yet here you are. Maybe the dreams are not true after all."

"I just had another vision, Mose," Jack said quickly. "It's Maria—Sam's girlfriend."

"You saw her?" Mose asked.

"Not quite," Jack replied.

"What did you see, Jack?" asked Harrison anxiously.

"Sam and Maria's child… she lived!" Jack said.

"Are you certain of this?" Mose exclaimed.

"I'm pretty sure," Jack said. "And she had a child, too!"

"King has a granddaughter?" Harrison said.

"In my vision, they were looking at old family photos," Jack said. "One of the pictures was of Sam and Maria, and they were together in front of the Administration Building."

"What about Maria?" Mose said. "Is she alive?"

"The woman said that her mother died while giving birth," Jack exclaimed.

"Then Maria's abortion down in the tunnels—that never happened?" Harrison said.

"Not if what I saw is true," said Jack.

"The Linhurst staff must have defied Slater's orders," said Mose.

"They were trying to save the child?" Harrison asked.

"They did save her," Jack added.

"We have to tell King," Harrison said. "It's the only way to stop him now."

Just then, the spirits above the reactor scattered in every direction as an explosion of light, wind, and thunder erupted in front of them. A blast of fiery red light appeared above the reactor and knocked Allyson to the floor. Harrison raced to her side and pulled her away.

King appeared as a full-bodied apparition—clear, crisp, and raging.

"It is time!" King boomed, his voice sounding like many voices.

A great wind began to swirl all around him, forming a vacuum that sucked in dust and debris from all around the station. The glowing green spirits fought to pull away from his powerful force.

Jack stepped forward, but Mose grabbed his arm. "Jack—wait!"

"I am the only one who can stop this," Jack cried out. "Let me do this!"

"Jack, we just got you back—please, don't go," Mose pleaded.

Jack gave Mose a look to say *trust me*, and Mose reluctantly released him. He turned and walked toward King, passing Harrison and Allyson.

"Jack," Allyson said weakly. "He's too strong. We have to find another way."

"This *is* the only way," said Jack. "It has been this whole time."

The spirits overhead struggled against King's energy, trying to escape the powerful force surrounding his glowing red body. Jack stopped within feet of the reactor and looked up. He suddenly recalled very clearly the night the spirits raced around the reactor, trying to get it started with Max Vidar. He remembered Heather taking King's hand before they disappeared into the beam of light that blasted forth from the station tower and into the night sky.

Yet here King was, attempting to take over the reactor and control the Linhurst campus. Jack's eyes were drawn to the amulet. The edges of the sun and peace symbol shimmered with a brilliant white light all around.

"You don't have to do this!" Jack yelled above the fury of the twister surrounding King.

King looked down at Jack, his eyes glowing like rubies on fire. "Where have you taken my energies?"

"Energies?" Jack puzzled.

"My human captors," King replied. "I need them to open the portal."

"Celia and Garrett are with us now," Jack called back.

"Return them to me! I am taking over this place!" King bellowed down, his voice monstrous and hollow. "After what those people did to me—what they did to *us*— Linhurst is mine!"

"But you have a daughter, King! She's alive!" Jack shouted.

"You lie!" King bellowed louder than ever, the vacuum and vortex around him growing more intense. The spirits were losing the strength to fight against him.

"She's alive, Sam!" Jack pleaded. "I saw her! In a vision, I saw your daughter and she was with a little girl."

King's rage intensified, rattling the walls and windows of the station.

"You lie! You cannot stop me!" King screamed.

"I know about Maria!" Jack yelled. "They tried to save her! I saw it!"

King looked down at Jack again, his face softening, the vortex calming a bit.

"Slater lied to you," Jack cried out. "He wanted you to think she died—that the baby died—but it's not true."

"Slater! He did this! Bring *him* to me!"

"Slater is in prison, Sam!" Jack replied. "He is paying for what he did."

King had no reply suddenly.

"Maria *did* die in the tunnels," Jack began again. "But it's not what you think. They wanted to save the baby—and they did, Sam. *They did!* The little girl is your granddaughter."

King's vortex slowed a bit.

"Her name is Maria," Jack hollered.

King remained still, the vortex and vacuum a slower but steady fury.

"She is still gone," King said with great sadness.

"You have to go," Jack pleaded softly. "You need to be with her—you just have to go to the other side!"

"That's it, Jack!" Allyson called behind him. "Help him be free!"

A spirit broke from the vortex and flew down in front of Jack. It was Frederick.

"He is too powerful," Frederick said to Jack, sounding tired and devastated. "We tried, but there's nothing more we can do—we are trapped here forever. It's hopeless."

Jack could see the look of utter despair on Frederick's face. Then Dorothy fought to break away from the vortex, followed by Gerald. They quickly gathered around Jack.

"You *are* the one," Dorothy said frantically. "You are connected to this thing. We can see it. You can release his grip on our energy."

Jack shook his head. He didn't understand. Then Frederick pointed up to King, who was staring blankly at the ceiling, his body glowing a dim red, his rage subdued, and his force pulling less on the spirits. He was obviously considering Jack's words.

"That's the key," said Frederick, still pointing at King.

That's when Jack saw the amulet again.

It doesn't belong to King. It was never his in the first place.

"The amulet," Jack said excitedly. "We have to get it from him."

"Yes, the amulet!" Dorothy exclaimed.

"My mother was with me that night," Jack began. "She left for the very last time in order to send the spirits on to the next world. The amulet is the key!"

Frederick nodded.

Dorothy smiled at Jack. "It belongs to you, Jack."

"No," Jack replied. "It belongs to you. It belongs to all of you. My mother knew it would set you free and it did. It will again!"

Dorothy nodded. She turned to Frederick and Gerald. "Tell the others!"

Then Frederick, Dorothy, and Gerald flew away from Jack and allowed themselves to be pulled back into the vortex. Only this time, they used the path of the cyclone to race along and tell the many spirits the news.

"We have to get that amulet," Jack heard a spirit say as it flew just feet away from him.

"Take the necklace!" another ghost shouted.

All the spirits were now focused on the amulet around King's neck. King could hear their chatter and see them fighting the vortex he had them trapped in.

"Ready?" Frederick yelled over the madness.

The spirits swirled intensely around the great monstrous body of King, allowing themselves to be pulled closer to him.

Dorothy, Gerald, Frederick, and others locked arms and formed one large ring spinning around King's gravitational field. Dorothy was nearest to King and stretched out her hand. As the trio drew nearer, she reached out for the amulet around his neck.

King's glow was a bright red again. He glared at the spirits coming for him, looking perplexed by their motion as he hovered steadily above the reactor.

Dorothy's outstretched fingers brushed the amulet, causing it to knock against King's chest. Jack watched in horror—if

King knew what they were up to, it would surely end their chance of getting hold of it.

Harrison, Mose, and Morgan stood in a close huddle nearby, watching with the same bated breath as Jack.

Allyson, however, was standing with purpose—she had her fingers placed on her temples, eyes closed, and was mumbling and muttering feverishly.

Just then, a great rumbling from beneath the station rocked the reactor. Jack turned his attention back to the spectral show, looking for the cause.

Gerald came around for another shot at the amulet, clumsily reaching out his hand and only brushing it lightly. King's rage intensified, his red-hot light growing. Long strands of fire shot out of his arms and flew around the building, spitting small flames and streaking burn marks across the station walls and beams. The twister around him began to increase in speed, causing the ring of spirits to move farther from him at once.

"No!" Dorothy called out desperately.

"I'm going in!" Frederick yelled. "On the next rotation, let me go."

"Are you sure?" Dorothy called out.

"Positive!" Frederick hollered back.

They sped a full rotation around King and, as Frederick neared the front of King, he shot toward the flaming ghost like an arrow from a bow. He was within inches of the amulet when King saw him coming and swung an arm out to swat him away. Frederick was knocked off his trajectory and tossed back into the vortex.

Dorothy screamed out in anger, blasted forth, and grabbed a piece of the amulet strap. The string snapped, and the amulet went flying from King's neck... straight toward Jack.

Jack ran forward, hands stretched out. The amulet landed in his open palms, seemingly in slow motion. He held the round piece of metal firmly in one hand, staring at the sun and peace symbol gripped tightly between his fingers. He hadn't seen it in two years and thought it had been destroyed in the blast that left the station tower, but there it was in his possession once more.

The cool metal against his palm made him feel as though his mother was with him again, and a sense of the world he once belonged to almost overpowered him. But he quickly realized it wasn't to be that way—he knew his mother was gone and had come to terms with it.

He looked closely at the edges of the artwork glowing brightly with white light as the amulet began to shake and rattle in his hand. The vortex and vacuum around King slowed—the monster was losing his power, his red aura glowing less brightly, the flames and fire dissipating.

"Return it to me!" King bellowed down at Jack.

"This doesn't belong to you," Jack said.

"It is mine!" King yelled.

"You stole this from the others who are ready to move on."

"It's mine!"

Just then, a white beam of light shot out from the amulet and blast toward the reactor. A round portal opened inside the body of the giant metal beast. That's when Jack finally understood the power of the amulet—it created doorways to the other side.

"Time for you to go," Jack called up confidently to King.

King's body trembled and shook. He raised his arms over his head and let out a furious roar. The station floor rumbled and quaked. Dust and debris rained down on Jack, and the lights overhead started swinging wildly. But something was different—King's energy was low and his glow dimmed.

"He has lost all power over us—now is our chance!" Dorothy called out.

"She's right! We must go!" Frederick called.

Several spirits turned and raced for the portal, dashing into its open mouth and disappearing to the other side. Then several more followed.

"AAARGH!" King bellowed. "Stop this!"

Jack held the amulet tightly in his fully extended hand, pointing the glowing beam from the sun and peace symbol at the generator, keeping the portal wide open. More ghosts flew through, some in pairs, others in whole groups. Soon, only a few remained in the station.

Allyson's voice grew louder as she mumbled and muttered a string of foreign words that sounded Latin or Greek.

"Go, Frederick!" Dorothy yelled.

"You first!" Frederick called back.

"How about *me* first?" Gerald yelped, then flew up and in through the portal.

King's rage intensified as he realized his sudden reversal of fortune.

"What have you done?" he yelled, his red glow fading to a dim green.

"I've set things right!" Jack shouted back. "You don't belong here. Now *you* go away!"

The generator rocked and shook, glowing a sudden bright white that illuminated the entire station.

"Your turn!" Jack called up to King.

King hovered listlessly above the rumbling reactor with the portal open wide from the beam of light firing from the amulet in Jack's outstretched arm.

"Why have you done this to me?" King asked.

"It's not about you—I've set them free," Jack said proudly.

"Thank you!" Dorothy and Frederick called to Jack in unison, then they locked arms and raced toward the portal.

Then Frederick and Dorothy flew at King, wrapped him tightly, and pulled him down toward the portal. King struggled, but he had grown very weak. With one last gasp, Frederick and Dorothy pushed him through the portal, and they followed him through to the other side.

They were gone. King was gone.

"Jack!" Mose called out from behind. "You did it! Let it go!"

Jack turned his head to see Mose standing just feet away from him, a look of awe on his face. Harrison and the others approached, looking just as surprised. Jack was relieved to see Celia and Garrett also standing there, holding onto one another for support.

"Jack, you can let go now," said Harrison calmly.

The amulet continued firing the beam of white hot at the generator. The portal was still open. And Jack couldn't seem to let go of the amulet—but not for lack of want or trying.

Jack also noticed that Allyson was still chanting, her eyes closed and her arms outstretched.

Maybe there's unfinished business to settle?

Jack tried to pull in his outstretched arm, but he couldn't bend it. His hand was gripped firmly around the metal symbol and he just couldn't let go. He even tried moving his body, but his feet were plastered to the floor.

"I can't!" he yelled to them in desperation.

Mose and Harrison raced over and grabbed his body, trying to pry him from the spot where he stood. Their efforts were completely useless—he wouldn't budge.

"What's happening to me?" Jack cried out.

Mose and Harrison were speechless and looked terrified as they struggled to move Jack.

Suddenly, a flash of light caught their attention. Jack looked up to see a large green orb shoot out from the portal and straight for Jack. Before he could discern what was happening, he was yanked from the floor and in King's grip again, then carried frantically throughout the station. The light from the amulet shot all around them like an out-of-control laser beam, tearing a portal through everything it touched.

Jack couldn't make out King's features, just a luminous green vapor—but the spirit was still strong, and it held him mightily.

"Return it to me!" King yelled from within the light, far off in the distance.

Jack struggled against him, pulling the amulet into his chest and shielding it from King.

"Come to us now, Maria!" Allyson suddenly called out, her voice echoing. "Maria, come to us!"

They suddenly stopped midair, floating high above the reactor. Jack looked down to see they were several stories up, just floating high above.

"Is it you?" King's voice called weakly from the light.

Jack looked down to see a woman's ghostly figure gently floating upward toward them from the portal. The doorway was beginning to close.

It was Maria's spirit.

"It is time, Sam," Maria said. "Come with me."

"Maria?" King repeated. "Is it really you?"

"Come with me, Sam. Free yourself." She put out a hand.

"No!" King's voice said from the light. "It's a trick—it's not you. You're gone. They're trying to trick me again!"

Jack continued to struggle against King as he could feel the monster loosening its grip.

"Sam, come with me," Maria said again, her voice calm and angelic. "You don't have to fight anymore."

"No! I won't believe it!"

King took off and raced Jack around the station in a flurry of sputtering light and flashes of violent green sparks. They were moving so fast Jack could no longer make out their surroundings. He began to lose consciousness from the dizzying speed, and he closed his eyes to contain his nausea.

"Sam, now!" Maria demanded.

Jack opened his eyes to see Maria's spirit following the maddening path King was carrying him on. She was soaring backward, staying just ahead of them. Her faded spirit clearly had a look of scorn, like a mother whose son would ignore instruction for the last time.

"Enough of this!" Maria yelled. "It is time you move on and quit this fight!"

She slowed suddenly and absorbed King's glowing green aura into her arms, and somehow pushed Jack away at the same time. She grabbed King tightly and made for the closing portal. Just when Jack thought he was free, a limb shot out from King's glowing orb and caught Jack in a tight grip as they flew downward.

"Let him go!" Maria yelled.

"I will not!" King hollered back from within the orb. "He's coming with us!"

"King…I love you," Maria said softly. "Please, do this for our little one."

"Maria?" King was aghast. "It is you!"

King released his grip on Jack and went full speed ahead with Maria on to the other side. Just as Jack thought he would pull away, he could feel his body being sucked into the portal along with them. He turned his body around and fought with all his might to pull himself from the force of the black hole, but it was no use.

The station disappeared from his view, then in an instant everything around him became bright white. Then he saw swirling colors in a tapestry of light streams. Jack felt as though he was floating on a cloud in an endless sea. A deafening but heavenly silence engulfed him. His limbs floated softly at his sides as if he was suspended in water. A light breeze brought a delightful scent into his nose.

A face appeared through the streams of color and light, followed by a hand. The open palm grew larger and reached out to him, coming just in front of his eyes. It gave his face a slight and comforting push and Jack began to float backward.

"Not yet," a voice said gently from the face, barely visible in the sea of white.

Jack tumbled backward slowly, spinning very slightly. He tried to turn his body, but he had no control. Then a new voice called out behind him.

"Release him!" Maria yelled.

Suddenly, Jack could see Sam and Maria, and feel himself flying away from them as if he was shot from a cannon.

The generating station reappeared, blurry at first, then in full view.

"There he is!" Celia cried out.

Jack exited the portal and fell helplessly toward the ground. The portal closed below him, sending rays of white light everywhere as Jack was careening ever downward.

"He's going too fast!" Celia screamed.

"Jack!" the group called out to him.

Then all went black.

Chapter 15

"Linhurst director Dr. Charles Moseley has declined comment pending further investigations into the power outages."

Jack could hear the female voice clearly coming from a nearby television.

"Nuclear power plant executives tell us that Roland Allister's actions and opinions are his own, and that his extraordinary claim about so-called spiritual energy providing the power for the Linhurst campus is very concerning."

Jack opened his eyes in time to see the smarmy executive in his disheveled suit on the television suspended from the wall in the corner of the room.

"I saw them!" Allister yelled into the camera as he was being led by Captain Hadaway into the Spring Dale police station. "There were ghosts everywhere! That's how they're doing it! We need to uncover their secrets!"

Hadaway guided Allister through the front doors of the station while other officers fended off the news crew. The shot cut back to the reporter.

"Allister has been placed on indefinite leave and is currently undergoing long-term medical treatment. As for the relationship between the nuclear power plant and the town of Spring Dale, we are told that Spring Dale Mayor Helowski is exploring other sources of energy, potentially leading to their ultimate decision to dismantle one of the two nuclear towers by year's end. This is Aurora Lux reporting from Linhurst Care Center. Back to you Bill."

"Thanks, Aurora. Another mysterious evening on the Linhurst campus, but at least Spring Dale residents have their power back. We'll stay on top of this story as more develops."

The screen went black.

"Jack, are you awake?" Henry asked gently. Jack looked to see his dad was seated close by his side, holding the TV remote in hand.

He felt sore and weak. His head ached. He looked to see sunlight pouring in through an open window in front of him, and he soon realized he was lying in a room with bright yellow walls, landscape paintings hanging on either side of him.

"How do you feel?" Henry asked.

Jack struggled to push himself to a seated position. He was in a room in the Linhurst Care Center where, through the window, he could see the tower of the generating station reaching out toward the sky. The building was sitting innocently as usual, like nothing of importance ever occurred inside its walls.

"What happened?" Jack asked.

"You took quite a spill, bud," Henry said. "I didn't see it, but they tell me you fell to the floor from the second story of the generating station."

Jack quickly recalled King racing him around the station, then releasing him after Maria pulled him through the portal. He couldn't remember anything after that.

"Celia?" Jack asked.

"She's just fine," Henry said with a smile.

"What about Garrett?" Jack asked.

"A few bumps and bruises, but Garrett is well," Henry said.

The door to the room opened, and Dr. Moseley appeared. "Jack, you're awake."

Jack gave a faint smile. "I'm awake," he replied, his voice hoarse. "How long have I been here?"

"Two days," Henry said.

Two days?! Jack's eyes lit up in shock.

"When you hit the floor of the station, you were knocked out cold," Dr. Moseley said. "That's when the portal closed. A corona of green light blasted out of the reactor and shattered the windows on the first floor of the station."

"That's going to be a costly repair, Mose," Henry said.

"I'm more concerned about Jack," Mose said, entering the room and standing at the foot of Jack's bed. "It's good to see you up and about."

Jack smiled at Mose. "I just heard something about Linhurst on the news."

"Thanks to Captain Hadaway—and with Danny and Tommy's help—we were able to keep the town's residents at bay."

"They didn't see anything?" Jack asked.

"Nothing we can't explain," Mose replied with a cunning grin.

Jack pushed the covers off his body and began to pull himself up.

"Whoa!" Mose exclaimed. "Easy, Jack! You've been out for a while."

"I want to see Celia," Jack insisted, lying back down as he began to feel dizzy all of a sudden.

"She is safe at home, resting up," said Mose. "I'll call her to see if she can come visit. For now, you need to take it easy."

Jack laid back on the soft pillow. His body ached. Then he remembered something.

"Does she still have the burn marks?" Jack asked.

"They've gone away," Mose replied.

Jack raised his arms and inspected them. They were free of any marks, just as they were a few nights before.

"I don't understand how he didn't get to me," Jack said.

"Those marks seemed to have been caused by the great energy Sam King generated," Mose said. "When he got hold of someone, I believe his energy created the marks. He was even able to use the energy to leave us the notes on the wall. I imagine something about the way you connected with the other side protected you from being harmed."

Jack looked at his arms again then back to Dr. Moseley.

"Take your time getting yourself up," Mose said. "I need to check on a few things first, then I'll ring Celia to come and visit."

Jack sighed and lay on his pillow as Dr. Moseley left the room.

"Jack, I'm glad you're all right," Henry began softly after a few moments. "What you did was very brave."

Jack looked him over to see the dad he remembered from years before—the one who believed in him and didn't have a leash on him. He saw the dad who actually cared to know him and give him his space at the same time.

Later that morning, Jack made his way to the lobby of Linhurst Care Center and found a seat near the large front windows looking out at the generating station. He watched as a few men worked to clean up the shattered windows Mose told him about.

Then he watched Danny Slater drive his car right up in front of the building and hop out—followed by Celia from the passenger's side. The pair made their way inside and walked right up to Andrea at the check-in desk.

"We're here to see Jack," Celia told her.

"Ahem!" Jack cleared his throat loudly.

Andrea stood up, smiled, then pointed to Jack sitting in the lobby. Jack gave them a small wave, and they headed over to him. He jumped to his feet, felt a little dizzy suddenly, and Celia rushed in to give him a hug and catch him before he passed out.

"Still a little weary?" she asked.

He nodded.

"Dude!" Danny began. "Can you believe what happened?"

Jack shook his head.

"I mean… what a night!" Danny replied. "It was just like two years ago."

"I think what Danny means to say is that he was happy to be such a help," Celia interrupted. "You know, Jack, I wouldn't have said this before, but it turns out that Danny did a lot to help set things right."

Danny blushed. "Just doing my job. Remember the note Captain Hadaway gave me? He helped me get this security job for Dr. Moseley."

"I don't understand," Jack said.

"After what my dad did here, I can't forgive him for it," Danny said. "It's been eating me up. I kind of see this job as a way to put right some of the bad stuff he did."

Jack's face lit up. He was suddenly proud about his decision to bring Danny to Dr. Moseley.

"Jack!" a voice called out behind them. They turned to see Harrison entering the lobby from the hallway leading to Dr. Moseley's office. He hurried toward them and leaned in to give Celia and Jack a hug, then boisterously shook Danny's hand.

"Charles told me you were here," Harrison said to Jack. "He called me the moment you awoke. How are you feeling?"

"Tired," said Jack. "But overall good, I guess."

"That was an intense ride," Harrison said energetically. "All the work I've been doing all these years, it finally proves everything I've been trying to investigate. Going back to the time I saw my mother. But it's so much to take in still."

Jack wasn't sure how he felt about Harrison's enthusiasm.

"We uncovered a lot here the other night," Harrison added.

Now Jack was simply annoyed—and Harrison's expression showed it.

"I've decided to keep all the footage and findings close to the vest," Harrison said apologetically. "Until we can do more investigating on campus, that is."

Jack loosened up.

"After meeting you and seeing your understanding of the paranormal, Morgan and I have completely reconsidered how we go about our work. We decided to find a way to be less expository and more investigative—really living up to our name. We decided that much of our work here at Linhurst will be for research purposes and less for likes and hits. Mose has contracted us to learn more about the reactor and how it works. Exciting stuff, right?!"

Jack was pleased to hear this. After all his experiences at Linhurst to date, and the lingering uncertainty about the future of the place, things were somehow beginning to look much brighter with Harrison on board.

"Oh, and there's one other thing," Harrison said. He pulled his phone, tapped and swiped a few times, then reached it out to Jack.

Jack took the phone and pulled it up close to see a smiling photo of a woman and a little girl.

"Is this who I think it is?" Jack asked, his voice breaking.

"Sam's daughter and granddaughter," Harrison replied, smiling from ear to ear.

"You found them!" Jack gasped. "But how?"

"I did a little investigation, only this time without the paranormal twist," Harrison said.

"They're just like I saw them in my vision," Jack replied, his voice shaking. He couldn't help feeling a bit overwhelmed by emotion at how happy they looked.

Just then, a woman burst through the front doors of the care center and raced across the lobby, making a beeline for Andrea at the check-in area.

"I've come to see a Dr. Moseley," she said frantically. "Is he here?"

"Do you have an appointment?" Andrea asked.

"No," the woman replied, sounding weak and breathless. "Does he work here?"

"I can see if he's available," Andrea replied. "Can I tell him the nature of your visit, please?"

"I had a brother who was a resident here," the woman said, voice trembling. "He told me I need to see Dr. Moseley."

"Is your brother a patient of ours?" Andrea asked.

"My brother died 23 years ago this week," she managed, then fainted to the floor.

"Time to get to work!" Jack said to Harrison.

AKNOWLEDGEMENTS

To all my family, friends and new fans who supported my first novel, *Freeing Linhurst*, thank you for the energy and support that inspired me to write the sequel and my second novel.

Thanks to Grady and Wyatt, whose excitement and awe kept me grounded and full of new ideas at every turn.

Thank you to Tracy Seybold for your help with the editing process.

Thanks to Beth Miner for your ideas and suggestions.

Thanks to Betsy Aikens for your keen eye and input.

ABOUT THE AUTHOR

Al Cassidy grew up all over the U.S. before settling down
in the Philadelphia area. He began in marketing &
advertising design—working primarily as a consultant
for non-profits—creating promotional materials, websites,
videos, illustration and more. After years of thinking about it,
Al finally took up writing and published his first story,
Freeing Linhurst, a tale he always wanted to tell.
He continues to design, illustrate, write,
and find ways to grow creatively every day.